Also by Tina Folsom

Amaury's Hellion (Scanguards Vampires, Book 2)

Gabriel's Mate (Scanguards Vampires, Book 3)

A Touch of Greek (Out of Olympus, Book 1)

Lawful Escort

Naked Shorts (Anthology)

Venice Vampyr #1

Venice Vampyr #2: Final Affair

SAMSON'S LOVELY MORTAL

(Scanguards Vampires, Book 1)

TINA FOLSOM

Samson's Lovely Mortal is a work of fiction. Names, characters, places, and incidents are the products of the author's imagination and are used fictitiously. Any resemblance to actual events, locales, or persons, living or dead, is entirely coincidental.

2010 Tina Folsom

Published in the United States

Cover design: Elaina Lee
Author photograph: Cheryl Grey, London

Printed in the United States of America

Acknowledgments

Many thanks to my critique partner Grace for her continued support, invaluable ideas, her laughter, and her friendship. And to my husband Mark for his patience, his love, and support.

A big THANK YOU to the readers and bloggers who help support my writing by spreading the word, recommending my books, and reviewing them.

ONE

"Let me suck your cock."

The vamp female tugged at Samson's pants. She freed his flaccid shaft from the confinement of his jeans and sucked it into her gorgeous mouth. He watched her red lips close tightly around him as she worked him frantically. Up and down she moved, the warm wetness of her mouth lubricating him.

With her hand, she cupped his balls and squeezed them in perfect rhythm with her sucking. She was talented, no doubt. He buried his hands in her hair and moved his hips back and forth, trying to increase the friction.

"Harder." His request was met with enthusiasm, her slurping sounds filling the dimly lit room.

He let his gaze sweep over her scantily clad body: hot curves, great ass, even a pretty face. Everything he could wish for in a sexual partner. Eager to give head, she would probably swallow too. Something he particularly appreciated. But despite feeling her tantalizing tongue run up and down his cock, despite the hard sucking motion, no erection was forthcoming. Her patience was wasted on him. Nothing moved.

Her head bobbed back and forth, her long brown hair brushing against his naked skin, catching in his pubic hair, but his body wasn't in it, almost as if she was sucking off somebody else, not him.

Samson finally pushed her away, humiliated and frustrated. If vampires could blush from embarrassment, his face would have been as red as the vamp's painted lips. Luckily, blushing was reserved for humans.

In lightning speed, he shoved his useless male equipment back into his pants and zipped up. Even faster, he fled her company. His only hope was that she would never know who he was. Good thing he was in a strange city and not back in San Francisco where he was as well-known as a pink horse.

A week after the embarrassing incident, his friend Amaury made a suggestion.

"Just give it a shot, Samson," he insisted. "The guy is completely trustworthy. He won't breathe a syllable to anybody about this."

His old friend couldn't possibly be serious. "A shrink? You want me to go see a *shrink*?"

"He's helped me a lot before. What have you got to lose?"

His dignity; his pride.

"I guess if you vouch for him, I can give it a try." And just like that, he'd caved. Was it desperation?

"And don't judge him from the outside."

The place was a joke. When Samson first entered the dark basement where the psychiatrist practiced, he wanted to run right back out. But the receptionist had already spotted him. With a saccharin-sweet smile and straightened back, she put her large chest on display.

Great, a shrink operating from a dungeon and a Barbie doll as the gatekeeper!

"Mr. Woodford, please come in. Dr. Drake is expecting you," her high-pitched voice invited him.

Once he'd made his way into Drake's office, he knew it was a mistake. Instead of a couch there was a coffin. One of the wooden side panels had been removed so a live person could lie down in it comfortably as if lying down on a chaise lounge.

The guy had to be a lunatic. No self-respecting modern vamp would want to be caught dead in a coffin! Vampires in San Francisco were mainstreaming, adapting to the human lifestyle. Coffins were out. Tempur-Pedic mattresses were in.

The lanky man rounded his desk and stretched out his hand to greet him.

"If you think I'm going to lie down in the coffin, you better think again," Samson barked.

"I see we have our work cut out for us." The doctor seemed unfazed by the rude remark. He pointed at the comfortable looking armchair. Reluctantly, Samson sat down.

Dr. Drake let himself fall in the chair opposite. As the doctor studied him for the first few minutes, Samson shifted nervously, hands clamped over the armrests of the chair.

"Can we get started? I believe I'm paying you by the hour." Offensive was better than defensive, he'd learned early in life.

"We started the minute you came in here, but then I'm sure you knew that." Dr. Drake's smile was noncommittal, his voice even.

Samson narrowed his eyes, trying to block out the implied reprimand. "Indeed."

"How long have you experienced these anger issues?"

The words were not what he'd expected. Maybe a question more along the lines of "So, what brings you here?" but not this direct assault on his already battered psyche. He should have asked Amaury more about the doctor's methods before agreeing to make an appointment.

"Anger issues? I don't have anger issues. I'm here for … the issue is … uh, my problem has to do with …" God, since when could he not say the word "sex" without being flustered? He'd never had any problems expressing himself when it came to sex. His vocabulary included many choice four-letter words he generally had no problem spurting from his lips whenever necessary.

"Uh-huh." The doctor nodded as if he knew something Samson didn't. "You think it's a sexual problem. Interesting."

Was the man a mind reader? Samson was aware that some vampires had additional gifts. He himself had a photographic memory. He knew that others of his kind could see the future or read minds, but he wasn't sure how widespread those talents were.

He needed to know whether he was at a disadvantage with this man. He didn't want to work with somebody who could read him like a book when he didn't want to be read. "Do you read minds?"

Drake shook his head. "No. But your problem is not uncommon. It's pretty easy to figure out. You exhibit signs of extreme anger and frustration." He cleared his throat and leaned forward in emphasis. "Mr. Woodford, I'm well aware of who you are. You run one of the most successful companies in the vampire world, if not *the* most successful. You are rich beyond belief—and trust me this will not influence how much I'll charge you—"

"Of course not," Samson interrupted. The quack would charge him what he thought Samson was willing to pay. It wouldn't be a first. He was used to people trying to inflate their prices because they knew he could afford it. But they usually tried only once. Nobody cheated him and got away with it.

"And at the same time, you haven't been seen in society for quite awhile, when you should be out there, courting beautiful women. I suppose your breakup with Ilona Hampstead had something to do with this."

"I'm not here to talk about her." Samson let out a quick breath. He refused to even say her name. She had no part in his life, not anymore, and the mere mention of her name made his fangs itch for a vicious bite. He cracked his knuckles, and wondered if that was the same sound he'd hear if her neck snapped. It would be music to his ears.

"Maybe not about her, but maybe about what she did. There can only be one reason for this. And we both know what it is. So, the question is now, are you going to trust me to help you?"

Drake's blue eyes punctuated his point.

"Do what?" Samson decided to stick with denial. It had worked so far.

"Get over the anger." The doctor was as insistent as Samson was stubborn.

"I told you, it's not an anger issue."

A knowing smile curved the doctor's lips. "Oh, I believe it is. Whatever she did, it angered you so much that it's putting a block on your sexual drive, as if you didn't want to make yourself vulnerable again."

"I'm not vulnerable. I never was. Not since I've been a vampire." The last thing Samson wanted to feel was being vulnerable. To him it was synonymous to being weak. If the doctor wasn't careful with his accusations, he'd soon find himself at the receiving end of Samson's displeasure. Maybe a physical fight would relieve his frustrations.

"Not in the physical sense of the word. We are all aware of your strength and your power. But I'm talking about your emotions. We all have them. We all struggle with them. Some more than others. Believe me, my calendar is booked solid with our fellow vampires who need help dealing with their emotions."

The shrink looked at him. No, he couldn't allow Drake to get this close. Emotions were a dangerous thing. They could destroy a man. Samson hauled himself out of the chair.

"I don't think this is going to work." The tightness in his chest bore witness to the effect Drake's words had on him, even though he was not ready to admit it. Not even to himself.

The doctor stood. "Ever since we've started mainstreaming," Drake continued, undeterred, "my practice has quadrupled. Adapting to the way humans live their lives has taken a toll on many of us. We now have to deal with emotional issues we kept buried for centuries. Literally. You're not alone. I can help you."

Samson shook his head. Nobody could help him. He had to get through this on his own. "Send me your bill. Good bye, Doc."

He stormed out, knowing the doctor had hit a nerve.

Well, sex was overrated anyway. At least it was what he was trying to convince himself of. There were nights when he believed his own lies, but it never lasted long. The truth was, he liked having sex— lots of it—but none of the sexy vampire women did it for him anymore. No matter how hard he tried, he couldn't get an erection.

He'd never heard of such a thing happening to any vampire. Sexual virility was part and parcel of being a vamp in the first place. Being impotent was a foreign concept in the vampire world. Only humans became impotent. If the news became widespread he would lose all respect from his peers. It was unacceptable.

So eventually he'd conceded, and a month later he'd made another appointment in the hope there was something the quack could do for him.

Samson blinked and wiped away the memories of the last nine months. Tonight was his birthday. He would try to have some fun.

As he strode from his wingback armchair to the wet bar at the opposite end of his elegant sitting room; his movements were fluid, his body tall and muscular, yet slender.

Samson poured himself a glass of his favorite blood type and downed it like a human would a shot of Tequila—minus the salt and lime. The thick liquid coated his throat and eased the thirst, dulling his hunger for other pleasures in the process. Good; no other pleasures would be satisfied tonight.

Same as the last two hundred and seventy-six nights.

Not that he was counting.

Only his thirst for blood had been stilled, the rest of his body's needs, while temporarily subdued, would go unmet. Sometimes he wished he could get drunk and forget about everything, but unfortunately, being a vampire meant he couldn't get drunk like humans did. Alcohol had no effect on his body. What he'd give for a little numbness right now.

He had expressly told his pals not to get him any presents or throw him a party. Of course he knew it was futile and only a matter of time until they would be at his door. Like pilfering barbarians, they would invade his home, raid his secret stash of quality drinks—consisting mostly of high-priced O-Neg—and waste his waking hours with old stories he'd heard a hundred times.

They'd given him a surprise birthday party when he'd reached the two-hundred mark, and it would be no different today, on his two hundred and thirty-seventh, with pretty much the same cast of characters.

In anticipation of the inevitable invasion of his privacy, he had dressed in dapper black pants and a dark gray turtleneck. Except for his signet ring, he wore no jewelry.

The clangor of the phone tore through the quiet of his home. He looked at the clock on the wall and saw that it was shortly before nine o'clock. Just as he'd thought, the boys were on their way.

"Yes?"

"Hey, birthday boy. How is it hanging?"

Not a good choice of words, definitely not.

"What is it, Ricky?" Despite Ricky's Irish heritage, he had adopted many California expressions and now sounded more like a beach-boy-surfer-dude than the Irish lad he was deep down.

"I just want to wish you a great birthday and see what you're doing tonight." Why Ricky had to keep up the pretense, Samson really didn't know. Wasn't he aware that his surprise birthday party was already out of the bag?

Samson cut to the chase. "When's everybody coming?"

"What do you mean?"

"What time are you guys going to surprise me with a birthday party?"

"How did you know? Never mind. The guys wanted me to make sure you were there. So don't leave the house. And if our other *surprise* arrives before us, keep her there."

Not again. He should have known. He bit back his anger.

"When will you guys ever learn that I'm not into strippers?"

Never have been, never will be.

Ricky laughed. "Yes, yes, but this one is special. She's not just a stripper. She does extras."

Would he be up for extras? Very unlikely.

"I think she'll do something for you, you know what I mean. She's good, so give her a chance, will you? It's for your own good. You can't go on like this. Holly said—"

Samson cut him off. So much for having some fun tonight. "You told Holly? Are you fucking nuts? She's the biggest gossip of the underworld! I told you in confidence. How could you?" His nostrils flared, and his eyes narrowed. With his fangs suddenly protruding from his mouth, he could have scared a champion wrestler from here till Tuesday. But Ricky wasn't a wrestler, and he wasn't scared easily. Not even till Monday.

"Careful how you talk about my girlfriend, Samson. She's not a gossip. And besides, she suggested that stripper. She's a friend of Holly's."

Perfect! A friend of Holly's. Sure, this was guaranteed to work!

Samson still fumed, but recognized it was too late to call the whole thing off. "Fine."

He slammed the phone down, not giving Ricky a chance to elaborate any further. Great! Now that Holly knew about his little problem, soon the entire underworld of San Francisco would know. He'd be the laughing stock of every party, the butt of every joke.

How long would it take her to spread the news—a day, an hour, five minutes? How long until the snickering behind his back started? Why not take out a one-page ad in the SF Vampire Chronicle himself to save her the trouble?

Samson Woodford, debonair bachelor vampire, can't get it up!

***

Delilah Sheridan's eyes hurt, but she continued scanning the rows of transactions for anything that looked out of place. Rubbing her stiff neck with her fingers, she longed for a massage, or at least a fifteen-minute soak in a hot tub, neither of which would happen tonight.

"Coffee?" John's voice came from behind her.

She pushed a strand of her long dark hair behind her ear. "No, thanks; I want to be able to sleep tonight. I've had insomnia the last few nights. I'm probably still on New York time." Her gaze remained fixed on her computer screen.

The night before, she'd barely slept despite the comfortable mattress. And the few hours she had been able to sleep, she'd been tormented by dreams which didn't make a lick of sense.

The large, spacious office was practically deserted. The only people left were the two of them. John Reardon was the chief accountant for the San Francisco branch of the nationwide private company Delilah had come to audit.

"Yeah, I know what you mean. It's not sleeping in your own bed, that's what does it, right?" John sounded sympathetic.

"At least they put me up in a corporate apartment rather than at a hotel. I don't get disturbed by the housekeeping staff."

True, she was staying in a comfortable condo which belonged to the company, but what did it matter when she couldn't sleep anyway? Before her trip to San Francisco she'd never had any problems with insomnia. On the contrary, she was known for being able to sleep wherever and whenever she put her head on a pillow. It didn't even have to be a pillow.

Delilah rubbed her eyes then looked at her watch. It was past nine o'clock. She felt almost guilty having stayed so late. John had insisted being there as long as she was. He didn't want to leave her alone at the offices. She guessed he didn't trust auditors not to snoop around. He got that right. Not that she'd call it snooping since she had all the authorization she needed. In fact, she had very specific instructions.

She wasn't just here to audit the branch office of the company, but to investigate some irregularities. Delilah was sure John had no idea about this. He'd been told that it was merely one of the usual audits Headquarters performed regularly.

"Sorry, John. I'm sure you're ready to go home."

She turned to him. Leaning against the edge of one of the desks, he lifted his coffee cup to his lips. His gray suit seemed ill-fitting, and the collar of his shirt looked frayed. He was quite tall and decent looking for an accountant. Boring, bland, but not ugly.

He probably didn't appreciate having to stay at the office this late. Well, she was beat anyway, so maybe she should call it a day, even though she knew she would probably toss and turn all night no matter what.

"Ready?"

A flicker of relief appeared in John's eyes when she nodded. It took him all of two seconds to slip into his jacket and grab his briefcase. He sure was in a hurry to get out of there. She couldn't blame him. He had a family waiting for him. And what did she have to go home to? It wasn't even home.

Not that home would have been any more welcoming than the corporate apartment. Nobody was waiting for her. No man, not many friends—not even a cat or a dog. After this assignment was over and she was back in New York, she'd go out more and date. That was the plan. It was an excellent plan, one she'd made during every one of her out-of-town assignments and then promptly dismissed when she'd returned home. This time she meant it, though. Really.

But for now, all she wanted was to get some takeout and go to sleep. John was kind enough to direct her toward Chinatown where she could pick up some food on her way back to the apartment. Even though she'd been to Chinatown before, her sense of direction was much less developed than her head for numbers. During the day she normally managed, but in the dark she turned into a lost cause when it came to finding her way.

It had started drizzling, and she didn't want to hang around too long. She ducked into the first Chinese restaurant she encountered. The place was virtually empty.

The woman at the entrance attempted to show her to a table, but Delilah waved her off.

"Just takeout, please."

The hostess handed her a menu. Delilah scanned it quickly, trying not to let her fingers linger too long on the sticky plastic cover. The menu presented too many choices. How many different ways could you cook beef? Beef with bamboo shoots, beef with mushrooms, spicy beef. Enough already. She would play it safe.

"I'll have the Mongolian beef with brown rice, please."

"Brown rice takes ten minutes." The Chinese woman was as friendly as a viper and just as pretty. If she thought Delilah would change her mind to white rice with her look, she was out of luck.

"That's ok. I'll wait."

Delilah sank onto one of the red plastic chairs near the door. This business trip was her first to San Francisco. As an independent contractor, she normally performed special audits up and down the East Coast and rarely travelled further afield.

When the head office's regular statistical checks had revealed that certain ratios in the San Francisco branch were off, they'd decided to use somebody who hadn't had any prior contact with the West Coast staff and hired an outsider. It was smart. Auditors could become too cozy with the staff they were auditing. A regular change of auditors was generally a good idea.

If anybody could find out where the problem was buried, it was Delilah. Her specialty was forensic accounting. It wasn't quite as exciting as police work, but it was probably the most exciting field in the accounting world, if there was such a thing. An oxymoron to some, but not to her. And besides, she was making a very decent living as an independent consultant.

This investigation should not present itself with too many difficulties. Certain ratios between assets and depreciation were off the charts and suggested that either somebody was completely incompetent or was trying to cheat the company. How, she didn't know yet, but she would find out soon.

Delilah was tired and knew she needed a good night's sleep, but she also dreaded going to bed. Some of her old nightmares had come back again and mixed with new ones. She hadn't had any in a few months, but upon her arrival in San Francisco a few days ago, her bad dreams had started to reappear.

They were normally always the same. The old French farmhouse they'd lived in over twenty years ago when her father had taken a two-year overseas assignment as a visiting professor. The lavender fields surrounding the property. The crib. The silence. And then the faces of her parents. The tears on her mother's face. The pain.

But this time the dreams had blended into other, more incomprehensible ones.

The Victorian house looked foreboding in the heavy rain. Light came from one of the windows; other than that it was dark. She ran faster and faster. Toward the house, to safety. She didn't dare look behind her. He was still there, still following her. Hands clamped over her shoulder. Then suddenly her fists pounded into a heavy wooden door. Something gave way. She stumbled forward and fell. Into warmth, softness, safety. Home.

"Mongolian beef, brown rice." The woman's voice pierced through the recollection of her dream. Delilah paid her tab and took the food. She stopped dead at the door.

Damn!

It had started raining in earnest. She had left her umbrella in the apartment, thinking she wouldn't need it today. Instead of opting for her trench coat, she'd only put on a light jacket. Well, that turned out to be a bad choice.

Everybody had told her how unpredictable San Francisco weather could be, and now she would find out for herself. The weather report had indicated no rain until the weekend. Could she sue the weatherman? Probably not.

She had no choice but to brave it. Delilah knew she wasn't far from the apartment, only about three blocks. Staying close to the buildings, she started running along the sidewalk then made a turn into the next street, and another one a block further. The apartment couldn't be far now. She looked around, but in the heavy rain she couldn't recognize anything. Was it another block more?

Her clothes were already soaked, and she would have to jump into the shower to get warm again. Where the hell was she? She turned another corner and found herself on a small side street. It didn't look familiar at all, but that wasn't her biggest problem, neither was the relentless rain. The problem was the guy coming toward her. Even though she couldn't make him out well, she would bet her retirement fund that he wasn't there to lend her an umbrella.

His imposing frame was silhouetted against the dim light of a streetlamp behind him. The chill of his look seeped into her body as a faint glimmer of light coming from a window appeared on the left side of his face. The scar puckering his skin didn't inspire confidence.

Delilah turned back to where she came from. Before she was able to take two steps, a hand clamped over her shoulder, jerking her back. The sudden jolt made her lose her balance. She slipped on the wet sidewalk, her legs buckling beneath her. Her food dropped onto the ground as she tried to fight for balance and brace her fall.

The guy's hand on her shoulder gripped harder as she screamed and tried to shake him off, crashing onto the sidewalk in the process. He bent down to pull her up. She yanked her head around. For the first time she could see his face clearly, clear enough to make an identification if need be. He was Caucasian and in his forties. Violence, and the intention to unleash it on her, was clearly written on his face.

Delilah couldn't allow him to drag her into some dark hole. Number one in survival training was never to let the attacker move the victim to a secondary location. She had to fight him off here, where she had a chance of getting the attention of a passerby.

Fat chance!

With this rain, nobody would be outside. Not even a dog.

He jerked her up, seizing her by the collar of her jacket now, having released the painful grip on her shoulder. Quickly, she stretched her arms back and slipped out of the jacket, leaving him holding onto it. Now she had a fighting chance.

He was startled, and she had a couple of seconds' head start. She'd been a sprinter in college, and it came in handy, even though the slippery ground didn't help—neither did the high heels of her shoes. Vanity would kill her one of these days.

With long strides she ran into the next street, her lean but strong legs pushing off the ground with a vehemence that was startling for her small body. He was close behind her. And faster. She had to run for all she was worth. Her breath quickened as her lungs demanded more oxygen.

Scouting the area ahead of her, she made a split-second decision and sprinted into the street to her right. A desperate glance over her shoulder confirmed that the brute was still chasing her.

Scanning the street, she spotted several Victorian residences on the other side. All of them were dark, except for one. It seemed oddly familiar with light shining through the windows in the front room. This was her chance, probably her only one. Not slowing down for even a second, she crossed the narrow street, ran up the few steps of the old Victorian and hammered at the door.

"Help! Help me!"

Frantically, she looked behind her while her fists continued pounding into the door. Her pursuer was less than half a block away and closing in, his face angry. If he reached her, he'd unleash his anger on her, and there was nowhere else to run.

TWO

Who the hell was banging on his door? Samson would have to teach his friends some manners. He realized it was raining cats and dogs outside, but it didn't give them the right to damage his door. They'd be sorry in a second. He was in a foul mood as it was, and announcing themselves like barbarians did not endear them to him.

He yanked the door open.

"Fuck off!"

A small figure with dripping wet hair and soaked clothes tumbled into his arms.

"Help me, please!" The female voice had an urgency to it he couldn't ignore.

Instinctively he pulled her in and slammed the door shut again.

"Thank you." The quiet mumble was almost inaudible, but laced with genuine relief.

She lifted her head and looked up at him. Big green eyes, long thick lashes, luscious red lips. Her white blouse was soaked, and she could have won any wet-t-shirt contest hands down. Not that he'd ever witnessed one. Her black-lace bra featured her breasts prominently: 34C, he guessed.

The stripper!

Of course, she was the stripper. So the guys had gotten him a stripper who would play the damsel in distress. It was different from the usual police woman or nurse, but still, it wouldn't work.

The last time his friends had surprised him with a stripper, Officer Nasty had tried a strip search on him, leaving him entirely unaffected. Not even the tease of a little bondage had gotten his cock to wake from its deathlike sleep. What made Ricky think this damsel in distress could do any better?

She looked pretty enough, almost innocent. At least he could play along for a few minutes, see if anything moved. Without getting his hopes up, of course.

"What happened?"

She smelled like a wet dog and something else, but he couldn't pinpoint it.

"Some guy attacked me." She stopped to catch her breath. "I have to call the police." She shivered and sounded believable. The woman had obviously taken some acting classes.

Nice touch.

"Well, why don't we get you into the warmth first and get rid of your wet clothes." That was surely the script she had in mind. What better reason to take off her clothes than because they were wet? He wouldn't mind warming her. With his body.

A crease appeared between her eyebrows. "Just a phone call, please. I can get changed at home, thank you." Her voice was clipped as if irritated.

Ah, so she wanted to play coy. Fine with him. He motioned her into the sitting room where a low fire crackled in the fireplace. She placed herself right in front of it and stretched her hands out toward the warmth. Her wet clothes clung to her body, emphasizing her tantalizing curves. Perfect proportions. Not too skinny, just enough flesh for him to have something to dig into. At least Ricky had picked somebody who physically appealed to him. It was a start.

"You'll catch a cold in those wet clothes," he whispered behind her. Her shoulders lifted, tension evident. She had obviously not felt him approach. What was wrong with her senses? As he cupped her shoulders with his hands, she shrieked and spun around. He recognized the glare in her eyes as a mixture of anger and fear.

"I have to go."

Now it was getting interesting. She was playing hard to get. Ricky was right, she was good. Maybe she could stir something up for him, just maybe. He enjoyed a good hunt as much as the next vampire. And he hadn't hunted in a while. Every woman had practically been handed to him on a platter, and as enticing as many of them had been, none had stirred him.

"Not so fast. I think you're forgetting what you came here for. Let's see what you've got to offer." He let her know that he was willing to play along. Just for the hell of it.

The damsel threw him another scared look and made for the door. Samson was faster and cut her escape route off. He was enjoying himself now. In fact, he hadn't had this much fun in a long time. Whatever Ricky was paying her, she was worth every dollar.

She breathed heavily, still pretending to be scared. He could almost smell her fear. It was exactly how he liked his prey. His hands dug into her shoulders to pull her close. He didn't care that her wet clothes would ruin his dry-clean-only pants and sweater.

"No, let me go!" Her desperate plea echoed in his vast home.

"You don't want to go." He soaked in her smell. Yes, wet dog, but something else too, something different. Was this little vampire vixen using some exotic perfume? It smelled delicious, tempting. A faint smell of lavender drifted into his nostrils.

Her terrified eyes looked up at him as she struggled under his hold.

"I'm sure Ricky paid you enough, and if not, I'm going to tip you generously." Money was no object. If she could do something for him, he'd be more than generous.

"Paid me?" Her voice was a high shriek, her panic underscored by the widening of her eyes. Beautiful eyes, their green shimmering in hundreds of different facets.

Had the cad not paid her yet? Well, he could take care of that later, but right now he wanted something else. A little taste of those luscious lips and that sharp tongue of hers.

There was something about her. She'd awakened his interest. Samson lowered his head and pressed his lips onto hers. She tried wiggling out of his embrace, but her attempt was weak at best. He'd known vampire females to be nearly as strong as vampire males, but the specimen in his arms had obviously decided not to use her strength against him.

Her lips were soft, deliciously soft. Samson slid his hand behind her neck to keep her in place while he used his tongue to tempt her mouth open. He wanted to taste her, feel that tongue of hers, but she kept her lips firmly pressed together, seemingly unwilling to surrender too soon.

The woman still struggled, trying to wrestle free of him. He didn't mind. In fact, the more she resisted the more he was aware of her body rubbing against his, and the more he wanted her. He continued his assault on her lips, sweeping over them with his moist tongue. He pressed her harder against him, running his other hand down her back to squeeze her cute little ass. Instead of her wet clothes, he felt the body heat buried underneath.

Her breasts were crushed against his chest, and her rapid heartbeat reverberated through his body. He enjoyed her unusual softness. And then he noticed something else. He felt himself react to her. Blood suddenly pumped into his loins, surging to his cock. His pants tightened uncomfortably. But he wasn't going to complain.

Samson released a moan of pleasure as he felt his hardening cock press against her stomach. She surely had to sense it too. He hadn't felt an erection in so long, and the realization that his old body still worked was a birthday present he hadn't expected. With his hand on her ass he hauled her closer into his body and ground his cock against her, letting her know that she'd achieved the impossible.

He would reward her plenty for it. Why hadn't his shrink thought of this? All he needed was a woman who pretended *not* to want him, and his hunting instincts would kick in. Reverse psychology was all it was. He'd have to fire Drake. In all those months the quack hadn't come up with anything helpful.

Suddenly her lips parted, and he didn't hesitate slipping his tongue in greedily.

Oh God, yes!

Her mouth, her taste—it was all so different from anything he'd tasted before. His tongue swept in deeply, searching for hers. It wasn't what he had expected. His body tensed as he explored her delicious mouth and played with her hesitant tongue, teasing her to give him more. He went deeper. Oh God, she was delicious.

With his hand on her neck he stroked her eagerly while his hand on her round ass couldn't stop caressing her and pressing her harder against him. His cock was rock hard and ready to burst. Samson couldn't remember ever having had an erection like this, not in the last hundred and fifty years anyway.

There was no way he'd let her go before he'd thoroughly fucked her. He wanted to bury himself in her for as long as he could and find the pleasure which had eluded him in the last nine months.

Samson swallowed more of her taste, gulped down more of her scent, and all of a sudden his nostrils flared.

Damn, what the hell was he doing?

Shit!

He wasn't kissing a vampire. She tasted human! His friends were killing him. They'd gotten him a human stripper! They should have warned him at least. He would hurt her if he wasn't careful. If he lost control, he could bite her and drink her blood. Those idiots!

And then he felt the pain, a sharp, stabbing und unexpected pain on his foot. He instantly let go of her and winced, hopping on one foot in an attempt to relieve the throbbing. She had driven her high heel into his Italian designer shoe with all her force.

What the fuck?

What had gotten into her? She'd kissed him back, she'd responded to him. There was no reason for her sudden outburst. And besides, Ricky had said she did extras. As he stared at her in disbelief, she glared at him furiously, and as if that wasn't enough, she slapped him right across the cheek.

Bam!

Stifled laughter behind him made him spin around in record speed. There they were: all his friends, watching him get hit by a woman. This would go down in the history books, the night Samson got slapped by a human female. What else was planned for his utter humiliation?

"What the hell are you doing, Samson?" Ricky asked.

"What do you think I'm doing? I'm having fun with the stripper you got me for my birthday." Since when was Ricky all prim and proper? After all, this was his idiotic idea.

"Stripper?" the woman yelled. "I'm not a *stripper*!"

Ricky shook his head, and the guys behind him couldn't suppress their stupid grins like they were a bunch of college kids and not full-grown vampires.

"Are you blind, man? This is the stripper." Ricky tilted his head to the woman in the short nurse's uniform and garter belt who stood amongst his friends. Samson's eyes ping-ponged between the nurse and the damsel in distress, then finally settled on Ricky. The truth was written on the redheaded vampire's shocked face.

"That" —Ricky pointed at the furious woman next to Samson—"is a seriously pissed off lady, to whom you owe a huge apology. I'd start groveling right now."

Good advice. Samson winced inwardly.

"Happy Birthday," Amaury, his oldest friend, said. If he was trying to diffuse the situation, he'd have to work harder at it, because it sure wasn't working.

"And congratulations," Thomas added, grinning, but he wasn't congratulating him on his birthday. His eyes were fixed on Samson's crotch. Nothing could escape Thomas' keen eyes, ever, especially when it came to a male body. Samson understood immediately, but it didn't make the situation any more comfortable. Eventually he'd have to face the woman he'd kissed so passionately, and it wasn't something he felt comfortable with. Especially not with the raging hard-on bulging under his slacks. A hard-on which did not want to go down, not as long as he had her taste on his tongue.

She brushed past him to get out of the room. He couldn't just let her leave. He owed her more than an apology. She had healed what his shrink hadn't been able to fix even after many months of weekly sessions. He had to do something, anything.

"Miss."

She continued walking as if she hadn't heard him. The guys parted to let her through.

"Please. I'm sorry. I didn't know. I thought you were the … I'm sorry. You must think I'm a savage. Please, Miss, let me offer you some dry clothes, something to warm you up. I'll have my chauffeur drive you home."

She stopped and hesitated at the door.

"Please." He didn't care that his friends were watching him beg. He would deal with them later. Strangely, all he now wanted was for her not to be mad at him. He didn't understand why he even cared;

after all, she was only a human. Finally, her shoulders appeared to drop as if the tension in them released.

Delilah turned and looked at him. She knew it was still raining outside, and the thought of dry clothes and somebody driving her home was tempting, especially since she wasn't quite sure if she would even find her way back to the apartment. Besides, the thug could still be lurking outside somewhere, and then she wouldn't be any better off than before.

Now that he was looking at her with his puppy-dog eyes, he looked warm and kind. He hadn't looked like that only minutes ago. She had felt as if she had been his prey. He'd looked like a hunter. His kiss had been experienced, hungry, hot. And unfortunately, exactly the way she liked it, which was why she hadn't been able to resist him and finally kissed him back.

Delilah had felt his body pressed against hers, his hands touching her intimately. He had aroused her. She assumed it was merely a reflex her body produced, but deep down she knew that no reflex in the world could make her open up to a man who attacked her unless she wanted him.

During his kiss she'd felt flames of hot fire shoot through her as if her blood had started to boil. Nobody had ever kissed her like that. None of the guys she'd dated had come even close to making her body melt like it did under his touch.

But this wasn't right. He'd just attacked her like a wild beast, because he thought she was some cheap stripper. There was no doubt in her mind as to his intentions. His erection was proof positive that had she not stopped him, he would have had her right there in the living room. It was not her idea of romance, no matter how long she hadn't had sex.

She glanced at the woman in the nurse's uniform. Disgusting! Her boobs looked fake, and so did just about everything else about her. She looked cheap, and Delilah was sure the woman wasn't just a stripper, but probably also a hooker. She could just about imagine what the tramp was hired to do.

So he had some crazy friends who gave him an even crazier birthday present. Unfortunately he had tried to unwrap the wrong present. Could she really be mistaken for a stripper that easily, or did the guy need glasses? Delilah looked down at herself and realized only now that her white blouse was completely soaked through, making it transparent, and her latest *barely there* Victoria's Secret acquisition shone through. She secretly cursed her love for black underwear. No wonder he thought she was a stripper. Maybe this was all much more innocent than she'd initially thought.

"Dry clothes you said?" she finally asked him. Despite the warmth in the house, she felt cold and knew her nipples were uncomfortably hard, almost aching.

The beginning of a soft smile twisted the corners of his mouth upwards, and he nodded. "I can get you a sweater and some sweatpants. You can dry off in the bathroom." He looked almost like a schoolboy now. "I'll be back in a moment."

She followed him with her eyes as he stalked up the stairs, strong legs taking two steps at a time, his tight backside shifting under the fabric. All muscle, no fat.

"I'm Ricky," one of his friends introduced himself. "Sorry; I guess it was all my fault. I told Samson to expect a stripper. He's normally a real gentleman. Please don't hold this, uh, occurrence against him." He was tall and good looking, with a boyish face of freckles and a full head of red hair. She detected a hint of an accent in his speech. Irish maybe?

"Absolutely," the next one chimed in. "I'm Amaury."

Amore? Like Italian for "love"?

What an odd name for a man. He stretched out his hand. She hesitated, but shook it nevertheless. His handshake was firm. "He's been under a lot of stress lately. Please forgive him." He was a large, burly kind of guy with dark hair reaching to his shoulders. But he wasn't a hippie. He seemed well-groomed, and his long hair suggested he wasn't of this era. Rather he looked like he belonged in a historic novel, riding a horse to save his favorite lady. His blue eyes were piercing, his smile disarming as it spread from his lips to light up his entire face.

Each of his friends tried to make excuses for him. They seemed to be close. A man who had decent friends like that couldn't be all bad. Of course, Charles Manson probably had friends too at some point, and it didn't make him a good guy. Same went for Jack the Ripper. The Zodiac Killer came to mind. And her imagination was galloping off again.

"He's really a great guy," another one professed. "Thomas. Nice to meet you, Ma'am."

Ma'am? Now that was formal.

His warm smile was in complete contrast to his attire: Thomas was dressed entirely in leather, his motorcycle helmet clenched under one arm.

A fourth guy was in the back. He seemed a little shy and just nodded at her. He was dressed in the same biker outfit as Thomas.

"That's Milo," Thomas introduced him and put his arm possessively around his shoulders. The presence of a couple of gay guys made her feel a little safer. How bad could things get if there was a gay couple in the room? At least she got the feeling that there'd be two guys who wouldn't hit on her and would potentially protect her.

"Nice to meet you. I'm Delilah." She shifted from one foot onto the other, feeling self-conscious about the fact that the men could see her bra. Her eyes looked for a safe place to pin her stare.

"Delilah? As in Samson and Delilah?" Ricky asked with a smirk on his face.

The guys chuckled. She caught how Amaury jabbed Ricky in the ribs with his elbow, apparently trying to shut him up.

"Yes, it's Delilah." What had one of the guys called her rescuer after she'd slapped him? Had she caught the name correctly? Could his name really be Samson?

"That's a nice name." Amaury's compliment sounded as if he wanted to fill the uncomfortable silence with something, anything.

"Samson, there you are," Thomas suddenly said, looking toward the stairs.

Delilah lifted her gaze and saw Samson walking down the steps. She couldn't take her eyes off him.

She shouldn't be gawking, but she couldn't stop herself even if her life depended on it. He was tall, well over six feet, and made a very impressive figure in his black pants and figure-hugging gray turtleneck sweater. His hips were slender, his shoulders wide, and he looked like he was no stranger to a gym. His dark hair was longer than was the fashion; it gave him timeless beauty. His hazel eyes demanded her full attention.

He glided down the stairs as if he owned the world, exuding a sense of confidence more strongly than anyone she'd ever encountered. With his every step, she felt drawn in by him even more, as if the closer he came, the less able she was to throw off the lines he was tossing out to reel her in. Yet, he was silent, not saying a single word as he approached.

Samson. The name suited him. This deadly sexy man had kissed her? What had she been thinking, pushing him away? Was she losing her mind? Obviously. There was no other explanation for it now. She knew what those lips could do to her, what those hands had awakened.

Just remembering those strong thighs pressed against her made her body temperature spike a few degrees. A few more seconds and she'd have a fever that was going to require medical attention. Or his attention. Preferably his attention, since a doctor could probably not help her with what she had: a severe attack of lust.

He stopped right in front of her, his gaze meeting hers. Delilah suddenly realized that she had been staring at him the entire time he'd made his way down the stairs. She was sure he had watched her examine him. Unable to tear herself away from him, she inhaled his purely masculine scent.

He handed her a stack of clothes, his hand accidentally touching hers as he did so, creating a spark of electricity in her.

"There is a guest bathroom at the end of the hall. Fresh towels are in the linen closet," he said, his voice soft and gentle.

"Thank you." Delilah felt her voice tremble, probably making her sound like a star-struck teenager.

As she walked down the hall to find the bathroom, she heard the men whisper, but couldn't make out what they were saying. She glanced back before she entered the bathroom and found Samson looking at her. Those hazel-colored eyes had followed her every move.

Samson turned back to his friends when he saw her close the door behind her.

"You guys are such assholes sometimes. I don't know why I keep hanging out with you," Samson accused them before snatching his cell phone from the table. He speed dialed.

"It's 'cause you don't have any other friends." As so often, Ricky had to state the obvious.

His call was answered instantly.

"Carl, please bring the car 'round in fifteen minutes."

"Of course, sir."

"Thank you." He disconnected the call and turned back to the gang.

"So, looks like things are looking up," Thomas remarked pointedly, grinning from ear to ear.

"She's human, you idiots!" Samson cursed under his breath, but loud enough for the gang to hear.

And the hottest thing I've ever touched.

"Well, *we* didn't send her here." Ricky threw up his arms in defense. "So, who is she?"

"How the hell should I know? She almost broke my door down, asking for help."

"I can play that, if that's what turns you on." Samson doubted the stripper's claim and ignored her.

"Okay, everybody to the kitchen, and leave me alone with her for a few minutes."

"With me?" the stripper purred.

No chance. Samson frowned. "No, with the human woman, damn it."

"Okay, okay."

He watched them as they disappeared through the dining room and into the kitchen at the back of the house. Amaury's palm had already connected with the woman's ass. Samson shook his head. His friend hadn't met a woman yet he didn't like.

If he left the guys alone for too long, they would probably drink him out of house and home. He could see his blood supplies dwindling by the minute.

Samson went to the wet bar and poured two glasses of brandy. He had gotten used to the taste of brandy and liked the warming feeling it caused in his chest when he tossed back a shot. Apart from that, it would pass through his system without effect. Being able to deal with human drinks was helpful whenever he met with humans in social situations.

Vampires mingled freely with their human counterparts who were oblivious to them being different. Some people were merely considered more eccentric than others. San Francisco was the perfect place for their kind. Practically everybody was a little weird, and nobody really gave a damn.

Vampire high society in San Francisco operated very much in the same way as the human high society of the city did. There were balls, the opera season, the symphony, gallery openings, ballet performances, recitals, and premieres of plays to be attended. Everybody who was somebody wanted to be seen.

Tonight Samson had something to celebrate. His hydraulics were working again; in fact, even better than before. His cock had been as hard as granite when he'd pressed his body against hers and had kissed her. How it had happened, he didn't know and didn't care, but at least he knew he was back. Damn, it felt good!

Samson turned to the door when he heard her steps. She wore one of his sweatshirts and sweatpants. Both were too large for her, but she had turned the sleeves over several times to make them fit. Damn, she looked cute. She had towel dried her long dark hair.

"Please, come in. Sit here. Warm yourself."

She inched forward into the room, her movements hesitant, her eyes clearly watching him to determine if it was safe to approach. "Thank you."

"Brandy?"

He handed her one of the glasses he had poured earlier. She reached out. Samson brushed her fingers with his when she took the glass from him. Cold. She sat down on the armchair closest to the fire and took a sip from her glass.

"Apologies; I haven't introduced myself to you. I'm Samson Woodford."

She looked up at him, and he realized that he was still standing. He took a seat opposite her to be eyelevel with her.

"Delilah, Delilah Sheridan."

Delilah? A beautiful name for a beautiful woman. A beautiful *human* woman.

Off limits.

Would she be his undoing just as the biblical Delilah had been his namesake's downfall? Yet another good reason not to touch her again.

"I must apologize. I've been rude, and it's inexcusable."

Inexcusable, yes, but arousing nevertheless. He wanted to feel it again: the heat, the arousal, her body. Even now, dressed in shapeless clothes several sizes too large for her, she looked more tempting than any female vamp he'd ever set eyes on. Her scent teased his senses, threatening to overpower his good manners once more.

"It was a misunderstanding. Your friends explained."

She seemed to be warming up. Her cheeks looked rosier now, probably from the warmth of the fire and the brandy she was sipping. If he could only lick the droplets of brandy off her lips, maybe his body would be appeased.

"How's your foot? I'm so sorry."

"It'll be fine. Not to worry."

If you kiss it and make it better.

"Thank you for helping me."

"Goes without saying. Again, I'm truly sorry for having acted like a complete jerk." Samson ran his hand through his hair. He recognized his gesture for what it was: indicating his nervousness, when he should have no reason to feel such a strange emotion.

"Where are your friends?"

Was she afraid of being alone with him? He had obviously scared her. He couldn't blame her. Being alone with the man who'd attacked her, kissed her passionately and ground his erection against her, could not be a situation inspiring confidence. Could she see that his cock started twitching again, readying itself for her? Samson shifted in his chair and crossed his legs.

"I've sent them to the kitchen to get the party started. I assure you, they will hear you if you feel the need to call for help. There's not one among them who wouldn't come running to help a woman in need of protection."

"Oh." Her surprised look gave him pause, as did the sudden blush on her cheeks. Maybe she didn't feel threatened after all. "I'm sorry I interrupted your birthday party. I should be going."

She made a move to get up, but he stopped her. "I've called my driver. He'll be here in a few minutes to take you home."

Delilah made a feeble attempt at rejecting his offer. "That's really not necessary. I can take a taxi."

"Please, allow me. It's the least I can do after all I've put you through."

She gave him a gorgeous smile. "Thank you. That's very generous of you."

"Tell me what happened out there." He tilted his head toward the window, looking out at the darkness.

She swallowed hard. "Some guy came after me in an alley. I ran and slipped, and he grabbed me. And then I ran, and he followed me. He was so close behind me when you opened the door."

She breathed heavily, obviously reliving her ordeal as she spoke.

"Are you sure he wasn't just helping you up when you slipped?"

She shook her head. "I'm sure. I saw his face; he wasn't friendly. He was chasing me."

Had she overreacted? Maybe the whole incident was completely innocent. Women sometimes read things into a situation which weren't even there.

"Can you describe him to me?"

"I only saw him briefly, but he was big, Caucasian, maybe in his early forties. There was a scar on his cheek."

"Do you think you'd recognize him if you saw him again?"

She nodded confidently. "Definitely."

A strand of damp hair caught on her cheek, and he had to use all his restraint not to reach forward to brush it out of her face. She wouldn't appreciate any more physical advances from him, not even the tender touch he craved right now.

Tenderness wasn't something for which any vampire was known, least of all Samson. Lust, passion—yes, but tenderness? He rather savored this rare feeling.

He heard the front door open. Carl had a key to the house, as did his friends, except for Milo. A few seconds later Carl made himself known at the door to the living room.

"Sir, excuse the interruption, the car is ready when you need it."

They got up from their chairs, and Samson regretted that he hadn't told Carl to take his time. He had enjoyed the woman's company and would have loved to enjoy her for a little bit longer. Enjoy her? What the hell was he thinking? It was better if she left now, before he did something really stupid. It had to end here and now.

"I'll get my clothes. I left them in the bathroom."

"Don't worry, I'll have them delivered to you tomorrow after they've been washed and pressed."

Keeping her clothes for a little while longer would allow him to once again inhale her scent.

"But, that's not—"

"—necessary?" He smiled. "Please allow me."

It definitely wasn't necessary, but his smile was so charming, Delilah couldn't refuse him. It seemed he absolutely wanted to make it up to her.

"Carl, please drive Miss Sheridan home. She'll give you her address. And make sure you escort her to the door and wait until she is safely inside. I don't want anything to happen to her," he instructed his driver.

"Yes, sir."

She was flattered. He wanted to make sure she was safe.

"Thank you so much." She stretched out her hand. "And Happy Birthday."

Samson smiled and took her hand, but instead of shaking it, he slowly guided it to his mouth and kissed it lightly without breaking their eye contact. "Thank *you*."

She felt a hot wave course all the way from her hand to her torso. God, he was handsome and a perfect gentleman—when he wasn't assuming she was a stripper anyway. That was maybe something she could get past easily.

Delilah hesitantly turned away and followed the driver who led her outside, sheltering her under a large umbrella as he escorted her to a dark limousine. As she let herself fall back into the comfortable leather seats, she sighed. What a night! The thought of the thug who'd tried to attack her still made her shudder, but as a result of it she'd met the sexiest and most attractive man of her life, so who cared about the first part of the story?

"Where to, Miss Sheridan?"

She gave him the address of the corporate apartment. For a second she wondered whether she should ask him to drive her to a police station instead, but dismissed the idea. She didn't want to spend half the night at a police station reporting the assault when most likely they'd never catch the guy anyway.

"Ah, that's just a few blocks from here. We'll be there in two minutes, Miss."

Delilah settled back into the leather seats again and closed her eyes. Samson Woodford. Tall, dark, and handsome. The star in any woman's wet dream. She touched her lips, the same lips he'd crushed with his. The brandy had obliterated his taste on her tongue, but she could still feel his body pressed against hers and his erection urging her to surrender to him.

Surrender. Give up control. The notion frightened and excited her at the same time. Of course, it would never happen. She would never see him again.

THREE

The stripper wasn't nearly as hot as Delilah, but she would do. Samson hadn't had sex in months, and he wasn't going to wait a minute longer. He heard his friends laughing in the kitchen. Had the show already started without him?

He strode through the door into the kitchen and saw Amaury licking red liquid off the woman's boobs. Blood. Her nurse's uniform was open in the front. They were like little kids, playing with their food. Vampires didn't generally feed off other vampires, which didn't mean they didn't like to pretend. His friend had obviously dripped some of Samson's supplies onto the woman and was now enjoying licking it off her.

"Stop monopolizing her. It's my turn now," Ricky complained and shoved Amaury to the side. Amaury grinned devilishly but made space for Ricky by concentrating on only one of her breasts instead of both.

"Share?" Amaury's suggestion was met with approval.

With a grunt Ricky slid his tongue over the stripper's breast which his friend had just vacated. He licked the remaining drops of blood, before closing his lips over her nipple. The woman threw her head back and moaned loudly as both men sucked on her.

"Yes, baby." Not that the two guys needed the stripper's encouragement.

Milo and Thomas watched with little interest.

"Last time I checked, it was *my* birthday," Samson interrupted.

Both Ricky and Amaury let go of the stripper's boobs. All eyes were on Samson.

"So?" Ricky asked.

"What?" he retorted.

"Well, everything working again?" Ricky emphasized his question with an unmistakable movement of his loins.

"I guess I'll have to do a tryout." Samson pointed at the stripper.

"Here, baby, have a lick," she offered and turned toward Samson, but he shook his head.

"Upstairs for a private performance." For his first sexual act after nine months of abstinence he preferred a little privacy. Not that he would normally care if his friends saw him fuck her.

Samson gave the guys a stern look. "You stay here—and leave me some of the good stuff, for God's sake! I've got some celebrating to do."

Samson followed the stripper upstairs. He didn't even ask for her name. It didn't matter. All he needed was a willing body to plunge into. Damn, had he missed sex. Finally, he would satisfy his carnal desire and be normal again. This was the best birthday present he could imagine. Maybe birthdays didn't need to be depressing after all. This could be a lot of fun.

Holy hell, had the human woman turned him on. She could raise the dead, and she had. For all intents and purposes his cock had been dead the last nine months. He'd turned into a complete and utter grouch, always irritated, always tense. No longer. After tonight, things would be back to normal again. Sex wouldn't control his moods anymore. It would just again become a normal part of his life.

The stripper was a vampire, which meant there was no need to be gentle with her. He wouldn't have to hold back. Just as well, given how tightly wound up he was. When he shut the bedroom door behind them, she turned to him and started her seductive striptease. Nothing he hadn't seen before. His friends had dragged him to strip clubs often enough, and very little could really surprise him. In his more than two hundred years as a vampire, he'd seen it all.

Piece by piece she peeled out of her white nurse's uniform. First the blouse fell to the floor, then her short skirt. In sleek movements she released her stockings from her garters and rolled them down, one by one.

Her hands went to her boobs, squeezing them together to emphasize their size. Bazookas. Samson wasn't really into women with huge breasts. He preferred a cute ass instead, but tonight it didn't matter. One by one she peeled her heavy melon-sized assets out of the tiny half-cups of her bra. He noticed them sag without the support.

She opened her legs to give him a good view of her pussy through her crotch-less panties. Shaved. Not particularly his style, but it would do. He motioned her to spin around to get a look at her ass. Her g-string hid nothing.

Slowly, she wiggled out of the strings that doubled as an excuse for panties, finally standing in front of him in the nude.

She didn't interest him, other than as a woman who'd provide him with some much-needed release. He wanted to get it over with.

Samson glanced at his four-poster bed, an antique he'd acquired back in the days when it was considered contemporary furniture. No, he wouldn't do her in his bed. Bent over the chaise lounge would do just fine. He'd flip her over, get her from behind and fuck the living daylights out of her. At least he wouldn't have to look at her face and could pretend she was somebody else.

A beautiful face flashed in his mind. Delilah. He could pretend it was Delilah.

Right, that was the plan.

Perfect plan.

The stripper wouldn't object. After all, it was what she was paid for. She'd do whatever he wanted her to do.

Excellent.

There was only one problem with his brilliant plan.

His cock had gone completely limp.

Dead.

Absolutely fucking dead!

Not a single blood cell rushing to it to rouse him, not a one.

Shriveled up like a prune.

What the hell was going on? It had been working fine only a few minutes ago, and now, with a naked woman waiting to be fucked, he couldn't get it up!

Not even an inch, not half an inch.

No movement whatsoever.

"What are you waiting for, big boy?" she teased him and batted her mascara-crusted eyelashes at him.

Samson glared at her. Was she mocking him?

She took two steps toward him and placed her hand over the zipper of his pants.

"Oh." She let out a disappointed sigh.

With lightning speed, he grabbed her wrist and pulled her hand off him. He pushed her away from him with his next breath.

"Fuck!"

The guys downstairs toasted each other when they heard Samson's voice from upstairs. In the old Victorian voices carried well.

"Now, that's either been one hell of an orgasm," Ricky began.

"Fucking hell!" Samson's voice came from above.

A few choice expletives followed. The guys looked at each other.

"Or none at all," Amaury mused.

They raised their heads toward the ceiling to listen for more, when they heard heavy footsteps on the stairs.

"None at all," Thomas confirmed.

"Oh bugger." That was Milo. "Poor sod!"

Samson had already stormed into the kitchen and overheard Milo's comment. He was fuming and ready to kill somebody. Thomas protectively stepped in front of Milo.

"Fuck!" With the power of a sledgehammer Samson slammed his fist onto the counter, cracking the granite countertop. It split into several pieces.

His eyes glared red, and his fangs were extended. He could barely control his anger.

"Amaury, get him some blood, now," Ricky ordered calmly, though he didn't take his eyes off of Samson.

"I'm already on it." Amaury handed Samson a glass with the lukewarm red liquid.

"Here you go, Samson, take a drink. You need it."

Samson snatched the glass out of Amaury's hand and gulped it down in one go, then glared at Ricky.

"You'd better make it clear to that stripper that if she breathes one word about this to anybody, I'll snap her pretty little neck in half. Is that understood?"

The feral look in his eyes confirmed that he meant it.

Ricky nodded. "We'd better be leaving. Guys!" He waved them out of the kitchen.

Samson could hear them in the hallway as the stripper came down the stairs.

"But he had a hard-on when that woman was here. I saw it. In fact, it was hard to miss," Thomas whispered loud enough for Samson's sensitive hearing to pick it up.

"I guess it would have worked with her. Shame she's a mortal," Amaury whispered back. Then his tone changed. "Hey honey, since we've hired you for the entire night, how about you come back with me. I have something you could squeeze in between those big tits ..."

A giggle was the stripper's reply.

Seconds later they were gone. The place was quiet again. Too quiet.

Amaury was right. It would have worked with her. Samson was positive. So why couldn't he get it up with the stripper? She had a good body, she was willing.

But she wasn't Delilah. She didn't have her scent or her beauty. Damn, her lips had been so delicious, and that timid tongue he'd finally coaxed out of her. Heaven. What a kiss, and what a pliable little body with just the right curves. He knew it hadn't been one-sided. He'd sensed her arousal. And then, when he'd come down the stairs bringing her dry clothes, her eyes had examined every inch of his body, and she'd liked what she'd seen. In fact, she'd licked her lips even though he was sure she hadn't noticed she was doing it. In her eyes he'd seen heat.

Fuck, he wanted her. Whatever it took, he had to have her.

Samson dialed a number. The call was answered immediately.

"Dr. Drake's office. How may I help you?" Barbie doll purred like a kitten.

"Samson Woodford. I need to see Dr. Drake."

"We're fully booked tonight. How about tomorrow at 1 A.M?" she offered, her voice much cooler now. He'd never shown her any interest in all the times he'd visited the practice, and she'd finally given up wasting her charms on him. Just as well. Samson couldn't stand her or her sugary smile.

"I think you can do better than that. Considering the outrageous fee your office charges me, I don't care who you have to cancel." This was a true emergency.

"One moment." There was a click on the line and a short silence before she came back. "He can see you in half an hour."

"Thought so."

Samson hung up, snatched his coat off the rack and headed for the door. He could walk to Pacific Heights. The night air would clear his head. He sure needed it.

He stalked through the night, his collar turned up, his hands buried deep in his coat pockets. The rain had eased. The streets were still busy with humans. He ignored them. After midnight the streets generally became more deserted, and more vamps would be out. But it was still too early for that.

Samson didn't understand why this human woman had affected him the way she had. True, she had a nice body and she was pretty, but he was used to beautiful women. As one of the most eligible bachelors in the city, he always had his pick of the cream of the crop.

He'd dated lots of beautiful women. Maybe "dated" wasn't the right word—he'd had sex with lots of beautiful women pretty much whenever he felt like it. There was always a steady supply of willing females, all vampires of course, to satisfy his carnal desires in the hope that maybe he'd pick one of them as his mate.

But then he'd picked one, and all his troubles had started.

Samson always supported some of the local charities and went to two or three charity balls a year. At one such ball he'd spotted a new woman in town. He'd heard her name mentioned before, but he hadn't yet seen her or been introduced to her. The moment he'd seen the tall redhead amongst the crowd, he'd fallen head over heels—in lust.

Rumor had it that Ilona Hampstead had come from a large coven in Chicago and was very well connected in the vampire world. She was the quintessential socialite and had decided to make San Francisco her home.

She played hard to get, and Samson's hunting instincts took over instantly. It took him more than a month to get her into bed. During that time he'd continued fucking every available vampire female to get over his frustration. But finally he had his trophy and wasn't shy about showing her off at every society event. She could be seen on his arm whenever he was out on the town.

The society pages were full with pictures, showing them at event after event. Contrary to common belief, vampires did show up in pictures. In fact, many were rather photogenic.

Despite his need for privacy, Samson enjoyed the attention and admiration of his fellow vampires for landing a beauty like her. While she was what he would call a high-maintenance woman, she did have her charms. She expected exclusivity, and he hadn't objected.

Over the next few months he fell in love with her, and somehow she became part of his life. He'd been alone for far too long, and the thought of having a constant companion he could trust appealed to him. All his friends assured him how great they thought the two of them were together, all except Amaury who kept his feelings to himself.

Their sex life was excellent, they had the same circle of friends, the same standing in society. They were the perfect match.

It was only a matter of time until rumors of an impending blood-bond were circulating, and the thought of forming a permanent bond between them excited him. Something was missing in his life, and she could fill that void, so he'd made up his mind.

Samson pushed away the thoughts of that fateful night when his world had come crashing down in one sweep. The past had no place in his life now. Only the present did.

He wondered whether the fact that Delilah was human had something to do with how he reacted to her. While he'd certainly had sex with human women before, back in the day when he was still a little wilder and more untamed, none of those had really interested him, so little so, that he gave up sex with humans altogether.

Sex with humans always presented itself with more danger than the payoff was worth. Amaury didn't share his opinion on this subject. But Samson felt that he'd always had to hold back and had never been able to truly unleash his power and strength on them without potentially injuring them. In the end it had felt like too much of a chore to continue with. Vampire females were easier to deal with when it came to sex. They could keep up with the strength and ferocity of their sexual partners and didn't break easily.

Samson knew it was madness to pursue the human woman, but he was desperate. He needed sex, and he needed it soon, otherwise he'd turn into a dangerous beast whose moods could no longer be controlled. He would become a liability not only to himself but also to those around him. He had worked too hard in the last two centuries to let all his achievements go to pot because of sexual frustration.

Less than half an hour after he'd left his home, he reached his shrink's office and stormed in. Time was of the essence. He'd never felt this kind of urgency before.

"Thank you for seeing me on such short notice."

Dr. Drake raised an eyebrow. "What's so important that you couldn't wait till tomorrow?"

"Something's happened."

He looked at him and the shrink's eyes flickered. "Oh. Tell me who she is and what she did."

"That's just it. I have no idea." Samson let himself fall into the coffin, stretching out his full length on the soft cushion.

His doctor stared at him in disbelief. Samson had never in all his sessions used the coffin and always insisted on sitting in the chair. Or paced impatiently about the room.

As Samson recalled the incident with Delilah blow by blow, Drake listened intently, taking in every word. At the same time he observed his patient's demeanor, breathing, and movements.

"What does it mean?" Samson asked eagerly.

"Interesting. And you said the stripper left you cold after that woman aroused you?"

"Like I said. As if I'd stepped into a freezer."

"Interesting." He steepled his fingers in front of his face with his elbows resting on his armrests. "In our session last week you mentioned something about missing something. Can you elaborate on that?"

"Now?" Samson shot him an exasperated look.

"I think it's important in relation to this event."

Samson huffed. "Fine. I just—I can't really put my finger on it. There was this void, no matter what I did, how much I achieved. It always felt as if I wasn't complete, as if an important part of me was missing."

"In what way?"

"Emotionally." Samson let out a sigh. "There was this yearning for something that would finally complete me. I believed that the blood-bond would have filled that emptiness. It had to."

"The blood-bond with Ilona? I doubt it."

"What makes you say that, doc?"

"A blood-bond is but a formal culmination of what's already there. The bond already exists. The ritual only formalizes it. The ritual can't complete you, if you haven't already found this completion in your mate."

"I don't get it. The ritual creates the bond. That's what I've been taught."

Drake shook his head. "A common misconception amongst our kind."

"I didn't feel the bond with Ilona, not like you describe it. I thought it would be obvious later, after the ritual."

"Trust me; you're not the only one who believes it. But if you didn't feel the connection to her before, then you weren't meant to blood-bond with her. It's not something you can force. In any case, I now understand better why you reacted the way you did when things fell apart with Ilona. It all makes sense now."

Drake got up and walked to the coffin.

"Comfortable?"

Samson's head jerked around, and suddenly he realized where he was. He instantly jumped up, putting distance between him and the offending coffin. "What the...?" He was losing it, definitely losing it. Not only did he not understand Drake's cryptic explanation, nothing in his life made sense right now.

"Uh huh."

"What? Damn it, what?" Samson needed an answer. What was he paying the quack for?

"I think I know what might have happened. By being confronted with a vulnerable human, you've allowed yourself to become vulnerable again and stripped away your layer of protection. And as soon as you were with the vampire female, that wall went right back up, and your dick went down."

"Thanks for the colorful illustration. I suppose you're charging me for this insight?" As if he needed a mental picture of his limp dick.

"Hmh, a mortal. I mean, it could work. It's entirely possible. Many of our kind have sex with humans. Of course, it would be dangerous— for her, at least, but if you were careful ... Well, yes, it could work."

Dumbfounded, Samson looked at him. What was the quack waffling about? Was he talking to himself? "Damn it, doc, what the fuck do I do now?"

"Listen, and just once do what I suggest. Just once. Find that woman again and have sex with her. Get it out of your system. I promise you: once you've had her, your body will remember what it was like and go back to normal. Trust me on this."

"But she's a mortal. Don't you understand?" The good doctor couldn't have forgotten this small detail that easily.

"I fully understand the implications, trust me. I understand the danger she'll be in."

"I'm not so sure you do. If I lose control, I could seriously maim her, possibly kill her. In the heat of passion, caution is my least concern. There's no telling what I'll do. Bite her? Suck her dry? Kill her?" The very thought was revolting. "After such a long abstinence, how can I be sure I can control my body?"

"What is she to you? Nothing, just a mortal, a human. Take what you need from her, and get on with your life. You need to have sex with her as soon as possible; otherwise, this window of opportunity might close again. Don't you see? It's like she was sent to you to help you. Do it, and stop worrying about the consequences. Heck, she might even enjoy it, considering your reputation ..." Drake had the audacity to chuckle.

Samson nodded. Maybe he could do that. He knew what he was capable of in bed. He'd always lived up to his reputation. He would be careful, try to be gentle so she would enjoy it. He'd have to make sure of it. That was the least he could do, give her a night of ultimate pleasure, a nice memory. And if his doctor thought it was that simple, maybe it was. For once he had to agree with his shrink. Damn, he wanted nothing more than to fuck her senseless, and now he had the doctor's order to do so.

***

Delilah sank into the warm tub and wished she'd bought bubble bath. She was in the mood for a long, hot soak, and bubbles would have been perfect. Her body ached from the tension. She tried not to think of the thug who'd grabbed her, but instead concentrated on her unlikely rescuer.

She hadn't really been able to savor his kiss since she'd been too preoccupied with fighting him off. Too late. She'd already screwed it up. With her luck, he would be finding a much more willing participant in the stripper who had obviously been hired for that purpose. Men could be such pigs.

If she hadn't been such a prude, maybe he would have sent his friends and the stripper packing and ... Oh, what was she thinking?

Dreamer. Hopeless romantic.

Gorgeous men like him didn't exactly fall for boring little auditors like her. And besides, she was a little too starved for some affection. Okay, maybe a lot. So maybe she hadn't dated a lot lately, okay, maybe not even a little. God, who was she kidding? She hadn't been with a man in over a year, and even before that she had barely dated.

Why would some man like he even be interested in her? He probably had all kinds of women swooning over him. He looked like the perfect eligible bachelor. Yes, she had noticed that he didn't wear a wedding band. And he was obviously well off. Living in an old Victorian in Nob Hill with a private chauffeur and limousine to boot just reeked of money, old money. Even as a non-San Franciscan she knew that Nob Hill was a very expensive area.

She'd noticed the elegance of the home with its rich furnishings, the old paintings on the walls, the expensive crystal he had served her brandy in. The bathroom she had changed her clothes in had shown the same elegant style. It appeared he had either bought the house in excellent condition or painstakingly restored every period detail of it.

But the money didn't even figure into her attraction for him. The man oozed sex appeal from every pore of his body. And she would love to lick it off him, every single drop of it.

Great!

Now she wouldn't be able to sleep all night. She'd be thinking of Prince Charming. Prince Charming who had kissed her because he thought she was a stripper. Would he even have tried if he'd known she was only some little auditor?

Work. She'd completely forgotten about it. She wanted to look at the files she had remotely sent to her virtual server without John noticing. Reluctantly, Delilah stepped out of the bathtub and dried off. A few hours of computer work would probably make her tired after all so she could get some sleep before she was due back at the office in the morning.

While her laptop booted up, she peeked in the refrigerator. Except for the leftovers of last night's dinner, it was empty. She popped the carton into the microwave for a couple of minutes.

Delilah logged into her virtual file server and pulled down the files. Long rows and columns of transactions stared at her. This could take a while. She dug into the leftover pasta, eating it straight out of the container.

Three hours later she was beat. Her eyes were hurting, and even rubbing them every two minutes didn't make them stay open any longer. Time for bed.

But her well-deserved rest wouldn't come.

She tossed.

She turned.

She lay on her side, her back, her stomach.

No use. Sleep wasn't meant to be. A sound startled her. In the dark she couldn't see anything. But she felt a heavy weight on her body, pressing her into the mattress. Hands touching her. Lips kissing. A hot tongue licking her neck. Not unpleasant, but unknown.

A body pinning her down, strong thighs imprisoning her. A hand sweeping her hair clear of her neck. A mouth kissing her neck. Until suddenly …

No!

Sharp razor-like teeth latched onto her neck and pierced her skin. Warm liquid ran down her neck. But the sensation wasn't painful. It was … pleasurable!

Then a loud repetitive sound.

Beep! Beep! Beep! The alarm. It rudely woke her. She jerked up. It was day. Her hand went to her neck where she had sensed the bite, but her skin was smooth, perfect like always. No wound. No blood. Just another bad dream.

At least she had slept, if not much. Probably only three or four hours in all.

A look at the clock told her she had to get herself over to the office, and pronto. She had finally found several transactions in the files she'd reviewed overnight that didn't make sense. She wanted to confirm her assumptions by accessing the original paper documentation in the office. She had a hunch that she was onto something.

After a rushed shower, Delilah dressed quickly and glanced at the clothes she had come back in. Samson's clothes. At least she had a reason to see him again. Okay, it was called an excuse. She could bring the clothes back to him. Maybe he would invite her in. She would try to stop by tonight after work and hope he was home. Home alone.

A look out the window told her it was still drizzling; she would be better off taking her umbrella to work today. While she searched for it in the hallway closet, she heard a knock at the door.

"Who is it?"

"Gregory, from downstairs. Delivery for you."

She liked the fact the building had a concierge service. It made her feel safer, especially after the attack the night before.

Delilah opened the door and couldn't even see Gregory's face behind the two-dozen red roses he carried.

"Good morning, Miss Sheridan." The strong scent almost overwhelmed her. They were beautiful and as dark red as blood.

"Wow! Are you sure they're for me?" She knew nobody here. Besides, it wasn't her birthday or Valentine's Day or anything special like that.

"Yes; the gentleman who brought them gave me your name. And this." He handed her a hanger with clothes wrapped in plastic. Her clothes.

Samson. How had he gotten her clothes cleaned and dried so fast? Was Samson downstairs? Her heart fluttered excitedly and her hands suddenly felt clammy.

"I believe there's a card with the flowers." Gregory sat the vase with the flowers on the side table in the foyer before he left.

"Thank you."

After she shut the door and hung her clothes in the wardrobe, she looked for the card. Why would he send her two-dozen red roses?

The card was handwritten in neat old-fashioned letters.

My sincerest apologies for last night. Will you do me the honor and join me for the theater tonight? May I pick you up at 7pm? Samson Woodford. P.S. My assistant Oliver is waiting downstairs for your response.

The butterflies in her stomach started to dance. She had to sit down. He was asking her out.

On a date.

A date!

What should she do first? Go downstairs and talk to his assistant, or finish getting ready for work? Oh God, she was flustered. The butterflies in her stomach were dancing. They would do so all day, she was sure.

A young man was patiently waiting in the lobby of the building.

"Miss Sheridan?"

"Are you Mr. Woodford's assistant? Oliver?" He was dressed in a dark formal business suit, just like Samson's driver the night before.

"Yes, Ma'am. He has asked me to wait for your response."

Her heart fluttered. "Please tell Mr. Woodford I'd be delighted to join him tonight."

"He will be happy to hear that."

She nodded at him and went to the double doors to make her way to work.

"Uh, Miss Sheridan?"

She turned, curious to see what else he wanted. "Yes?"

"Mr. Woodford has also asked me to offer to drive you wherever you might need to go."

"Oh, that's not necessary. I'm just going to work. It's not far. Thank you."

"Please allow me. The limousine is right outside."

He gallantly opened the door for her and led her to the car. Why was Samson spoiling her like that? Or was she dreaming again? This couldn't possibly be real.

Delilah gave Oliver the address of the office and settled in for a smooth ride. The noise of the city didn't penetrate the car. It was almost like a little safe haven. What luxury. Somewhere, sometime she would have to pay for this luxury—in a cosmic kind of way. Nothing was free. Not in her world.

***

Even though it was already daylight outside, Samson was still up. He was tired, but he didn't want to sleep yet. He had to know if Delilah would accept his invitation to the theater.

After getting back from Dr. Drake's office, he'd spent the rest of the night reviewing reports from the different branches of his company, Scanguards.

When he'd been turned into a vampire at the start of the nineteenth century, he'd realized very quickly that even a vampire needed money to live. On a whim, he'd started hiring himself out to protect travelers at night. It turned out security was a profitable enterprise. It also meant there was always a large supply of lowlifes and criminals from which he could feed, while protecting a wealthy traveler or an expensive shipment.

Later, he'd turned his one-man enterprise into a company and hired other likeminded vampires. As a vampire, he finally achieved the success which had eluded him as a human. It was ironic that, as a vampire, he was able to protect the very lives so many of his fellow vampires wanted to destroy. It was Samson's way of preserving his humanity.

Now his nationwide firm provided security guards and bodyguards to corporations, celebrities, foreign dignitaries, and other individuals. While he'd kept the company's headquarters in New York, he'd decided to withdraw to San Francisco to live a quieter and more normal life. As normal as life could be for a vampire.

Many of his employees were fellow vampires, mostly working as night guards or bodyguards. He'd groomed several human managers who became the daytime face of Scanguards and dealt with the public.

Very few of his human employees knew, or had ever seen, Samson. And Samson wouldn't recognize many of his human employees if he met them on the street. He liked it that way.

He kept out of the day-to-day running of the business, but liked to keep up to date by reviewing all important reports from the various branches. He would only intervene if things started sliding. There were always little problems somewhere, but he trusted his managers to take care of the small stuff. He wasn't a micro manager.

Ricky, Amaury, and Thomas all worked for him. Ricky was in charge of vampire recruitment, Amaury dealt with real estate, and Thomas was chief of IT. Their friendship didn't get in the way of work—well, most of the time at least. Milo had started hanging out with them since he and Thomas had become an item almost nine months earlier.

The blackout shades in Samson's lavishly decorated bedroom were drawn as he sat on his four-poster bed and flipped through the reports, every few seconds glancing at his cell phone. He'd sent his assistant Oliver off to Delilah's apartment over half an hour ago and had still not received a text message back.

Oliver was human and acted as his eyes and ears during the day. He was one of the very few humans who knew Samson was a vampire. Samson had saved Oliver from a life of crime, and his prodigy repaid him with loyalty and dedication.

Carl, who was a vampire, was his driver, butler and personal assistant at night. Samson's personal employees earned more than many managers in large companies did. It wasn't that he was extraordinarily generous, but he knew human and vampire natures very well. If staff were paid extremely well and treated even better, they were loyal. And loyalty was paramount to him.

What took Oliver so long? Was Delilah not up yet? He looked at the antique clock on the mantle. It was past eight o'clock, and he was getting extremely tired. As a vampire he was able to stay up during daytime, but at a somewhat diminished capacity. His senses weren't as sharp, and his energy level was lower than normal. Of course he couldn't go outside, because the rays of the sun would burn him to ash. But he could move about the house as long as no direct sunlight touched him.

A humming sound alerted him to a message on his cell phone. He looked at it.

She said yes.

Yes! Yes! Yes!

Samson couldn't remember when he'd last been so excited about seeing a woman. Or excited about anything for that matter. He'd make sure it would be perfect. How he wanted her! He could already imagine the things he'd do with her, the way he'd touch her, how he would plunge into her until he was completely spent. This would be his real, if belated, birthday present to himself.

FOUR

Delilah shook her head, trying to contain her irritation over John's reluctance to comply with her request.

"No, the electronic records won't suffice. I'll need the backup documents for these transactions," she insisted and looked up at John who hovered over her desk, a gesture she interpreted as intimidation. It wouldn't work on her, despite the fact that she hated it when people she barely knew got so close to her.

The training she'd had on how to deal with difficult clients taught her not to show her emotions on her face. While she watched sweat accumulate on John's brow, her own face remained unwavering, just the way she'd practiced often enough in front of the mirror. She didn't need to see her reflection; she knew exactly how her facial muscles felt when she did it right.

"We don't have them here. They're all at a storage facility down at Oyster Point."

Not a good enough excuse. Not that any excuse would work on her.

"Where's Oyster Point?"

"In South San Francisco."

"Well, that shouldn't be too much trouble then. Get them up here this afternoon."

Even though she wasn't familiar with San Francisco and its surroundings, she knew where South San Francisco was, since she had passed it on her way from the airport. It couldn't take longer than twenty minutes to drive to the facility in Oyster Point.

"I'll request them, but I can't guarantee that they'll send them up this afternoon. It's an outside vendor we use for this, and I don't have any influence over how fast they work." He shrugged his shoulders.

"Fine. Just get them here. If they're not here this afternoon, I'll want them tomorrow morning first thing. It's already Friday tomorrow, and I really don't want to spend my entire weekend in the office. I suppose you don't either."

She gave him another determined look, making sure her unyielding mask was still in place. If she had to threaten him with weekend work, so be it. It didn't mean she had any intention of working this weekend. She was hoping to do some sightseeing on Saturday and Sunday. The plan was to wrap up the audit on Wednesday the following week. She was confident that by then she would have solved the mystery hidden in the books.

What she had discovered so far was promising. It appeared somebody was manipulating depreciation entries in the books. She trusted her gut feeling which told her something was fishy. It was done very methodically, and it appeared that it had been going on for close to a year.

Only a year—strange. Delilah looked at the dates on her screen again and confirmed the time frame. Why would records for the current and previous year already be in storage? Most companies would only send records older than three years into storage. She didn't like the sound of it, not a bit.

The reason she wanted the original documents from John was because she needed to see who had first initiated and then authorized the transactions. The computer entries didn't show it. Keying was done by low-level employees, approval was generally a level or two higher.

Delilah was fully aware that even though it was strictly against company policy, many employees would share logons when they were in a crunch and things had to get done. Therefore, while she knew whose logon had approved the transactions in question, only the original paperwork would confirm who was really behind it. And whoever was initiating these transactions was going to be in trouble once she wrote up her report.

"I'm going for some *dim sum* up in Chinatown. Do you want to tag along?" John's offer came out of the blue.

Delilah was reminded that the night before she hadn't gotten to enjoy her Chinese takeout and now felt a craving for it. She gave him a grateful smile.

"Actually, that'd be great. I'm starving."

"Let's go then."

She snatched her jacket off the coatrack near the door and followed John out. Even though she'd already been in San Francisco for almost a week, this was the first time John had asked her to join him for lunch. All other days he'd always seemed in a hurry during lunch break, rushing out of the office as soon as she left for her own break.

Dim sum would be a welcome distraction and hopefully make the day go by faster. She couldn't wait till seven o'clock and her date with Samson. What would she wear? She hadn't really brought anything dressy. Maybe she could stop by a boutique after work and buy something suitable?

She walked up the steep streets into Chinatown next to John. He seemed to be quite fit, even though he didn't look it.

"Have you had *dim sum* before?" he asked.

"Sure. I have it all the time in New York. But I think our Chinatown is not quite as large as yours." She figured she should make small talk with him.

"I read somewhere that San Francisco's Chinatown is the largest in the US. Not sure if it's true, but it might be." John seemed surprisingly chatty. "Lots of shops here, and if you go a few blocks up toward Stockton, there are actually some quite decent food shops. Down here it's mostly knick knacks and souvenirs. Tons of tourists."

"Yeah, I noticed. I've been through here at midday before, and the sidewalks were so packed you couldn't even get through." She looked down Grant Street, the main drag in Chinatown. The place was teeming with tourists and merchants.

"It'll get even more packed this weekend. It's the Chinese New Year, and there'll be a parade on Saturday night. You might want to watch it. I normally go with the kids. They love it. There'll be a dragon and all kinds of fun stuff."

"Maybe I'll check it out."

She followed John into the tacky-looking Chinese restaurant. It was busy with mostly Chinese customers, which was always a good sign. The hostess led them to a table. The red tablecloth was covered with a glass plate which she wiped down quickly.

"To drink?" She was curt almost to the point of being unfriendly.

"Tea," both of them said in unison.

"I bet you can't wait to get back home and sleep in your own bed," John mused.

Delilah smiled. "Absolutely." *Not.* After meeting Samson, she wished she could extend her stay to see where things would lead. But it wasn't in the cards.

"Must be tough to constantly have to travel for your job."

Delilah nodded absentmindedly. She had never thought it tough. Actually, it was a blessing to be gone so much. At least she wouldn't have to admit how lonely she really was in her little apartment in New York. When she was on the road and staying it hotels, she could pretend to others what an interesting life she had. Nobody would get to know her well enough to see through her and find out just how little she had to go back to.

She had no brothers or sisters, well, not anymore anyway. Her mother had had trouble conceiving, and Delilah had begged to have a little brother or sister for years when she was a child. When her mother had suddenly gotten pregnant again at the age of almost thirty-five, the entire family had been ecstatic. A little over a year later their world had collapsed, and her baby brother was gone. Her mother was never the same after that.

Her father was almost ten years older than her mother and was now in a home for Alzheimer's patients. He didn't recognize her any longer, and while she took care of him financially, she'd stopped seeing him. She was just a stranger to him, and it hurt her every time she saw him.

Her mother had died two years earlier. It was a blessing that her father didn't know. Alzheimer's had already claimed too much of his conscious self for him to know that his beloved wife of over forty years had died of cancer. The doctors kept her up to date on his condition on a regular basis, but there was nothing else she could do.

He seemed comfortable, and the home she had chosen for him was one of the best. No member of her once-happy family was left.

"Delilah, did you want some of these?" John pulled her out of her depressing memories.

The waitress showed them a platter with little dumplings.

"Oh, sure."

She dipped a dumpling into the soy sauce and devoured it. "This is delicious. Do you come here often?"

"At least once or twice a week. It's pretty convenient for the office. My wife hates Chinese food, so I normally get my fix during the week," he admitted and laughed. "Oh, which reminds me: my wife wanted to know what time I'm going to be home for dinner tonight. She was going to cook her special dish."

Delilah caught John's oddly curious look.

"Well, I was planning to leave the office at five o'clock tonight."

She could probably get some clothes shopping done in less than half an hour, then …

"Five o'clock. So early? Any plans?" His question was so casual, she almost didn't hear it.

… then take a shower, shave her legs, do her toenails …

"Actually I'm going to the theater." Maybe pink for the toenails? Was red too aggressive?

"That sounds like fun. What are you going to see?"

She loved the stage and always got excited when she knew she'd see a play. But this time the reason for her excitement had a different name.

"I don't really know." Delilah averted her eyes, afraid they would reflect her excitement about the upcoming date. She didn't really care what she was going to see, as long as the man sitting next to her was Samson Woodford.

"What do you mean, you don't know?" John looked confused.

"An acquaintance is taking me out, and I completely forgot to ask which play we're seeing." An acquaintance—she wanted Samson to be much more than that, at least an acquaintance she could have sex with. Lots of sex. Lots of good sex. If he was as good in bed as his kiss promised, there'd be lots of great sex.

Was it getting warmer in the restaurant?

"Too spicy?"

"What?" Delilah lifted her gaze to meet John's inquisitive stare.

"The dumpling." He pointed at her plate.

"Yes, yes. I think I put too much hot sauce on it."

It was probably safer not to think of sex anymore while out for lunch with John. Or in the office during the rest of the day for that matter, especially since there was no air conditioning in the building.

***

Samson wished he could see his reflection in a mirror, but since vampires didn't reflect in mirrors, he had to make do with Carl.

"How do I look?"

"Dashing." Carl wasn't a vampire of many words.

Samson fiddled with his shirt collar. "Too much? Shall I change into something less flashy?"

He wore dark slacks and a simple white shirt with the top two buttons open, no tie. He wanted to look casual, but not too casual. He fidgeted with his shirt collar again.

"If I didn't know any better, sir, I'd say you were nervous about tonight."

"Have you ever seen me nervous, Carl?" Samson deflected.

"Never, sir. Not a single time in the almost eighteen years I've been working for you. You are confidence personified. Which makes this rather strange, if I may say so."

Point taken.

"Has it been that long already?"

"Indeed."

Samson remembered the dark October night well when he'd had made the fateful decision. Save Carl or let him die?

"Do you regret it?" Samson did. He regretted having subjected Carl to a life as a vampire, but back then, he'd only had a few seconds to make a decision. Carl's attackers had left him bleeding to death. Had he not turned him, Carl's life would have been over.

Carl raised his eyebrows. "Regret that I work for a gentleman?"

Shaking his head, he replied, "I'm no saint. We both know that."

"None of us are. But you are a gentleman. I believe your mother, God rest her soul, would be proud of you. She must have been an extraordinary woman, having raised a son like you."

Samson smiled. "You would have liked her." He paused. "Carl, have you ever thought of doing anything else? I mean, did you never want to start a different career?"

"There's nothing I'd rather do than work for you."

"I'm glad to hear that. You know, I would be quite lost without you. My household and my life would be a mess if I didn't have you."

"Thank you. Shall we, sir?" Carl motioned toward the front door; as always, trying to keep him on schedule.

"And you're sure this is fine?" Samson felt his forehead crease in a frown.

"Yes, sir." Carl nodded and helped him into his coat, before opening the front door. The rain had stopped again, and it looked like it would be dry, for a few hours at least.

As Samson settled into the back seat of the limousine, he wondered how he should play it. Casual and sweet? Aggressive? Sexy? Damn, he had no idea what would work on her. Apart from her name and where she lived, he knew absolutely nothing about her. Well, Oliver had also reported where she worked, but he had no idea what she actually did. The building where Oliver had dropped her off housed more than twenty different companies. Maybe he should have instructed Oliver to run a background check on her so he would be armed with a little bit more than his charm to get through the evening. And get her into bed. His bed.

He knew he had to be careful since he'd already screwed up the night before, acting like a jerk. Maybe a sweet-and-charming approach would work best with her. He would try that first. Light conversation, lots of laughter, nothing heavy. It was a good plan. He could do that.

The ride was short, almost too short for him to collect his thoughts. He stopped Carl from getting out of the car.

"Thanks, Carl; I'll get her myself."

Samson stepped into the dark street and went into the lobby. He loved the winter months, because sunsets were early, and it gave him longer nights and more opportunities to be outside.

The lobby attendant announced him on the phone. Samson waited patiently, settling in for at least a ten-minute wait. He knew what women were like. Certainly the vamp ladies he'd dated had always left him waiting, as if it was an unwritten rule never to be ready on time. Human women surely were no different.

The lobby was adorned with a large mural, and he admired the artwork. He hadn't been here for a long time. His company owned a couple of condos in the building. They used them for out-of-town business associates, but he never visited any of them himself. Amaury was in charge of dealing with all of his real estate holdings.

"Samson."

Delilah's voice made him turn on his heels. She had taken less than two minutes to come down. Was this really her? She looked even more beautiful than he remembered. The night before she'd been soaked, but now her long dark hair hung from her head like silk. Her face was clear, and if she used any makeup, it wasn't visible. Her green eyes sparkled. She wore a black swinging skirt and a violet top tied on one side. He couldn't wait to untie that knot and unwrap her from it.

"Delilah." He took her hand to his mouth, planting a soft kiss on it. "Thank you for accepting my invitation." Her scent engulfed him instantly and wrapped itself around him like a cocoon.

She gave him a ravishing smile. "I'm glad to see you."

"Shall we?" He offered her his left arm, and she hooked her hand in it. Wanting to feel more of her, he placed his right hand over her fingers, pressing down gently. She was soft and warm. Tonight those fingers would touch him in all the right places, just as his hands would learn every inch of her body.

"What are we going to see?"

Samson had no idea. He'd asked Oliver to get him the best tickets to whatever was considered the best show in town and had completely forgotten to ask him what it was. He had put the tickets into his jacket pocket without even looking at them.

"It's a surprise."

"I love surprises."

She would get plenty of surprises with him. Hopefully all good ones.

He helped her into the car and addressed his driver.

"We're ready, Carl."

As the limousine pulled away from the curb, Samson opened the bar in front of him. He pulled out a small platter with sushi and canapés.

"I figured you probably haven't eaten yet."

"Thank you; that's so thoughtful of you." Delilah blushed, and the color looked good on her. Maybe he could find other ways to make the blood rush to her cheeks.

"Champagne?" He was already opening a bottle and poured two glasses, handing her one. He touched his glass to hers and looked at her.

"So I may make a better impression on you tonight than I did last night." He gazed into her eyes.

"You already have."

Her admission was unexpected. Could he now go straight from sweet and charming to sexy and smoldering? One portion of his anatomy certainly put a "yes!" vote in already.

Down boy!

Samson shifted in his seat and pointed at the canapés. "What would you like?"

She stretched her hand toward a piece of sushi. He shook his head, took the piece, and guided it to her mouth.

"Open," he urged her in a soft voice.

She obeyed instantly, and he gently placed the small piece of sushi into her mouth. His finger briefly brushed her lips as he did so, and it wasn't accidental. She swallowed.

"Aren't you going to have any?"

"No; I've had an early business dinner," he lied, "and besides, I'd much rather feed you." Not that he wouldn't have loved the idea of her feeding him, but sushi wasn't exactly on his menu. No solid foods for a vampire. He noticed desire growing in her eyes as he looked at her mouth. He imagined those lips on his naked skin. How would his skin react to her mouth brushing over him?

"May I have another one?" Her voice was smooth, silky, temping. Did she know this was foreplay?

He placed a canapé into her mouth and provocatively let his finger linger at her lips until she responded to him by closing them over the tip of his finger. In slow motion he withdrew his finger and let it slide over her closed lips.

He could already feel his body respond to her. Ten more seconds, and she would give him another raging erection.

"Do you like my choice of food?" It wasn't his choice of food he wanted to discuss. "I could get you anything else you wanted." The question of what else was implied. Preferably a portion of his body. Preferably the one which was currently begging for more space in his pants.

"No, this is quite perfect." Her eyes roamed over his body, sending a tingle of anticipation into his loins.

"More?" How many hours would she be able to keep up with him before she'd collapse in his arms, naked, hot, and exhausted?

"I'm quite hungry today." She was playing his game, and he liked it. There was nothing shy about her. She showed him what she wanted and wasn't embarrassed about it. A sign of a strong woman. He couldn't wait to find out what she would be like in bed—if he ever made it to a bed with her and didn't fall over her someplace else. Which was a definite possibility.

"I guess I'll have to keep feeding you. I don't want anybody to start a rumor that I don't feed my guests. Nobody is going to leave my company hungry. For anything."

She responded by licking her lower lip, and it looked like she didn't even know she was doing it. His gaze was involuntarily pulled to her breasts as soon as his peripheral vision noticed a change in them: her nipples had hardened and were pressing through the fabric of her top. His cock responded in kind and tilted in her direction.

When he gave her the next canapé she held onto his hand, and as soon as she'd swallowed the food, her lips opened again. Slowly and deliberately she pulled one of his fingers into her mouth and licked it clean. He drew in his breath. She sucked on him gently, and her eyes locked with his.

She did the same with the next finger. Samson felt his cock strain toward her, asking to be next in line to feel those luscious lips. When she released him, he traced her lips with his moist finger.

"Delicious." Delilah shifted, changing the way she crossed her legs, drawing his eyes to her smooth calves. He admired the gentle curves of her flawless flesh.

He wanted nothing more than to kiss her, but he had to wait. For now he wanted to bring her body temperature to boiling point and enjoy the view of her hardened nipples. Unfortunately, it was his own body temperature which was rising. Maybe he should ask Carl to turn on the air conditioning.

The ride to the theater was too short, especially since he was having so much fun. How he would make it through the two-hour performance he had no idea. He was in the right mood to give the tickets to the next passerby and take her back to his house immediately. But he was worried that his uncontrolled desire for her would scare her and make her retreat. He couldn't risk it.

"Sir, we're here." He heard Carl's voice as the car came to a stop.

Delilah watched Samson intently as he helped her out of the car like the perfect gentleman, almost as if the few minutes of erotic play hadn't happened. He was deadly sexy, and the touch of his fingers on her lips had aroused her more than she would want anybody to know. If a simple touch did that to her, she'd be heading for the abyss shortly.

She could barely believe how bold she'd been in the car. She wasn't normally the type to go after a man, but all her inhibitions had gone out the window as soon as he'd fed her the first piece of sushi. Potentially the whole situation could have been embarrassing, especially if he had withdrawn his fingers. But he hadn't. He'd participated.

On the marquee of the theater she saw that the play they'd come to see was the musical *Wicked*. She'd heard good things about it and had wanted to see it when she was back in New York.

As Samson led her through the crowd, his hand rested possessively on the small of her back. It was a commonly accepted gesture for a date, but after what they'd shared in the car, it felt more sexual than anything—and she didn't want to change a thing about it.

They were seated in the middle rows of the orchestra with a great view of the stage. His shoulder brushed against hers as they sat next to each other. He reached over to hand her the playbill. Their hands touched as she took it, and it sent a wave of fire through her core, low in her belly. She'd never met anybody who could send such sensations through her body with a simple touch. She couldn't look at him for fear he would see in her face how aroused she was.

"I hope you'll enjoy this." She felt his whisper close to her ear and wasn't sure he meant the show. Or was she the only one with a one-track mind? She turned to him to try to read him. No, she wasn't the only one. The wicked glint in his eyes confirmed it.

"I think I will."

His mouth was only a couple of inches from hers. How easy it would be to kiss him.

"I'll make sure of that." She would hold him to his promise.

The house lights dimmed, and slowly the chatter of the audience ceased. Everything went quiet in anticipation. She could almost feel the electricity prickle between them, when she suddenly felt his hand on hers. The sexiest man she'd ever met was holding hands with her in the dark of a theater. The touch conjured up images of hot, steamy sex, and she felt her body temperature spike as a result.

Samson kept holding her hand during the entire first act and only released it when there was occasion to clap. She noticed him looking at her from the side several times, but she didn't return his gaze. She was too worried her good manners would desert her like the rats leaving a sinking ship, and she'd jump his bones right there in the theater. She didn't need or want an audience for what she wanted to do with him.

When the lights came up for intermission, he let go of her hand.

"It's gotten warm in here." She fanned her face with her hands.

"Downright hot. Would you like a drink?"

What she needed was to splash some water onto her face before she spontaneously combusted. Or maybe a cold shower to douse the flames she felt shooting through her belly.

"That'd be great."

They got up and made their way through the crowd toward the bar. Samson was right behind her, his hand on her waist guiding her in front of him. When she reached a bottleneck at the door, she stopped abruptly, unable to get any further. His body suddenly molded itself to her back. His chest felt strong and hard, and his hand, which had rested on her waist, now slid around her stomach to hold her close to him.

"I guess we're stuck here for a little while." Despite his comment, he appeared unconcerned about the hold-up. His hand lay intimately low on her stomach, his fingers leisurely tracing the seam of her panties through her skirt. Subtly she pressed her body into his and felt the rigid outline of his erection against her lower back. His hand on her stomach held her in place so she couldn't rub herself against him any further. Had he noticed what she was doing?

"Delilah, we'll have to be patient." She felt his warm breath on her neck and his lips almost brush her skin. His words told her he'd caught her naughty movements and knew exactly what she was up to. Why didn't she feel embarrassed about her brazen behavior?

"Patience is overrated, don't you think?" Her retort elicited a chuckle from him, but he didn't release her from the intimate position she was locked into. On the contrary, it felt as if he pulled her closer into him, or was his erection growing? His fingers seemed to slip slightly lower, provocatively pressing against the top of her mound.

"I'm sorry, are you getting too hot?" His voice sounded almost innocent, when his hands were anything but.

"I like it warm."

None of the other theatergoers could see his response to her admission, but Delilah could feel it.

Samson slowly rubbed his thumb against her sex, the thin fabric of her skirt barely providing any barrier. His nostrils picked up her scent: the sweet scent of her arousal. She surprised him with how far she let him go, and if there weren't that many witnesses around, he'd fuck her right here, standing up.

All it would take was to hitch up her skirt, strip her of her panties, and she'd be his for the taking. Without even touching her, he knew she was already wet—wet enough for him to slide in without resistance. What if he pulled her aside and found a dark corner somewhere in the theater? Would she be game?

Before he could form a plan, the bottleneck dissolved, and he had to release her from his intimate embrace. They moved into the bar.

"What would you like?" He had a hard time making his voice sound normal again. In his own ears he could only hear the lust and desire his body had difficulty getting under control.

"Just some water, please." As he ordered, Delilah excused herself to find the ladies room and left him at the bar. His eyes followed her. She had curves in all the right places. How could a woman like her still be unattached? Were all those human guys out there blind? Just as well; at least he wouldn't have to fight off the competition. She would be all his soon—very soon.

"Wishful thinking." The voice behind him was one he hadn't wanted to hear ever again. Should he ignore her and leave?

"I said—" she repeated.

Samson spun around. "I heard you the first time, Ilona." His voice had the razor-sharp edge to it which he always employed when dealing with enemies. He glanced at the tall beauty in front of him. She was dressed to the nines, her long red hair artfully draped over her naked shoulders. The tight corset of her dress accentuated her breasts, and the dark green of her gown complemented the color of her hair and skin. She was stunning, but he wasn't fooled, not anymore.

"A little tense, are we?"

"None of your concern. Shouldn't you be heading for a costume party somewhere in Hell?" Samson took the bottle of water the bartender handed him and paid.

"Definitely tense. So it's true then?"

He gave her a sharp look, unwilling to even guess where she was headed with her insinuation.

"Go play your games with somebody else. You should have realized by now that I don't care for your company."

"You once did. In fact, you craved it. Don't you remember?"

Oh, he remembered. "I don't recall much about that time, given that I was temporarily insane back then. So why don't you move along. There must be plenty of rich guys in town you haven't bedded yet. Or have you slept your way through them already?"

"At least they can get it up." Her light tone belied the venom in her words. She sipped nonchalantly on her glass of wine.

Samson hissed under his breath. How he would have liked to snap her little neck. He could almost hear the sound it would make when breaking.

"You should be careful about the lies you're spreading," he warned her in a low tone. "Lies can kill people. Even people like you."

"They're not called lies if they're true. So, it looks like I broke you."

Damn Holly! She really spread gossip faster than anybody he knew.

"Don't flatter yourself. It doesn't become you." He never wanted to feel Ilona's touch again. The very thought disgusted him. How he could have ever enjoyed her evil hands on him, was a mystery.

"If you come back to me I can fix you," she hummed, obviously convinced of her seductive powers.

"You can't fix what's not broken." True. He had been broken only a day ago, but now, thanks to Delilah, everything was working just fine.

"Liar."

"I wouldn't touch you if you were the last woman on earth. So, leave me alone."

Samson turned, and she put a hand on his arm. He whipped back around and shot her a venomous look, jerking his arm away from her.

"Darling, sorry to keep you so long," Delilah's voice suddenly chirped next to him. He felt her warm hand on his arm, instantly relaxing his taut muscles. Gratefully, he turned to her.

"Here's your water, sweetness." In the corner of his eye he could see Ilona's surprise. She stood there frozen as she watched them, while he placed his hand on Delilah's back to pull her away.

"Thank you." He kept his voice low as they walked through the bar area.

"It looked like you wanted to get away from her." There was an unspoken question in her voice.

"I did."

"Somebody you know?"

Should he tell her? It wouldn't do any harm. "Ex-girlfriend."

"Oh. She's beautiful." Delilah sounded deflated.

"Only on the outside." Samson knew what she felt. Women, whether humans or vampires, were predictable in one way: they always compared themselves to other women. He had to stop her from worrying about it. He pulled her into a corner and looked deep into her eyes.

"You are more beautiful than any woman I've ever met. And if there weren't so many people here, I'd show you just how desirable I think you are."

His fingers stroked her cheek softly. He wanted to kiss her, but not here, because he knew he wouldn't be able to stop once he started. Instead he pulled her hand to his mouth and kissed her fingertips. Her skin was warm and sweet. He nipped at her index finger and pulled it between his lips, closing around it and letting his tongue play with it.

"Samson ..." Her voice was but a whisper.

He watched her as she closed her eyes and inhaled deeply, until he let go of her finger. He was more than satisfied with the effect he had on her. She responded to each of his seductive movements, and he wasn't even using vampire mind control. That's right, he wasn't! He hadn't even noticed. Every interaction with her had been completely and utterly devoid of any mind control on his part.

Vampires used mind control to place thoughts in their intended victims' minds to allow them to approach them and feed from them, and then later, to wipe their memories clear so they wouldn't have any recollection of the events.

Since Samson didn't feed off humans unless it was an emergency, he rarely had the need to use mind control. He drank blood acquired through a blood bank and was content with it. It wasn't quite the same as the warm, pulsating blood coming straight from a human's veins, but it was sufficient to satisfy his hunger and nourish his body.

Of course, when he'd been a new vampire, and there had been no such thing as a blood bank, he had taken blood directly from humans. Sometimes he'd taken too much and had accidentally killed humans. Over the years he'd learned to control himself better. When blood had become more readily available on the commercial market, he'd switched to it.

He hadn't used mind control in a while, and it hadn't even occurred to him to use it on Delilah, though he wanted to make absolutely sure to have sex with her tonight. Using mind control would have ensured him that.

But her response to his touch had given him absolute certainty of the fact that he didn't need to use his vampire skills on her.

"We should go back to our seats. We don't want to miss the second act."

"No, we wouldn't want to miss anything." The husky tone in her voice told him she wasn't talking about the play. Samson felt his pants tighten instantly. This was not the time to have another erection, but alas, he had no control over it. Better to hide in the dark of the theater.

He looked at her from the side as they quietly watched the second act. He wanted her so much, it was painful to wait. In the dark, he reached for her hand and found her willingly accepting his touch. He needed more. It was stupid to feel like a schoolboy, fumbling in the dark, but he couldn't help himself. Hesitantly he guided her hand to his thigh where he left it. Would she pull it back?

He couldn't follow the action on the stage when there was a much more exciting mystery unraveling right next to him. As he let go of her hand, his body was tense. It was the moment where she was free to pull her hand away, or to leave it where it was, burning through the fabric of his pants, sending shockwaves of heat through his body.

Delilah did neither—her hand didn't pull away, but it didn't stay where he'd placed it either. Instead, her hand gently moved along his thigh, up and down, stroking him, moving higher up now. Damn, she was killing him! His hard-on was straining against his pants, and he had no way of shifting in the tight space to make himself more comfortable.

Her warm hand moved up to the apex of his thighs. He was almost ready to come right there and then—when would this damn play be over? Samson held his breath until he noticed her look at him. She chuckled silently. What was so funny?

Delilah leaned into him, and he felt her mouth close to his ear.

"You shouldn't play with fire if you can't take the heat."

Bloody hell, she was playing him like a fiddle, turning him into putty in her hands. And she knew it all too well. He'd always thought of himself as being the predator, but she'd turned the game around, switching into his customary role. He couldn't wait to turn the tables on her later.

"Payback's a bitch." And he would thoroughly enjoy it.

"Shh!" a voice from behind reprimanded him.

Samson took hold of her hand again, stopping her from caressing him any further, but still keeping it on his thigh. He could handle that—just about. He hadn't had this much fun with a woman since he'd been a teenager and human. As a vampire, everything to do with sex had been hot and heavy without real fun and games. Well, this was hot and heavy too, but at the same time he could sense the humor in it all. He wondered whether she could awaken his lighter side and make him feel carefree and relaxed again.

He couldn't remember when he had last joked with a woman, but with Delilah, everything seemed so easy. She didn't take herself too seriously; it made it almost easy to forget what he was. She treated him like a normal man. Of course she would. She had no idea what he was. It didn't matter, not tonight. Tonight he'd take her to his bed, and he would be just a man, a man who wanted her. He would forget that he was a vampire.

FIVE

Ilona threw her shoulders back and sailed out of the theater. She'd lost interest in staying for the second act. Could anybody blame her? She hadn't seen Samson since the breakup. And to see him after such a long time in the company of a human threw even her for a loop—especially since she'd heard that he was suffering from erectile dysfunction. So what was he doing out with a human woman? Like a mere mortal could ever satisfy a man like Samson. What a ridiculous notion!

Ilona was friendly with Dr. Drake's receptionist and therefore knew about Samson's sessions with the shrink. Not that she cared if he could get it up or not; she certainly had no interest in him anymore, particularly since it was clear that he would never blood-bond with her.

She shot past a waiting couple who'd waived down a taxi, and ripped the passenger door open.

"Excuse us, but—" Ilona ignored the man's protest and snarled at him. She felt better when he flinched and pulled back.

She let herself fall into the backseat and, without thinking, she gave the taxi driver an address as she slammed the door shut.

Only when she leaned back into the seat, did she realize that the address she'd given him was not hers. She sighed. Maybe it was better not to go home, considering the mood she was in. Her subconscious seemed to know what she needed anyway.

Distraction.

Less than ten minutes later, she stood at the door of the apartment, having been buzzed up to the top floor. She barely had time to straighten her dress when the door opened.

Amaury gave her a once-over. As always, he looked sexy as the devil, which was exactly what she needed tonight.

"Look what the cat dragged in," he drawled.

She walked straight past him into the open-plan living area. "I never knew you to be one for clichés."

Amaury shrugged his shoulders and let the door fall shut. "Things change. But I see you haven't." No. She was still as gorgeous and as coldhearted as ever. Some things never changed.

He watched her as she leaned against the bar. "How have you been, Amaury?"

Raising his eyebrow, he didn't bother answering her question. "What do you want, Ilona? Did you break your vibrator? Or why else would you be here?"

She pursed her lips. "Are you always this crude?"

"Only with you, darling, 'cause that's how you like it, don't you?"

"And?" She paused. "Are you planning to deliver?"

Amaury looked at his wristwatch. "I have an hour to kill. It's an option." He could do with some sex. He could *always* do with sex.

"If you only have an hour, we'd better not waste time by chatting as if we were old friends." She parted her lips, allowing her tongue to dart out. She licked her lower lip, and he followed her gaze as it dropped to his groin.

Amaury knew what she saw: a vampire ready for some action between the sheets. He was always ready. Merely talking about sex could get him aroused. It was both a gift and a curse.

It wouldn't be the first time he bedded Ilona and probably not the last one either. She had a great body, and she liked her loving rough. Rough worked for him. Especially with a woman like her.

"Why tonight?" He wasn't ready to let her have her way yet. The longer he'd stall her, the more randy she would get. And a randy Ilona promised a great fuck.

"What do you care? I'm here, aren't I?"

He could tell she was hiding something, pretending this was like any evening for her, but he sensed her frustration. Deep down. Something had ruffled her feathers. That's why she needed him: she needed the tension released. He knew just how.

Amaury took several steps toward her, stopping inches from her. "What are you wearing underneath this frock?"

"Nothing."

Just like he'd told her after their first sexual encounter. He let out an appreciative grunt. He preferred his women to come prepared. No use wasting time by dealing with pesky underwear. He never wore any himself.

"Since we both know that you don't like sucking cock, let's just get to the main event, shall we?"

He didn't give her a chance to respond. Instead he hauled her over his shoulder and carried her to the couch. She didn't show any rejection to his treatment, and he didn't expect any. He dropped her facedown onto the soft, cream cushions.

Amaury let himself fall onto it right after her and pinned her underneath him. He ground his loins into her, pressing his erection into her thigh.

"Missed my cock, did you?"

"Arrogant bastard," she hissed and tried to push him off.

He grabbed her wrists and let her struggle for a while. "Yet you keep coming back. I guess there's something you want from me. And we both know it sure isn't my charm—which only leaves my cock."

He knew it was all a game for her, pretending she didn't really want this. But the scent of her arousal betrayed her. He absorbed her smell, making it obvious to her what he was doing.

"How rough would you like it this time?" He did not allow her to avoid his gaze. She'd have to tell him what she wanted, and then he'd decide whether he'd give it to her or not. Maybe he would, maybe he wouldn't. It depended on his mood.

Ilona pressed her lips together, and he couldn't suppress a grin. As always, she wasn't prepared to ask for it. Just as well.

"I guess I have my answer then. Maybe a slap on your ass will loosen your tongue."

An interested flicker animated her eyes.

Exactly as he'd suspected.

"You savage!" Ilona's voice didn't carry enough anger for him to even consider it a protest. More of an invitation, actually. Not that he needed one.

A second later, he rolled to the side and flipped her onto her stomach. Holding her wrists with one hand, he used his other one to lift up her dress.

"Let's see if you lied to me, or if you're truly wearing nothing underneath. You know how I can get when somebody lies to me." Too many lies, and they would unleash a beast within him.

A hitched breath was the answer. And then a comment. "I know."

Provocative.

Amaury knew instantly what he would find underneath the green silk of her evening gown. So he readied himself to deliver her punishment.

His hand pushed up the fabric, up over her knees, her thighs. He stopped for a second when he reached her round cheeks. As he pushed the fabric over her ass and let it bunch at her waist, he took in the sight. Creamy, delicate skin. Pale.

Almost naked, but not quite. Wearing a thong qualified as a lie.

Slowly he stroked a hand over her ass. His finger hooked under the string and lifted it. A moment later he let it snap back onto her skin. He *tsk*ed.

An expectant sigh came from Ilona. "Oops, forgot I was wearing that."

Another lie.

She wanted it badly. And he'd deliver. He wasn't one to disappoint a woman in bed. And besides, he'd just gotten in the mood for something bad.

His hand lifted from the smooth skin of her buttocks.

"No more lies tonight." His order was followed by his palm connecting with the right cheek of her ass in a short but stinging slap.

She moaned into the cushion as he gave her a second's reprieve before he delivered the next slap onto the other cheek. His palm prints only showed for a few moments then disappeared. On a human woman they would have remained longer, not on the vampire female beneath him.

He nudged her legs apart with his knee. When she didn't comply quickly enough, he paddled her ass once more. Left and right. Again. Instantly her thighs spread, but the thong obstructed the clear view of her pussy. It had to go. After all, he was a visual type of guy.

"No more thongs." He ripped the piece off her, discarding it on the floor.

"Yes," she whispered, her voice colored with the arousal his senses were already bathing in.

He lowered his hand and slid it between her thighs, drenching his fingers in her cream. She jerked when his hand found her clit and rolled it between his thumb and forefinger.

But he only let her enjoy it for a second, before his finger dove into her slit. The motion almost lifted her off the sofa.

"You need it bad," he commented.

"Yes, real bad." She sounded breathless.

"I've got just the thing for you." A pretty big thing.

Vampire speed was a good skill to have when wanting to free one's cock quickly. This was the moment when it definitely came in handy. His erection jutted out proudly as soon as he'd lowered the zipper. He didn't bother taking his pants off completely.

He knew he was big, larger than the average vampire. Many women wouldn't be able to accommodate him immediately, but Ilona had been fucked sufficiently by countless men; she was well used to an extra-large helping of cock. And he was ready to dole out her serving. Inch by iron-hard inch.

Centering himself behind her, he grabbed her hips with both hands and plunged into her heat. Slick, hot, and wet, she welcomed him. He moved in and out of her, taking her moans for what they were: encouragement.

"Harder!" she screamed, sounding angry.

"Don't you give me orders," he bit out and thrust deeper, then followed it up with a slap on her ass. And another one. He was in the driver's seat, and he'd make it clear to her.

"Oh God, yes!"

Amaury grinned devilishly. He knew exactly what she needed. And what he wanted.

"I think you need your ass fucked, so you know who's in charge in my bed." A warning he was willing to turn into reality.

He felt the muscles of her sheath tighten. No, he wouldn't let her come, not yet. He pulled out instantly and held her still.

"Damn it, you bastard! What the fuck do you think you're doing? Fuck me, now!" She was like hell on a runaway train, scratching and clawing at him.

"Oh, I'm gonna fuck you. On my terms." But her well-used pussy wasn't enough for him.

He dipped his finger into her slick heat and coated it with her cream. As he slipped it out, he ran it up the crack of her ass until he found her other hole. She went completely still. His finger rimmed the puckered hole, moistening it with her juices.

Within seconds she relaxed, and he felt her arch upwards and push herself against his finger, tempting him to enter. He didn't need any coaxing. His finger drove into her narrow sheath, her muscles securing him tightly.

Letting go of her hip, he reached underneath the couch, recovering the jar of lubricant he kept there for events like this and dug his fingers into it. Smoothing a generous amount over her hole and working it into her with his fingers, was almost as pleasurable as fucking her.

But not quite.

Already now she was panting heavily, moaning every time his fingers moved in and out. Two fingers now, preparing her for his massive cock, stretching her.

"Tell me now, or I'm going to leave you hanging. Tell me what you want."

A moment's hesitation. He didn't expect any less. Then, "I came to have my ass fucked. You're happy now?"

Happy? Amaury was never happy. Satisfied? Yes. Satisfied, he could do that. And he'd be well satisfied in a few minutes.

"Then you've come to the right place."

He eased out his fingers and placed his cock at her dark passage, nudging forward. The tight ring guarding her entrance relaxed, and the lubricant allowed him to slide in. Just an inch. Then another one.

Ilona's moan turned into a scream. "Yes!"

And then he thrust past the entrance, deep into her, feeling the tight muscles clench around him as securely as if she'd grabbed him with her fist. Amaury knew she didn't feel any pain as he sensed only her pleasure. Good. In either case, he wouldn't have pulled out. Not now. Not when her muscles delivered just the pressure he craved. It would be a short fuck, but a damn good one.

He pulled back, then plunged deep. And again, finding the rhythm that drove him wild and promised release.

"Yeah, you like me to fuck you like that, don't you?" he urged her to surrender. "That's why you keep coming back. 'Cause nobody can give it to you like that."

"More!"

"I've got more. Lots more." And he pumped harder, driving his shaft in deeper, faster. Several more frantic strokes, and he knew he would lose it. Her body was too tight, too hot. It was too much.

"You have the tightest ass I've ever fucked."

His hand slipped to her pussy, finding her clit instantly. One touch, and her over-sensitized body erupted. The moment he felt her muscles spasm, he lost control and joined her in her climax.

His semen shot into her in short bursts, mimicking Ilona's spasms. Seconds later he collapsed onto her.

"And don't you ever try to order me around again." Truth be told, he welcomed any excuse to spank her—it got him hornier than hell.

"As long as it gets me what I want …"

"Let's not kid ourselves, Ilona. Neither one of us will ever get what we want."

She huffed. "Like you have any idea what I want."

"You are not that different from me, even if you don't want to admit it. But if you believe that you can fill your empty heart with money, power and meaningless sex, you're more delusional than I am. It's not going to warm your cold heart. You can ask me. I'm an expert at it."

He sure was. Amaury closed his eyes to the pain he remembered, then swallowed it away. Cursed to sense other people's emotions, he was devoid of feeling love himself. Loyalty, friendship, anger, even guilt, pain and lust—he had no trouble feeling. But love? There was no place in his shriveled up heart for it.

"You're wrong. Money and power will get me a long way to where I want to be."

Amaury rolled off her and shrugged. "If you want to delude yourself, be my guest. It doesn't change anything about the facts."

She turned her face to him. "Do you really believe I give a damn about what you think?"

He let out a bear laugh. "Of course not. All you give a damn about is my cock. I'm not the one who's delusional."

She slapped at him, but he caught her arm without effort.

"Looks like somebody needs another spanking." And another quick fuck.

Amaury looked at his watch. He could spare another twenty minutes before he had to do some work.

***

When the final curtain at last fell and the clapping subsided, Samson looked at his gorgeous date.

"Are you trying to cause a disturbance in the audience?" he teased her.

"Now, how would I do that?" Delilah asked innocently, her big eyes looking up at him.

"Looking at me like that is a start." If she continued like that he'd drag her behind a curtain and take her right there.

She shook her head. "No, let's just keep the record straight. You started it."

"You didn't stop me."

"I'm just a weak woman."

He laughed heartily, drawing the attention of several theatergoers onto him. "Oh, a woman you are. Weak, you're definitely not. I bet you can bring any man to his knees."

"What makes you think that?"

"I'm a living example of the power you have over men." He moved his head much closer to hers.

"Shall we get out of here before *you* cause some sort of disturbance?" Her giggles were refreshing.

He laughed and pulled her out of her seat. "Where do you want to go?"

"How about we'll just go with your plans? You did have something else planned, didn't you?"

Undressing her in the next dark corner was the plan.

"What if you don't like what I've planned?" He was enjoying teasing her.

"Try me."

As in taste? In a heartbeat.

Samson licked his lower lip. There was a hell of a lot of things he wanted to try, and tasting her was just the beginning. "I think I will. No. Scratch that. I *know* I will."

With his arm around her waist, he led her to the stairway. The theater had almost emptied, and they were the last ones to walk down the broad staircase leading to one of the side exits. The sound her high heels made on the stairs echoed through the air.

They were alone. He could press her against the wall and take her right there in the stairwell. Her moans would echo through the empty space, bounce off the walls, the sound amplified. But it would be over too soon. No, he had to distract himself and get her to his house where he could keep her all night.

"Why do women torture themselves and wear high heels like that?" Samson was certain his voice was colored with pure lust.

"Because women don't like to be short."

He chuckled. "It's called petite. And men like petite women. Brings out the protective instinct in them."

She playfully punched him. His abs were rock hard. He laughed to cover up his true feelings; did she have any idea what her touch did to him, and how close his control was to snapping?

"If you want to wrestle, it can be arranged. But I have to caution you, I don't give up easily."

And with you, I'll wrestle naked.

"Neither do I."

"That should make for an interesting match." The hot look he gave her was sure to tell her just how interesting a little naked wrestling match between them would be. And what the winner would get.

"Place your bets."

"My money is on the girl."

"How come?" She seemed utterly surprised at his choice.

"I know the guy's weakness." He winked at her.

They stepped out into the street. The stairs had led them out of a side exit into a small alley. Samson could see the main street a short distance ahead of them.

"Watch out for the puddles," he cautioned and navigated her around a large pool of water left by the rain from the previous day.

"What? You mean you're not going to throw down your coat and let me step over it?"

He loved the way she relaxed him with her lighthearted jokes.

"Saville Row, sweetness. I don't think my tailor is going to appreciate it if he finds out."

Samson turned her toward him and pulled her into his arms. "So, is that what you're looking for, an old-fashioned Prince Charming?" Delilah had no idea how old-fashioned he truly was, or how old for that matter.

"I don't know what I'm looking for." Her voice trembled. Her face was still flushed, but he doubted it had anything to do with the heat in the theater. Her smile was gone from her face, and her gaze collided with his.

"Try me." Slowly he lowered his head and approached her mouth. Her parted lips beckoned with the promise of pleasures his body was craving. He needed that kiss, and he needed it now.

"You two, against the wall!" a menacing male voice cut through the silence and destroyed the moment. Somebody would have to pay for this.

With lightning speed, Samson jerked his head in the direction the voice originated and stared at a big thug and the nozzle of a handgun. He felt Delilah shudder in his arms and protectively held her closer. The heat of her body seeped into his, and despite the dangerous situation, he allowed himself to enjoy her closeness.

Samson knew he had to act fast, and he couldn't use his vampire speed or fangs to defeat the assailant. He wouldn't allow anything to destroy the evening he'd planned with the woman in his arms. He couldn't risk for her being frightened or suspect that anything about him wasn't quite what it seemed to be. His secret had to be guarded.

"Didn't you hear what I said? You, against the wall!" the thug repeated. "I want the girl, now!"

Samson instantly realized that their attacker was human and therefore easily controlled. Delilah gasped, and his hand went to her head to pull her face into his chest.

You will not pull the trigger.

He used the only weapon available to him, his mind control.

You will not shoot.

"Delilah, please do as I say. Get behind me."

He pushed her behind his broad back. He could feel her shaking.

"Oh, God, no," she whimpered. "He'll kill you."

Not likely. It wasn't exactly easy to kill a vampire, especially not with a gun. Even if the thug shot at him and hit him, his body would expel the bullet, and the wound would close up quickly.

Only a few things could kill a vampire: a wooden stake through the chest, exposure to sunlight, and some major injuries to his body resulting in severe blood loss. If a vampire got caught in an explosion, it would most likely kill him, as would a fire. But the man only had a gun which represented no danger to Samson.

Nevertheless, he had to be careful. Delilah was with him, and he couldn't risk her getting hurt.

"Hey, idiot. I want the girl. Give her to me, and I'll let you live. No need to play the hero."

Samson reached one arm behind him to calm her. "Close your eyes, sweetness, and everything will be fine." He kept his voice calm and soothing. No need to worry her any more than she already was.

You will not shoot. You will not attack us.

He knew he could defeat him in an instant, but how would he explain this to her? How could he explain his superhuman abilities without causing any suspicion? He was in a bind. He could control the thug not to shoot for quite a while, but even that would cause suspicion eventually.

The man watched him intently and suddenly took a couple of steps forward. Samson could see his face clearly now, including the scar on his cheek and the small tattoo on his neck. Very unusual, very distinctive. Knowing that he would recognize him if he saw him again, Samson formed his plan. There was no need to kill him now. It was sufficient to chase him away and have his men deal with him later.

"What do you want?" Samson asked him calmly.

"Are you deaf? The girl." The man's voice was a snarl.

"Not an option."

"Then I'll kill you." He looked as if he wanted to pull the trigger, but didn't. Samson used his confused state to lunge at him. With a high kick of his right leg he hit the weapon out of the thug's hand. The man looked at him, stunned and shocked.

Run! Run now and don't come back!

And like a frightened rabbit he ran out of the alley. It was over.

Samson turned and crossed the distance to Delilah with three large strides.

"Everything is fine," he assured her as he pulled her into his arms. "He's gone."

She shook like a leaf. "He didn't hurt you, did he?"

"No. He didn't get a chance."

"How did you learn to kick like that?"

He held her at arm's length from him and looked at her face. "Didn't I ask you to close your eyes?"

"I peeked." She buried her head in his chest. "You shouldn't have taken such a risk. He had a gun."

"The alternative wasn't an option. Nothing happened. He was just some no good thug."

Delilah shook her head.

"What?"

"I recognized him. He was the same guy who attacked me last night."

The realization hit him like a freight train. "Are you sure?" Samson put his hand under her chin and urged her to look at him.

"Absolutely sure."

Damn it, he shouldn't have let him get away. It couldn't be a coincidence that it was the same guy. Something was wrong. Seriously wrong.

Effortlessly, he lifted Delilah into his arms to carry her out of the alley.

"I can walk."

"Indulge me." Feeling her body so close to his calmed him.

He saw the limousine immediately as they exited the alley. Carl was leaning against the car, waiting for them. When Carl saw them approach, his look became concerned, and he immediately opened the car door.

"Something the matter, sir?"

Samson lifted her into the car. "We were attacked. Get us home, Carl, quickly, please."

He slipped into the seat next to her and took her hand into his, before he pulled out his cell phone with the other. The car was already in motion when the call connected.

"Ricky, we were attacked." He made his voice sound as calm as possible in order not to worry Delilah even more.

"Who was attacked?"

"Delilah and I, outside the theater."

Ricky interrupted him. "You were on a date with the human woman?"

"Would you listen?" He started to get annoyed. "Delilah recognized him as the same guy who attacked her last night. I'll have Carl fax over a sketch of him later. He shouldn't be too hard to find. He's got a tattoo on his neck and a scar on his cheek. He's probably a member of a gang. Have the boys comb the city for him as soon as you get my description."

Absentmindedly, he led Delilah's hand to his lips and kissed her fingers tenderly. He needed to feel her to make sure she was alright.

"Was he a vampire?" Ricky wanted to know, his voice quieter now.

"No, definitely not."

"Demon?"

"None of that, just a regular lowlife." Hopefully Ricky understood that this meant the guy was human. He couldn't exactly say it while Delilah was sitting right next to him, listening to his side of the conversation.

"And you let him get away?" Ricky's accusation rang in his ear.

"What do you think? I couldn't risk Delilah being hurt." Was Ricky high on something? He knew full well that he couldn't just have killed the guy in front of her without exposing himself.

"You could have wiped her memory clean. Ever thought of that?" Ricky kept his voice low so Delilah couldn't hear him. He was right, but somehow Samson didn't have the heart to use his powers on her.

Something stopped him. He didn't want anything to taint his relationship with her.

Relationship?

How had that strange thought entered his mind?

"I'm not listening to any more of this. Do what I told you to do. And another thing: he dropped his gun in the alley next to the theater. Retrieve it and trace it. Carl will show you where we were." He was pissed and ended the call.

"What's wrong?" Delilah sounded worried.

He immediately realized that he shouldn't have been so harsh on the phone, but instead should have reined in his temper. He didn't want her to be concerned. Gently he pulled her closer, putting one arm around her shoulders and taking her hand in his.

"Nothing. It's just Ricky. He's a little stubborn sometimes. You won't have to worry about anything anymore. That man can't hurt you."

Samson kissed her hand. Delilah loved feeling his lips on her skin. It soothed her. She snuggled closer to him and hoped he wouldn't think she was too needy, but his strong body made her feel safe, and that's what she needed right now.

"Shouldn't we go to the police?"

"The police never do anything about these things. Let Ricky handle it: he works in security. He knows what to do." His voice was determined as if he was certain what the right course of action was. A man who took charge.

She looked up at him. The whole incident hadn't fazed him at all. While she had shaken like a tree in a hurricane, he was calm and collected, almost as if occurrences like these were common for him.

"You probably think I'm crazy, but until this thug has been apprehended, I want you to stay at my house."

She gave him a startled look. "Your house?"

"I know what this suggestion must sound like, especially after … you know … but I don't want you to be alone. Somebody is obviously after you, and until we know who and why, I'd feel much better, if you were under my protection."

Delilah wondered whether he was suddenly embarrassed to mention the little erotic games they had played. Could this damn incident have killed his mood? She assumed as much. It seemed that now he felt obligated to protect her. She would have wanted to stay with him tonight, but not to be under his protection. No, she wanted to be pinned under his sexy body, his naked body.

"You want to protect me?"

"Of course I do." Samson gave her a strange look.

"Is that all?" She was certain that her disappointment showed. She'd never been good at hiding her feelings. As she looked into his eyes, she could detect a flicker in them, and then he suddenly smiled.

He shook his head. "No, that's not all. If I only wanted to protect you, you'd be staying in the guest room."

Something in her stomach made a somersault. A smile formed on her lips. "And I'm not staying in the guest room?" She was eager for his answer and held her breath.

"You can, if you insist." His thumb stroked along her jaw and his stare was fixated on her lips. "I certainly would not want to force you to do anything you don't want to do, but I was hoping I could convince you to choose my bed instead." His voice was sultry and full of desire. No man had ever spoken to her like this. His eyes suddenly looked much darker as he lowered his head toward hers.

His bed. Had he really said his bed or was she hallucinating? "Will you be in it?" She felt hot, unbearably hot at the thought of sharing his bed. She had trouble swallowing.

"As long as you want me to." His hand on her chin pulled her closer to his face. "Last time I kissed you, I forced myself on you. I don't want this to be the case tonight. So I beg you, Delilah, please kiss me."

As she brushed her lips against his, she could feel him inhale sharply. The instant her lips touched his, everything around her seemed to disappear and melt into the distance. She barely felt the movement of the car or the leather of the seats. His arms pulled her into a tight embrace, and his lips gave her all the attention she wanted, nibbling on hers and sucking on her as he hijacked her kiss. She felt his tongue slide gently over her lips, so tentative she thought he'd never invade her mouth with it, until he finally did, and did so with a masterful sweep. His tongue encircled hers, demanding she play with him, dance with him.

His kiss sent scorching hot flames through her body, so hot she thought she'd dissolve from the inside. The fire burned deep in her belly, sending warmth and moisture trickling from between her legs, pooling in her panties which would be soaked thoroughly within seconds. She was a quivering mess in his arms. She shivered violently at every passionate assault of his tongue on her mouth, unable to control her reaction to him. She hoped he wouldn't notice how lost she was in his arms, how completely and utterly under his spell. Abruptly he pulled away.

"Are you okay?" Samson's voice sounded concerned, but also breathless and rough.

"Please don't stop," she begged and pressed her mouth onto his. Without missing a beat, he continued where he'd left off.

His hand moved down to her lower back, shifting her and draping one of her legs over his thighs. He softly caressed her firm cheeks before moving down her thigh to the seam of her skirt. She felt how he stroked her naked skin and how his hand traveled upwards underneath her skirt. Higher, and higher still. His fingers reached the seam of her panties where they hesitated for a second, until she moaned almost inaudibly. As if he'd waited for her sign, he slipped his hand underneath the fabric, stroked her bare skin and squeezed her gently.

Delilah knew this man was a virtual stranger to her, and it wasn't normal to allow him to touch her like this when she barely knew him, but she couldn't stop him. She didn't want to. His touch aroused her, and she hadn't felt that aroused in a long time. She couldn't deny her body the pleasure he was promising. As his hand slipped lower to search out the warmth and moisture which pooled between her legs she released another moan.

If he continued for much longer, she'd come in the car. She had to pull herself together, try to get some control over her body, but how could she? His hands promised pleasure she hadn't felt in a long time, and her body's response was automatic and uncontrollable. Even if she had wanted to resist him, she wouldn't have found the strength. Why did she allow him to touch her so intimately?

Another sigh escaped her mouth just as he separated his lips from hers.

"We're here." His voice was as breathless as she felt, and his eyes were dark when she looked into them, almost as if his pupils were fully dilated. The hazel color was completely gone.

She looked around. Carl held the car door open. She hadn't noticed that they had stopped or that anybody had opened the door. She had completely and utterly lost all of her senses with just one kiss.

SIX

Carl stood waiting patiently while Samson took out a pad of plain paper from the antique bureau in the living room and sat down. Delilah watched him as he started drawing an image on the paper. His movements were swift. Within minutes, the picture of a man leapt off the page. Samson raised the sheet for her to see.

"Is this close enough?"

She couldn't believe her eyes! The drawing showed the spitting image of the criminal who'd attacked them. In addition to the face of the man, Samson had drawn the image of the tattoo: two circles with a cross in the middle. "It's as if you'd taken a picture. How did you do that?"

"Photographic memory," Samson explained and handed the paper to Carl. "Fax this over to Ricky. He's waiting for it. And then ..." He looked at her. "Carl can pack up some of your things and bring them here if you tell him what you need for the next few nights."

Next few nights? She liked the sound of that. "That'd be great. Just bring everything." Delilah fished for her key in her bag. When she glanced up, she looked into Samson's face, frozen in apparent shock, eyes widened. His adam's apple moved as he swallowed hard.

"Everything, Miss?" Carl asked politely, but she ignored him.

Looking at her gracious host, she laughed. "You should look in the mirror and see your face!" She got herself under control. "Priceless." His shocked face, thinking she was planning to move in, was quite a sight to behold. But she couldn't let him suffer any longer.

"Sorry; it's not what you think. I'm in San Francisco on a business trip. I only have a small suitcase and my laptop, so I figured Carl might bring the whole lot. If that's ok?"

Samson exhaled visibly. "You had me there for a second; I didn't see that one coming." He looked relaxed now. "Carl, will you get Miss Sheridan's things please and put them in the guest room?"

Delilah handed Carl the key to the apartment. He turned around to leave.

"And Carl, could you also stop by the supermarket and get some food for Miss Sheridan? I think my fridge is pretty empty."

"What would you like, Miss?"

"Delilah?"

"Just whatever you eat," she answered. She really didn't want to make any trouble. When it came to food, she wasn't fussy.

"Sir?" Carl looked a little lost.

"Just get some fruit, milk, coffee, cereal, yogurt, bread, the usual," his boss instructed him. "And thanks, Carl."

"Good night, sir, good night, Miss."

A second later Carl was gone. She was still looking to the door when Samson's arms wrapped around her from behind, pulling her into him.

"Were you trying to shock me?" He started nibbling at her ear lobe.

"Did it work?"

"What do you think?"

His lips wandered to her neck, softly brushing her skin until goose bumps started forming.

"Cold?"

How could she be when his hot hands stroked across her belly? "Hot."

And getting hotter by the second.

"Thought so." Samson sounded suspiciously smug.

He left one hand wrapped around her waist and moved the other one higher, traveling deliberately up the middle of her torso through the valley of her breasts until he reached the neckline of her top.

"What were you trying to do to me in the theater?" He stroked his fingers along the line where her top stopped and her skin began. Her skin tingled when his fingers touched her.

"Get a reaction out of you."

Samson pressed her harder against his body, rubbing his cock against her lower back. He had a full-blown erection and made no secret of it.

"This kind of reaction?" He wanted her to acknowledge his hard-on? She could do better than that.

Her hand trailed back to run down the side of his hip as she rubbed her buttocks against the hard outline of his shaft, eliciting a not-so-subtle groan from him. It felt too good not to, so she did it again. "I wanted to see whether you'd have the same reaction as when you thought I was a stripper."

So Delilah *had* noticed that he'd had a hard-on when he'd kissed her the previous night. And despite the effect she knew she had on him, she had accepted his invitation. Brave. "Satisfied?"

"I think you'll need to do a little more to satisfy me."

Samson accepted the challenge. His hand traced her neckline. Slowly he slipped it underneath her top and caressed her breast. He cupped her firm peak. Her *very responsive* peak.

"That's a start. Samson?"

"Uh huh?" His hand was busy teasing her nipple and turning it hard.

"The stripper last night." He felt her hesitate. Her question was unspoken, but he knew what she wanted to hear.

"I didn't touch her. I sent her away. There was no way I could touch another woman after I kissed you. It didn't feel right." Not entirely true, since he'd certainly tried, but the result was the same. He hadn't touched the stripper.

Delilah tilted her head back, and he seized the opportunity to sink his lips onto her exposed neck. Her tempting neck. He could feel her hot blood running through the throbbing vein right underneath her pale skin. So delicious. So trusting.

"All night after you left I was wondering whether you'd allow me to kiss you and touch you. Or if you'd fight me again."

She gave him an answer by taking the hand that rested on her waist and slowly pushed it lower. He couldn't resist the open invitation. With a swift move he pulled up her skirt and slid his hand underneath.

He let her scent guide him to the warm moisture pooling at the apex of her thighs, touching her drenched panties with his hand.

"Is that what you want?"

"Yes." She moaned and widened her stance for him. Effortlessly his hand slipped into her panties and traveled to the moist folds of flesh marking the entrance to her body.

"You're so wet." He let his admiration color his words.

"That's your fault." Her voice was even more of a turn-on than she could know.

"Last night I was dreaming of being inside of you, of feeling your muscles tighten around me when you come. I couldn't think of anything else. I could barely get through the day." He had barely slept. Rather he'd been daydreaming about her, about the things he wanted to do with her.

"I didn't fare much better after how you made me feel last night."

Delilah tilted her pelvis toward his hand in silent invitation.

"Tell me, did you touch yourself, imagining it was my hand?"

His fingers played with her warm flesh, parting the plump lips and spreading her cream. She let out another moan, but didn't answer him.

"Did you make yourself come?" He was eager to hear her answer.

Delilah shook her head. "No."

"Why not?" He eased one finger into her inviting slit. She was so tight, he was sure she hadn't been fucked in a while.

"I wanted you to do it."

And he would. "Like this?" He used his thumb to find her clit and caressed it, while his finger slowly slipped back and forth, in and out.

"Oh God, just like that." Her head dropped against his chest.

"You feel so good. Even better than I've imagined."

"Hmh." Her body started rocking with him in a tantalizing rhythm. His second hand came to aid, allowing him to spread her flesh and expose her engorged nub to his eager fingers, pinching her lightly to send more sensations coursing through her body. She was so easy to read, reacting so directly to each of his ministrations.

"I'm not going to stop until you come right here." He breathed into her ear. "I want to feel your orgasm rock through your body, and I want to be the reason for it." The thought of making her come excited him more than pleasing a woman had ever before. At this moment he wasn't concerned with his own pleasure, he just wanted to experience hers. Now that he knew that he would have her, he could wait and enjoy the anticipation.

"Can you do that for me, come for me?"

His cock was firmly pressed against her lower back, and he knew his erection would still be there later. It wouldn't come down, not with feeling her body the way he was. With every movement she rubbed herself against him, seemingly oblivious to the sensations she sent through his body.

"Oh God," she moaned breathlessly. He massaged her clit, following the movements of her body, speeding up as her rhythm sped up. Now two of his fingers plunged into her and moved rhythmically in and out, making her sigh louder, while his finger on her engorged button moved relentlessly, never slowing down, never tiring.

Samson noticed when her breathing changed, her body tensed and her movements became short bursts. He relished the way her body reacted to his touch. His fingers were drenched with her juices, and the scent made his already-hard cock yearn for release.

"That's it, sweetness, just like that."

She rode his fingers like an experienced and eager rider. Her skin was flushed, her pulse had quickened, and he could virtually smell the hot blood rushing through her veins, right underneath her skin where his lips latched onto her neck, suckling gently.

But he wouldn't bite her. No. This was for her. For some inexplicable reason he wanted to be the best lover she'd ever had. He wanted to thank her for what she'd done for him, for the way she aroused him.

"Yes; come for me." His hands moved faster, matching her rhythm. He could sense the shudders going through her body, the waves, and then her interior muscles clenching around his fingers in short spasms, raining more cream onto his hand as she came. Slowly he stilled his hand to let her ride out her climax.

Samson slipped his fingers out and brought them to his mouth, licking her arousal off them, well aware that she watched him with bated breath.

"Mmh, you're delicious." He'd never tasted anything better in his life. This wouldn't be the last time tonight that he feasted on her.

"Oh my God!" Her voice sounded husky as her knees suddenly buckled.

He caught her and brought them both down on the couch. He turned her in his arms to gaze at her face. She looked flushed, her skin glistened.

"Satisfied now?" He smiled.

"You're amazing." She met his look and pulled his face to hers. Her lips approached his and met them in a passionate kiss.

"Does this mean you're going to share my bed tonight?"

"I thought we'd already cleared that hurdle."

"I don't recall getting a definite answer from you. Even though, I could venture a guess."

"Maybe I'll just show you my answer."

Her hand went to the bulge underneath his pants, cupping it. He felt her fingers slowly trace his hard cock from the tip to the base and back again. He inhaled sharply. It appeared that his selflessness in pleasuring her would pay off.

"I think I get the idea."

"Let me just make it a little clearer, so there's no misunderstanding later."

Delilah tugged at the zipper of his pants and pulled it down slowly. Her hand easily slipped inside. Samson felt the soft skin of her palm pushing his boxers aside and finding his erection straining against her hand. She wrapped her hand around him, gripping his hard shaft tightly. A drop of moisture had already oozed from its tip. With her finger, she slowly spread the moisture over the head, massaging it in. He couldn't remember ever having been touched this gently.

She would be a very attentive lover, he knew now. She would be just the right medicine for him. One on which he could easily overdose if he wasn't careful. Dr. Drake had neglected to tell him how much sex he should have with her. Surely he hadn't meant just once?

"Oh, God, woman, you're torturing me."

Delilah gave a soft giggle. "I don't believe you know the meaning of torture."

She moved her hand up and down his erection, keeping her grip firm, as if she knew how he liked it. No tutoring needed.

"I do now." Samson sighed.

"Take me to bed before we embarrass Carl when he gets back."

He swept her up into his arms and walked up the stairs. This time she didn't protest being carried. He liked the feel of her small body in his arms. As he carried her into his bedroom, he noticed her giving her surroundings a brief glance. The four-poster bed, the floor pillows in front of the huge fire place, the paintings.

He noted with joy that nothing held her attention for long. Instead her eyes moved back to him, giving him another of her gorgeous smiles. His worldly possessions didn't seem to influence her. He believed he could have carried her into a shabby hut, and as long as there was a bed, she would have smiled at him with the same anticipation in her eyes.

Samson lowered her onto the bed, quickly stripping her of her shoes before he reached for a remote on the bedside table. One click and the fireplace ignited, starting a small fire. The lights on both bedside tables were on and provided a soft glow in the room. He let his eyes glide over her, savoring the moment.

"Beautiful." He meant it. To him she was the most beautiful creature he'd ever touched. And now she was in his bed. Ready for him.

Moments later he joined her and took her into his strong arms again. Her body felt so right.

"I forgot to mention: though I can guarantee your safety here, I can't guarantee that you'll get any sleep tonight." He made no attempt to hide the desire in his voice. "In fact, I guarantee you that you won't." Not a wink of sleep, not as long as he had any energy left. And as a creature of the night he had energy in abundance.

Her long lashes fluttered as she looked up at him. "Don't make promises you can't keep." He knew she was teasing him. He felt his skin burn when her fingers travelled to his shirt where she eased one button open and let her hand slip in to touch him. What soft hands.

"Is that a challenge?" He was definitely up for it, more than she could even begin to understand.

"What are you going to do about it?" He knew what *she* was doing about it, because he was at the receiving end of it. And not complaining either. She'd opened two more buttons of his shirt and now liberally caressed his chest. He was not about to stop her.

"This." He kissed her cheek. "And that." He kissed her neck. "And that."

Samson crushed her lips with his, invading her like he'd done before, but this time more fiercely, more passionately. Nothing could stop him now. She was his, and she wanted him of her own free will. The thought made him feel powerful and stoked his passion for her even more.

Delilah responded to him so willingly and completely, giving her body over to his in the most trusting way he'd ever seen a woman react to him. He didn't understand it, but he soaked it up. Her body molded itself to his with an understanding he couldn't even begin to comprehend. Even though he was a complete stranger to her, her body seemed to trust him. He could feel how it cried out for him when she writhed against his every touch. Always asking for more.

Samson interrupted their passionate kiss and pulled back to look into her eyes. They matched his in passion and desire. This human woman had fire, more than he'd ever seen in any vampire female.

"I want you," he murmured, barely recognizing his own voice, so low and dark.

"You have me." Did she really mean it? He was going to find out.

Her hands trailed over his chest, barely touching, yet making his whole body shiver at the electric sensation of her caress.

It was time to unwrap her. He undid the knot of her top taking all of two seconds, before he peeled her out of it. Delilah wore no bra this time. He gasped at the sight of her naked breasts. They were round, firm, and their peaks were topped with hard pink nipples that begged to be touched again. He would answer that particular call anytime.

His hands squeezed her breasts gently, and his fingers tugged at her nipples, sending visible shivers through her body.

"Oh yes!" Her voice was breathless and just a whisper.

He lowered his head, brushing against her sensitive skin with his lips. Her back arched to move toward him.

"So impatient." He teased her skin, but knew he was just as eager as she was.

"Please."

His lips found her nipple and slowly sucked on it. As his tongue swept over it, she wiggled under his grip. She wanted more. He moved to her other breast, licking her with his moist tongue, kneading her with his hands, feeling her twist under him. Sweet torture. It was payback for what she'd done to his cock earlier.

"You taste good enough to eat."

"I thought you've already had dinner."

Samson smirked. "I skipped dessert."

Because I'm going to devour you instead.

She gave a soft chuckle of approval.

Her breasts received the attention they demanded as he sucked harder, getting to know every inch of them with his lips, his tongue and his hands. His eyes had already made a mental image of them, burned into his memory forever.

Her scent engulfed him. It had been there all evening, the faint scent of lavender on her skin mixed with the scent of her arousal. He'd picked it up in the theater and fought it as best he could. No longer. He was ready to take it all in and let it wash over him.

They undressed each other, both of them impatient now, unable to wait any longer. Finally all their clothes lay on the floor, and their naked bodies embraced. Her curves fit perfectly into his body. Custom made just for him.

Delilah's hand touched his erect cock, caressing the velvet-steel length of him. He was close and desperately needed release.

"I don't think I can wait any longer." He'd held onto his control as best he could. "Especially not if you touch me like that."

"Would you rather I didn't touch you like that?" Her voice sounded more innocent than he knew she was, evidenced by the fact that she continued with her wicked caress.

"Don't you *dare* stop." It wasn't a threat: it was a demand he knew she only too willingly gave into.

"Where do you keep your condoms?"

"Condoms?" Samson didn't immediately understand, until he realized she thought he was human. Humans used condoms. He couldn't tell her that she didn't need to worry about disease or pregnancy with him, so what should he do now?

"I'm sorry, I completely forgot. I didn't really plan this …" It was an innocent enough lie.

Delilah smiled. "And there I thought you were trying to seduce me from the minute I got into your car."

"I was, but I guess I didn't really think I'd be successful." Of course, he thought he'd get her into bed. At least he knew he would have tried anything to succeed. Even mind control?

"You don't strike me as the guy who'd give up easily."

"I don't, but it doesn't mean I always get what I want." Actually, most of the time he got what he wanted. Just not lately.

"Tonight you will. I brought a condom."

"Does that mean you've been planning to get me into bed all along?" he said mock-shocked, but in reality he was relieved their evening wouldn't be cut short due to lack of protection.

"A girl's got to try."

He kissed her. "So where are those condoms?"

"In my handbag. I think I left it in the living room."

"I'll get it."

Samson rushed downstairs, grateful for the short interruption. He was thirsty and needed to get some blood if he wanted to make sure she was safe from him for the rest of the night. He couldn't let his thirst for blood get in the way of his sexual satisfaction. He sped into the kitchen and gulped down a large glass of blood. As he closed the fridge, he realized that in the morning she would see the blood in there. He couldn't let that happen. Quickly he wrote a note to Carl, put it into an envelope and secured it to the fridge door with a magnet. He would see it when he came to bring the food.

Samson found her handbag, snatched it, and dashed back up the stairs two at a time. She was waiting for him. As she pulled out a condom from her handbag and handed it to him, he couldn't put it on fast enough. Instead of joining her on the bed, he pulled her toward him by her ankles until her legs dangled over the side, and her buttocks rested on the edge of the mattress where he stood.

He looked at her as he spread her legs and positioned himself at her center. Slowly. Deliberately. He pulled her legs up and rested them against his shoulders. She was waiting for him, waiting for him to make a move. His cock at the moist entrance of her body teased her to increase her awareness of him.

Samson inhaled her scent and then slowly pushed forward, plunging into her.

She moaned loudly, joining his groan.

He felt her tight muscles around his cock closing in on him. No, she hadn't been fucked in a while. He would do the honors of fucking her from now on. He pulled back so only the very tip of his hard shaft was still submerged in her.

"More!" she begged.

Samson thrust back into her, deeper than before. And again. Their bodies slammed together, hard, deep. His cock took on its own will, plunging into her and pulling back in a rhythm he knew would put him over the edge. He needed to get control of himself, to slow it down, to make it last.

He reminded himself of who she was: a human, a vulnerable mortal with hot blood pulsating through her veins. Delilah deserved better than him fucking her like a beast. He released her legs and lowered himself on her, hovering above her. Instantly she wrapped her legs around his hips and pulled him close to her.

He lowered his lips onto hers and kissed her. She tasted like a beautiful flower in a meadow full of lavender. Images of a warm summer afternoon drifted into his mind. He was dancing with her in a meadow of lavender with the sun shining onto him without burning him. He felt the warmth of the rays on his skin, not hurting, but caressing him. What was happening? He could clearly feel the sun, smell the lavender and see the meadow. Was he hallucinating? He blinked and the image disappeared as quickly as it had appeared.

His rhythm slowed, and with more tenderness he thought he was capable of, he moved inside of her, slowly and deliberately, soaking up the sensations their intimate joining conjured up in him. He gazed into her green eyes and felt tenderness overwhelm him.

"This is wonderful." Never had sex felt this tender to him and conjured up such loving feelings in him—not even back when he was human. This woman made him want to feel with his heart, not just his body.

Samson sought her mouth again, tasting her sweet nectar. He was instantly transported back into the sun where he basked under its rays.

What was she doing to him, giving him these strange visions? Or was his abstinence from sex to blame for the images in his head?

Even though he didn't know what was happening, he didn't fight it, but let himself be carried away—until he suddenly felt her muscles spasm around his cock, squeezing him as she came.

"No, not yet." But it was too late. He couldn't hold back and came as she milked him until he was spent.

"Delilah." He recognized the smile on her face as that of a satisfied woman. He would make sure that he'd see that smile all night. Her lips were still moist from his last kiss. Gently he brushed a strand of her hair from her cheek and followed it by kissing the spot.

A contented sigh was her answer. "Samson."

He could have stayed on top of her all night, but instead rolled off and stripped himself of the used condom. He didn't like the separation from her and instantly pulled her back into his arms. Draping her over his body, he kissed the top of her head tenderly. He couldn't say anything else. For once in his life he was speechless.

Delilah lifted her head and looked at him, but no words came to her lips. Instead, she buried her head in the crook of his neck. He tenderly stroked her hair. There was no need for words. He'd never felt the need to hold a woman the way he held her. He'd never felt the need to cuddle with a woman after sex, so why with her? He had no answer to his question, and for now he didn't need any.

Samson put his hand under her chin and pulled her face up to him. Without a word, his lips found hers, kissing her longingly. He knew by morning her lips and the rest of her body would be sore, sore because he wouldn't be able to stop. Just this one sexual act with her had shown him he needed more of her. He wasn't even close to being sated.

Why? Maybe because he was so starved for sex, or maybe because her body felt so good. Whatever the reason, and he didn't really care at this point, he needed more.

Samson could feel himself getting hard again and wanted to join his body with hers.

"Could you please hand me another condom?" he asked her as he released her lips.

"I only brought one."

"One?" Disbelief overrode his instant panic. He looked at her. "Did you think one was going to be enough?"

"Well, I didn't know …" He caught her glance at his erection, and the knowledge that she liked what she saw made him feel like a proud peacock, increasing his hardness even more.

"Ye of little faith!"

He touched his finger to her nose and laughed. "I'm not going to be able to spend the next six hours in bed with you without touching you. I don't have that kind of self-control, believe me."

"So, what now?"

"Would you hand me that phone from the nightstand please?"

Delilah reached for the cordless phone on her side of the bed and handed it to him.

"What are you doing?"

He dialed a number. "Putting in an order." He listened for the call to be answered.

"Carl. I forgot something," he started, and she seemed to realize what he was about to do and blushed. Her pink cheeks were the cutest thing he'd ever seen. He grinned sheepishly. "Could you please stop by the all-night drugstore and pick up a box of condoms for me?" He paused, not knowing how to answer Carl's question that followed. "I don't know." Maybe Delilah did. "What size?"

"Extra large." She laughed out loud.

"Did you get that, Carl? Yes, make that a dozen, and just leave them in front of my bedroom door when you come in. That'll be all for tonight. And no interruptions tonight whatsoever. I don't care if there's an earthquake—I don't want anybody calling or dropping by. Let the guys know, too. Thanks Carl."

Samson put the phone down, barely listening to Carl's reply.

"Extra large, huh?" He grinned at her.

"A dozen?"

He shrugged. "Well, I figured I can always get more for tomorrow night, but if you think a dozen isn't enough for tonight, I'll call him back." He made a half-hearted attempt at picking up the receiver again before Delilah stopped him by tickling him at his sides and under his arms. He laughed and turned to her to pay her back. He rolled around the bed with her. As he started tickling her, her giggles grew louder and more uncontrolled.

"I can't believe you asked your driver to buy you condoms."

"He'll get over it." Maybe she thought it was an embarrassing thing, but Carl probably couldn't care less if he bought dental floss or condoms.

She settled down after her giggling spell, and he pulled her back into his arms again.

"Kiss me," she demanded.

"It's going to be at least half an hour till the condoms arrive. I'm not sure how safe it is to kiss you right now. It might make it very hard for me."

She pointedly looked at his erection. "I don't think it can get any harder." Neither did he. And as if to prove her point, she wrapped her hand around his hard-on and caressed him gently.

"I guess I lost that argument." He smirked and gave into her request.

Delilah loved the way Samson kissed her: tender, passionate, like a man on fire. Without holding back. No man had ever kissed her the way Samson did; he made her feel like she was the only woman in the world. She shuddered at the power he had over her body and mind, and at the same time, let herself fall without regret.

He'd given her more pleasure in an hour than she'd had the entire last year, and if a man could bring her to such heights, she couldn't hold back. She still expected to wake up from a dream and find herself alone in the apartment, daydreaming. It was incredible that a man as handsome and desirable as he would give her the time of day, or night, for that matter. But everything felt too real, so it couldn't be a dream.

"I think we should find something else to do until Carl gets here," he suggested suddenly, his voice strained. Disappointment swept over her. Why hadn't she packed more condoms?

"It's not that I don't love kissing you, but I can tell you right now what that'll lead to in about two minutes. And you don't want to have to fight me off when I can't control myself any longer."

"I don't think I'd be very good at fighting you off."

"It would be fun if you at least tried." It sounded like something which could indeed be a lot of fun.

"Ah, a man who likes to hunt." She gave him a knowing look.

"Especially when the prey looks so delicious." His eyes told her just how delicious he found her.

Delilah let her finger slide over his lips. "Go on; catch me if you can."

Samson playfully closed his mouth, but she pulled her finger back.

"Not fast enough."

She'd let him catch her, but not just yet. He'd have to work for it a little first.

"Give me another chance."

Her finger went back to his lips, teasing him with her soft touch. She watched him intently trying to figure out when he would snap his mouth shut. His poker face gave no indication. His tongue reached for her finger, slowly and sensually licking it as if he had no intention of snatching it. Another flick with his tongue, and suddenly his mouth rocked forward, engulfing her finger and snapping shut.

Samson held her hostage and sucked at her gently before releasing her.

"You let yourself be distracted by my tongue—that was your downfall," he warned her, his eyes flickering. "Never take your eyes off the hunter. You never know when he might strike."

He pulled her down onto his chest. "How about a kiss for the victorious hunter?"

"Since when does the prey kiss the predator?"

"Never heard of Little Red Riding Hood?"

"She didn't kiss the hunter." But she would kiss Samson. He'd caught her. He deserved his prize.

"But she kissed the wolf. What if I was the wolf? Would you kiss me?"

"What version of Little Red Riding Hood were you reading as a kid?"

"The adult version, of course!" He flipped her onto her back so quickly she barely knew what was happening. A second later she was pinned underneath him. She didn't complain: in her opinion, it was a good place to be.

"Since you're not going to kiss me of your own free will, I have no choice but to torture you."

He jumped off the bed and picked her up in his arms.

"Where are we going?" What kind of torture?

"Into the bathroom for some water torture." He smiled, and his eyes twinkled like a rascal who was planning a prank. Torture suddenly sounded like something she had to try.

His bathroom was windowless and enormous. In addition to an oversized vanity with two sinks, there was a large Jacuzzi-type tub and a huge walk-in shower. The toilet was separate behind a wall.

"I'm kind of looking forward to this water torture you're promising."

"Are you telling me I can't scare you with anything?"

"I guess not. But if you want me to pretend...." She could playact a little if it turned him on. Not that she thought she needed to. Just being herself with him seemed to turn him on.

Samson set her onto her feet and switched on the water in the shower. Once he'd tested the temperature, he gave her a little shove toward it. "After you, my lady."

Delilah stepped into the shower and felt him right behind her. The water started raining down her torso, and she soaked up the warmth.

"Close your eyes," he ordered. "I want you to only use your sense of touch—nothing else."

"Hmm." She closed her eyes, curious about what he had in mind.

His hands touched her shoulders and painstakingly slowly ran down her arms, pausing in the crook of her elbows before connecting with her wrists. Samson encircled them and pulled her arms up, then eased her toward the tile wall of the shower, pressing her against it. He placed her hands flat onto the wall before releasing her.

"Don't move." His order was spoken calmly and with the confidence of a man who was used to his orders being followed. She'd obey: as long as she enjoyed what he was doing. A couple of seconds later, she was certain she'd obey for however long he wanted her to.

His hands went back to her shoulders before descending over her shoulder blades, down her back and over her hips, stopping just short of her round cheeks. Instead, he ran them down the side of her thighs.

Hot flames shot through her under his touch. The fact she couldn't see what he was doing only intensified the sensation.

Delilah heard him shift behind her and suddenly felt both of his hands on her ass making circular motions before moving upwards again. She breathed heavily.

"Lower." She yearned for his hands on her backside again.

"I'm afraid I make the rules here. Are you ready to give me a kiss yet, or do I need to torture you longer?"

"More torture." The choice was easy. If this was torture, what would happen if he decided to shower her with pleasure instead?

His hands went underneath her arms and slowly traveled down her sides to her hips before moving inwards and down the middle of her ass. She moaned when she felt his hand rest in between her legs. Hoping he wouldn't notice, she tilted her pelvis backwards to force his hand to her front. He pressed her back toward the wall.

"No, no."

Seconds later she felt something warm and slick on her ass. His tongue was licking every inch of her backside. Samson knew how to torture a woman. She felt how hot liquid surged to her already moist flesh and started oozing from her. Finally she felt one hand reach underneath her, probing her moist folds.

With his other hand, he pulled her hips toward him and widened her stance. Delilah felt him turn, and finally his face was right underneath her, in between her legs. He'd positioned himself with his back against the tile wall, his legs stretched out in front of him, his face at her core. With both hands he clasped her ass and pressed his face into her sex, letting his tongue slide over her warm flesh.

"Oh God!" she yelped.

He held her firmly so she couldn't escape, while his tongue played with her clit. His strokes were masterful and relentless. She knew the only way he would stop was when she came. And she wanted to come … right in his mouth.

His tongue was skilled in finding the right spot and the correct pressure to apply to her to make her gasp at every stroke. His moans mixed with hers, telling her how much he enjoyed pleasuring her. Never had she met a man so selfless when it came to pleasing her.

His hands gently stroked her ass, and his tongue teased her in a rhythm that made her body tingle. She felt her body heat up, burning from the inside as if it was a volcano ready to erupt. The molten lava in her core boiled to the surface, and in one big explosion her body released all its tension, shooting waves of pleasure into her every cell.

Delilah braced herself against the tile wall, her legs shaking, when she felt him get up from underneath her and cradle her in his arms.

"How about a kiss now?"

Delilah turned and opened her eyes, finding herself staring into his, which had turned from its hazel color to a dark gold.

"Anything you want." She meant it. He didn't even have to ask.

His lips merged with hers, and he took her and smothered her in a long and passionate kiss. His hands pressed her against his naked body, and she could feel his hard cock against her stomach. She wondered how difficult it had to be for him to touch her like this while he had to wait for Carl to come back with the condoms.

There was something she could do to ease his need. Delilah pushed herself away from him, earning her a startled look from him.

Samson was about to protest the interruption when he felt her hand sheathing his cock.

"Do I get to torture you too?"

"Under one condition. Continue kissing me." He'd never felt anything like it with anybody else. When he was submerged in her kiss, she transported him to another world, a world of sunshine and warmth. He was getting addicted to it. The images were so vivid he could almost sense the sun on his body and smell the flowers in the meadow. Yet he had no idea why he had those visions with her.

He sought her lips again and was instantly transported back into the summer meadow. She slid her hand up and down his erect cock, tugging on it harder with each movement. Her hand was soft and warm, and the water trickling down on them made every movement smooth.

Delilah knew how to excite him. Just feeling her breasts crushed against his chest, her lips on his and her tongue dueling with his, aroused him more than any vampire female ever had. But the touch of her hand—it was something out of heaven. The way she ran her hand over him, squeezed him with just the right pressure and moved his skin back and forth, was as if she could read his mind, knowing instinctively what he wanted and what brought him closer and closer to his climax.

"Delilah."

Her hand squeezed him again, faster now and harder. In a desperate attempt to steady himself, he dug his hands into her hips and pressed one thigh in between hers. But the onslaught of sensations her caress sent through him was too much. His breath quickened, and his body tensed as he felt his seed shoot through his cock and spray against her stomach.

He braced himself against the wall behind her and buried his head in the crook of her neck, trying to hide from her that his legs shook like those of a teenager experiencing his first sexual encounter. This human woman drove every sane thought out of his body.

"I think that's all the torture I can take for now." It wasn't what he'd wanted to say. He'd wanted to tell her what he felt when he was with her, but he couldn't. He barely knew her. She would think he was crazy. And besides, it would never work: he was still a vampire. He shouldn't even feel the things he felt with her.

Samson tried to convince himself that the reason he felt like this was because he was so starved for sex. It would just be tonight until he had stilled his hunger for sex. After that she wouldn't mean anything to him, he was sure. For certain there was no good reason why he would want her any longer than that. After all, he was just following doctor's orders. And who in their right mind would continue taking medicine once the illness was cured? Who indeed?

SEVEN

Delilah stopped in front of the painting over the fireplace in Samson's bedroom. The scene of a stately home surrounded by expansive grounds and a small pond drew her in. There was something oddly familiar about it, almost as if she knew the place.

She felt Samson stop behind her.

"When did you paint this?" she asked him without thinking.

"How did you know I painted this?" His voice sounded as surprised as she was herself. For some inexplicable reason she knew he'd painted it. She could see Samson standing in front of an easel, paint brush in hand, shirt and pants dirtied by various colors of oil paint.

"I don't know. But when I look at it, I know you painted it." She astounded herself by the certainty with which she said the words.

"I did. It's my ancestral home. My family came from England."

"It's beautiful. Is the home still in your family's hands?" It was more a castle than a home, but the warmth Delilah felt when she looked at it made her realize it had been a true family home with love and laughter.

She turned to him and saw the pain in his eyes for one second, before he planted a smile on his lips.

"No, not anymore. They lost everything after some unwise investments. The family became penniless, and everything was sold off. That's what brought me, uh, my ancestors to the United States. Their only son came to this country in the late eighteenth century to make a name for himself."

"And did he? Make a name for himself?" Delilah asked with interest. She loved history, especially when it was connected to somebody she knew personally.

"Yes and no. He was successful in business in the end, but he never saw his parents again. It was the biggest regret of his life, having to leave them behind. Never to hug his mother again, never to converse with his father about the things that mattered to a young man."

There was pain in his voice. She felt a sense of loss slam into her chest.

"You say it as if you knew him. It was over two hundred years ago."

Samson blinked then gave her another smile. "I'd like to think that I know him. It's what I would have felt in his situation. Losing family is the hardest thing to get over."

She understood all too well. "When did you lose yours?"

"Too long ago."

He pulled her into his arms and kissed the top of her head. She felt his need for tenderness and molded into him, wrapping her arms around his back.

"Come, join me in my favorite spot."

Samson pulled her down onto the large floor pillows in front of the fireplace. Delilah rolled onto her stomach and gazed into the flames. Shadows created by the fire danced on her bare skin. Her long dark hair was sprawled over her shoulders. Some of the strands were wet from the shower.

His body was turned toward her, and his head rested on his hand as he admired her beauty while he played with her hair. He enjoyed running his hand over her bare ass, caressing her more tenderly than he'd ever caressed a woman before. Her skin was deliciously soft and flawless.

"You said you're on a business trip. How long will you stay in San Francisco?"

Samson dipped his head to kiss the delightful indentation at the base of her back.

"Till Wednesday. I'm taking the red-eye back to New York."

He felt a sharp stab in his chest. Indigestion? Not likely—vampires didn't get indigestion.

"New York? I used to live in New York. Tell me what you do there." He wanted to get her talking so he could get his mind off what he really wanted to do—bury himself in her again, and again, and again. Maybe nibbling his way over the swells of her ass would take the edge off. He did just that, letting his lips graze over her delicate skin.

An appreciative moan was her response before she spoke again. "I work as an independent consultant. I travel a lot for my job."

"What kind of consultant?" He wasn't really interested, but he still hadn't heard Carl come back and knew he had to kill the time somehow. As much as he wanted to go down on her again, he didn't think he'd have enough self-control left to stop himself from plunging into her this time. There was no way he wanted to piss her off by sleeping with her without a condom, since he figured she was the kind of woman who'd just ditch him if he did something against her will.

Of course, as a vampire he could always force her, but he didn't want to. He wanted her to come to him of her own free will. He had the feeling that sex with Delilah was much more satisfying when she wanted him. The thought of forcing her gave him a strange sense of guilt.

"Financial stuff. It's really not that interesting."

It sounded like she didn't want to talk about it. Being the hunter he was deep down, he felt the challenge rise to get an answer.

"Try again." To encourage her, he placed soft kisses on her sexy ass.

"What?" She turned her head back to him and gave him an inquisitive look.

"Let me get this right. You don't want to tell me what you do?" Samson propped himself up.

She cringed. "Because it's really not that interesting. And once I tell you, you'll think I'm boring just because of what I do."

"Issues, issues. There's no way I could ever look at you and think you're boring." His eyes deliberately scanned her naked back and ass. No, boring was definitely not the right adjective to describe her.

Luscious, hot, sensual, but not even those words could really capture what he saw.

"You're going to laugh."

"Have a little faith in my abilities to control myself."

"I'm an auditor."

"An auditor?" he repeated before he felt a stifled laugh build in his chest. He tried to suppress a grin, but too late. She was worried he'd find her boring because she was an auditor? That was just too funny.

"You can audit me anytime."

"I could count and measure all your parts to make sure everything's where it should be."

"You'd better have a real large measuring tape on you."

A second later a pillow hit him in the face.

"I knew it! Go ahead, make fun of the little auditor—but it won't be original. I've heard every joke before."

Samson snatched the pillow and threw it right back at her, starting a pillow fight. He knew she wasn't mad at him when he heard her giggle. Delilah rolled and hit him with another pillow which he immediately appropriated before immobilizing her by pinning her down underneath him. She panted. He kissed her before he released her again.

"What made you want to be an auditor?"

"It was just something I was good at." She appeared reluctant to talk about her career choice.

"But you didn't know that before you started the job. There must have been something that interested you."

"It wasn't really interest in the job, more like … I don't know, the fact that I could be in control of something."

The answer surprised him. Delilah didn't strike him as a control freak. "I'm not quite sure I get that. What do you mean by control? Did you want to be the boss?" She was a strong woman. He could certainly see her as a leader in her field.

She shook her head. "Nothing like that. I wanted to control risk, to make sure things didn't go wrong."

"But is that really what you do now? Control risk?" As if she was afraid of something. What could she fear?

"In a small way, yes. I make sure things get fixed when they go wrong. I find the culprit and correct the situation. It eliminates risk in the future."

"Why is that so important to you?" Samson was curious now. Why was a gorgeous woman like her interested in such a seemingly mundane field? Shouldn't she be interested in something more feminine?

"Because some outcomes can hurt people. If I can reduce risk, I can reduce bad situations." Interesting concept.

"And people won't get hurt?"

She nodded.

"Couldn't you help people better if you'd become a doctor instead?" It seemed like a much more straightforward path to helping people if that was what she wanted to do.

She waved him off. "God, no! I get nauseous at the sight of blood. Figures I can handle, blood I can't."

Samson swallowed hard. If she couldn't handle blood, it could definitely be a problem later when ... What the hell was he thinking about? There wouldn't be a later. She'd never have to deal with blood. He wouldn't bite her.

Time to change the subject. Fast.

He pinned her down once more, imprisoning her wrists and lowering his head. Her breath mingled with his. "You're the most exciting woman I've ever met." Too abrupt a change of subject? Maybe, but she didn't seem to care.

"Is that why you're hard again?" His erection was hard to miss, pressed against her warm thigh.

"And the most perceptive. And if Carl doesn't show up here in the next ten minutes I don't know what I'm going to do with you." He underscored his statement with an exasperated breath.

Delilah rubbed her thigh against his hard-on, tempting him even further.

Little minx!

"Make that five minutes," he corrected himself and moaned.

Samson loosened his grip on her wrists, and she freed one hand to put it on the back of his neck. "Maybe I can help you pass the time." She pulled him down and touched her lips to his. As soon as he felt her soft skin and then seconds later her moist tongue slip into his mouth, he was completely lost. For a few seconds he gave into her, returning her passionate kiss, but the urge to penetrate her was getting to be too much. With all his remaining strength, he pulled himself off her and rolled onto his back.

He sat up and moved away from her. "Okay. Here's the deal. You stay right over there." He pointed to one end of the floor pillows. "And I will stay on this side."

"And then?"

"We'll talk. Maybe I should loan you a robe."

"A robe? So you're done looking at me?"

"Not even close. But it might be fun to rip it off you once the condoms get here." He could already imagine the scene. Damn, was his mind not capable of thinking of anything else but sex, or rather, sex with Delilah? He had the feeling it might take longer than one night to get this out of his system.

***

Carl pulled the limousine into the garage and got out. In two trips, he brought both the groceries and all of Delilah's personal items into the foyer, including the flowers Samson had given her. The house was quiet except for the low voices he could hear coming from upstairs. His hearing was as sharp as Samson's. In the kitchen he saw his boss' note immediately. When he read it he raised his eyebrows. His boss thought of everything.

Without hesitation he moved all blood from the main fridge into the smaller one in the pantry and locked it. Delilah would not find anything out of the ordinary, and their secret would be safe. He didn't like the idea that the woman was staying in the house, but he would be the last man to question his boss' decisions.

Carl was absolutely devoted to Samson. His loyalty was unsurpassed, and he would give his life for him should it ever become necessary. After all, Samson had revived him when a gang of criminals had robbed him of his human life. Granted, he was now a vampire, but in Carl's books it was better than being dead.

Carl finished filling the fridge with human food before bringing Delilah's luggage, as well as the bunch of red roses, into the guest room. He knew she wouldn't be staying in the room: he could hear them both in the master suite.

He paused in front of the door and set the box of condoms down when he heard Samson laugh. He hadn't heard his boss laugh like this in a long time. He was finally happy, at least for a moment. And it would only be for a moment. What Carl had found amongst Delilah's things when he'd packed for her concerned him. He needed to bring it to Samson's attention.

He lifted his hand to knock at the door, but hesitated.

He remembered Samson's explicit instructions of not wanting to be disturbed tonight, and despite his concerns, Carl didn't have the heart to disrupt him. Samson needed a night of fun and games. It would have to wait.

Carl left the house, knowing his boss would have already heard him on the stairs. There was no need to let him know he'd executed all his wishes.

As soon as he was back in the car he dialed a number.

"Yes, Carl?" Ricky answered instantly.

"We need to talk. It's urgent."

"I'm with Amaury. We're down in Dog Patch, behind the old mill." Dog Patch, part of the Potrero Hill neighborhood of San Francisco, was one of the shadier neighborhoods in San Fran and not a place where humans liked to hang around after dark. Vampires, on the other hand, did, because it was away from the curious eyes of humans.

"Fifteen minutes." Carl pressed harder on the accelerator, and the car shot down the hill heading for the Embarcadero.

***

"What do you mean? Was he armed?" John Reardon hissed into the cell phone. He nervously paced on this patio, constantly glancing back at the house, hoping his wife wouldn't overhear him.

"I don't know what happened, but I'm telling you: I'm out."

"That wasn't the deal, Billy. I've already paid you." John's voice was panicked now.

"And I've earned my money, but the bitch keeps on getting help. You told me she didn't know anybody here, and suddenly she's with this guy who defends her with his life? I'm telling you, there was something creepy about that guy. Don't mess with her."

"Damn it; just give it one more try. I'll see her in the office tomorrow, and I'll find out what she'll do in the evening. I'll make sure you'll get her alone. Please, help me out."

He heard Billy inhale sharply several times until he finally spoke. "If you weren't married to my sister, we wouldn't even be having this conversation. Okay," he paused again, "but this time you'll tell me the whole story. Then I'll decide if I continue to help you. I'm not gonna risk my neck for you blindly anymore. Family only goes so far."

"It's better if you don't know too much." As much as John wanted his brother-in-law to help him get him out of the mess he was in, he thought it safer if Billy didn't know everything.

"Bull. Start talking or I'm out." Billy's various brushes with the law had given him a badass attitude.

"Promise me you won't tell Karen anything about this." John didn't want his wife to know what he'd done. They were fighting enough about everything as it was.

Billy grunted in agreement.

"I cooked the books. It was really simple at first, just some accounting entries, and I wrote down equipment to scrap value. After that it was easy to sell it and pocket the extra money. It helped. We needed the money after we bought the new house." John knew it was no justification for stealing, but he'd really had no other choice. The interest rate on his mortgage had spiked, and he couldn't make the payments anymore.

"That's it? Sorry, but that's not enough reason to get rid of the auditor," Billy declined flat out. "You don't even know if she's going to find out." If Billy only knew what was really going on, but he couldn't trust him to keep his mouth shut.

"She'll find out; she's one of the best. I've checked her out."

"So she finds out, and you're gonna get a slap on the wrist. Big deal."

"I'll lose everything." John still couldn't tell him about the man who was blackmailing him. No. He was too afraid of him to even mention him to Billy, as if the man would find out somehow. "Please, Billy. Do it for Karen."

There was a long pause during which he almost thought Billy had disconnected the call.

"Okay, but this is the last time. If she gets away again, you're on your own. And you'll owe me another grand."

"Thanks, Billy." John flipped the phone shut. Billy was the least of his problems. At least he could manipulate his brother-in-law into almost anything. And with a rap sheet as long as his arm, Billy had enough resources at his hands to make things happen. Plus he was always in need of money.

John dreaded the phone call he had put off all evening.

Once he'd started cooking the books he'd thought his troubles were over, but then one day he'd received a phone call from a man who knew what he was doing. The man had started blackmailing him. In exchange for his silence he'd asked for access to the company books. John never asked what the man wanted, figuring the less he knew the better.

Now, with the unexpected arrival of the auditor from New York, he was worried that she'd find what he'd done. His career would be finished. Not only that: he would be criminally prosecuted. But that wasn't even the worst. The man had told him to get rid of the auditor, or he in turn would get rid of John.

John had never seen him and only spoken to him on the phone. He didn't even know his name, but he knew the man meant business. Whatever his blackmailer was up to, it was a much bigger fraud than the few thousands John had embezzled. Why else would he need John's logon and password to the company's systems? And why else had he requested to take care of the auditor?

As John dialed the number, he secretly hoped he would get his voicemail, but he knew chances were not good. No matter what time of the night he called, the man picked up, whereas during the day he often reached only his voicemail.

"What is it?" the familiar male voice answered.

"She got away again."

"I know."

"How?" John didn't feel comfortable that he was already aware of his screw-up.

"I have eyes and ears everywhere. You should have gotten her when you had a chance. Now she's being protected, and I'm going to have to take care of it myself. Idiot!"

"I'm sorry."

"Oh, you will be when I'm done with you. I need another week, and if you can't get her or any other auditor out of those books until then, I'm going to have to find somebody else to do your work. Do you understand me?" His voice was sharp.

John shivered. "Yes. There won't be any more problems. I promise."

"Good."

A click on the other end, and the call was disconnected. Nothing was good. John instinctively knew it. One day soon, the shit would hit the fan, and he would be standing right in front of it. It wasn't a pretty picture.

"John!" he heard his wife's voice behind him as she stepped out onto the patio. "Did you not pay the credit card bill last month?"

He turned to her and saw her holding the bill in her hands. She looked more than annoyed.

"Of course I did. I always do." Had he paid it? He couldn't remember whether there'd been sufficient money the previous month.

"Then why are they charging us a finance charge and interest on this one? That can't be right! I'm gonna call them."

John snatched the bill out of her hands. "I'll take care of it. I'm sure it's just some clerical error. I'll call them first thing in the morning."

"Good, because I hate it when these credit card companies cheat honest people like us. It's appalling!"

He watched her go back into the house and ran his hands through his hair. How long could he keep this up? He heard his youngest fussing. If he didn't have the kids to worry about he would just hightail it out of town with his wife. But with two kids in tow, how far would they get? And besides, who'd say Karen would even come with him once she knew what problems he'd gotten himself into?

EIGHT

Samson pulled out a condom from the box and put it into the pocket of his bathrobe before he turned back to face Delilah.

"You want me to do what?" A grin was already forming on his face. He liked her suggestion. In fact, he liked it very much.

"Catch me, and if you do, maybe I'll let you rip the robe off me." She laughed and jumped over the bed and off on the other side. She wore a long robe of dark-green silk he had loaned her. It was too long for her and presented a tripping hazard. Not that he needed the unfair advantage he had over her.

"It'll be a short chase," Samson warned her without malice. "And, I always win."

"I'm fast."

Damn, she was cute. And playful.

"I'm faster."

Effortlessly he jumped over the bed as he saw her take off around the armchair and then run over the floor pillows in front of the fireplace. He took a different route but took his time. He didn't want the hunt to be over too soon. He always kept two steps behind her, making sure she was almost in reach, but giving her the feeling she could get away if she wanted to.

Her giggles filled the room which, for too long, had not seen or heard any smiles and laughter, let alone the intoxicating reverberations of Delilah's voice.

Delilah rounded the armchair again, and Samson stopped right opposite of her. She made an indication to the right, but then veered left. She jumped over the chaise lounge as if it was a hurdle, and he had to admire her agility. The way she could spread her legs would come in handy eventually. He could think of more than one use for her nimbleness: how her long, shapely legs would wrap around him, how he would draw them up to his shoulders. His cock went rigid at the thought.

Samson licked his lips and went after her as she headed for the bed and jumped onto it. That was exactly where he wanted her. He seized her ankles and pulled her down, making her fall face forward into the soft pillows, almost knocking the wind out of her.

"Got you." He jumped onto the bed like a tiger capturing its prey, pinning her underneath him. "I've come to claim my prize."

He pulled her hair to the side to reveal her neck and face. She was breathing heavily. Realizing that he was probably crushing her diaphragm with his weight, he rolled to her side, pulling her with him. He neatly tucked her cute ass into his groin and molded his chest to her back. He enjoyed playing with her, yet he'd never been the playful type. Never had a woman's body felt so good to him. It had to be the fact he was so deprived of sex.

"I let you win," Delilah insisted, still out of breath.

"I won fair and square." Samson smirked while he pulled her silky robe aside, exposing her legs. How could a small woman like her have such long legs? He let his hand run down her smooth thigh, admiring her perfect form.

"What do you want?"

It was plain and simple. "You."

"You already have me." Did she realize what she was admitting to him?

He eased the robe off her shoulders. "So, all this is mine?" The word "mine" sunk deep into his chest, feeling utterly right as he pressed his lips onto her shoulder. Without bringing out his fangs, his teeth scraped at her skin. He felt her shiver. "Did you know that a lion bites his lioness during mating to claim her as his?"

The thought of claiming her whipped through his mind like a bullet ricocheting in a confined space.

"Is that what you're trying to do?" She didn't pull away.

"Don't tempt me, or I might just do what a lion would do."

Samson had to stop looking at her neck where her artery pulsated under her skin. The only way to forget about the blood flowing in her veins was to satisfy another hunger, one that made his cock throb uncontrollably.

"Who says I would stop you?"

Samson pulled in his breath at the tempting thought, before he slid her robe down further and unwrapped her from it within seconds. He quickly shed his own bathrobe and pulled her back to his chest. Her sweet ass lined up perfectly with his hard shaft. If ever he'd seen a woman with the most perfect behind, it was Delilah. Just looking at her, knowing that in a few seconds he'd bury himself in her while enjoying the view of those delightful round cheeks, filled him with desire.

He fumbled for the condom and slipped it on. "I've never been so hard in my life than with you." So constantly hard, so constantly wanting.

"Anything I can do for you?"

Samson pushed himself between her legs, felt for her entrance and rammed his cock into her up to the hilt. "Yes." He moaned loudly. "You can let me fuck you till sunrise."

Or longer.

Delilah pulled her knees up higher to give him better access, and he seized her hips and pushed harder. She was so wet; he effortlessly slipped in and out despite his size. From his position behind her, he had complete control over her. She was vulnerable, yet all he could hear were her sounds of pleasure, moans escaping from her lips with every thrust he made. It was like music to his ears. A concert of magic sounds appeasing his body in a way no other sounds ever had.

Her face showed signs of ecstasy; her breathing was short and huffed, her body pliable, responsive.

"Give me more." More? This human woman wanted him to fuck her harder? He would break her. He shouldn't do it. It was too dangerous.

"More," she begged again until he could hold back no longer. He felt his fangs come out, and his body harden. His vampire self wanted to fuck her. Damn it, he'd been holding back for so long, he had neither the willpower nor the self control to stop the transformation. She wanted to be fucked. What was he waiting for, another invitation?

But he couldn't let her see him like this, no, not with his fangs extended and his eyes glowing red. She would be scared of him if she saw him like this. His hand went in search for the broad silk belt of her robe. He found it and pulled it up.

"Close your eyes and I'll fulfill your every wish." He tried to control his voice and put the belt over her eyes. She was startled at first, but to his surprise let him proceed tying the knot behind her head.

"I won't hurt you, I promise."

"I know." It was incomprehensible why Delilah trusted him. But he knew that she did. He could feel it.

Samson gave her one last thrust from behind before he pulled himself out of her. Then he turned her onto her back and lowered himself onto her, centering himself.

"Delilah, sweetness, wrap your legs around me."

He plunged into her and rode her hard, harder than he had before, harder than he should with a human. Hell, he shouldn't have sex with a human in the first place. Too late. He was already in too deep, literally and figuratively. And he wasn't going to stop—no. Stopping now, when he had everything he wanted, was not an option. Giving up making her body hum with pleasure, and his in return? No. No man ever could—and a vampire even less. He was driven by his desires, more an animal now than a man.

His fangs hungered for her neck and the blood it promised beneath her pale skin. Skin so vulnerable, so breakable, so delicious. He soaked in her scent of lavender and knew what he needed, but couldn't get it. He couldn't kiss her, not now, not with his fangs extended. Damn!

Her muscles were so tight around his shaft Samson knew she would milk him any moment. He knew he'd be ripping the damn condom to shreds when he did but he didn't care. No more holding back.

"Oh, God, yes." Delilah met each of his thrust with an equally powerful reaction, their bodies slamming together so forcefully, he thought he'd break her into pieces. But he kept on impaling her on his hard shaft, filling her tight sheath perfectly.

Then suddenly her muscles squeezed him tighter as she came, too unexpected for him to stop the approach of his own climax. He could literally feel the waves crashing through her body. In a ripple effect they ignited what seemed like dynamite in his own cells, making him explode with the force of an atomic bomb. His head veered toward her neck, his fangs ready to rip her vein open and drink her blood.

Take her! She's yours!

At the last second, he jerked his head into the other direction and buried his fangs into the pillow as he collapsed on top of her.

Samson exhaled heavily, once, twice, three times. He'd almost bitten her, almost. This was getting too dangerous for her. Yet, at the same time, he knew he couldn't stop. He needed more of her, and there weren't enough hours in the night left to truly get his fill of her.

He felt how she pulled her blindfold off and turned her head, but he kept his own buried in the pillow. Slowly his fangs receded into his gums, and he could feel the tension in his jaw ease.

"So, you were holding out on me the first time," she said, panting as heavily as he was.

Samson raised his head, knowing his fangs had fully retreated, and the red glow in his eyes had subsided. He would look completely normal to her again—or as normal as he *could* look after the most mind-blowing orgasm to date. He was sure he had a stupid grin plastered on his face. The kind of grin a sixteen-year-old boy would have after his first sexual encounter.

"You're going to curse me tomorrow when you see all the bruises I've left you with. You're so breakable."

"I'm not any more breakable than any other woman."

But a lot more breakable than a vampire female.

And a lot tastier.

Her lips beckoned, and he couldn't resist. Tenderly he kissed her, capturing her upper lip and gently sucking it into his mouth.

"You amaze me. It feels like you're two different people, one wild and one tender."

"Hmh." She had no idea how accurate her assessment of him was, so instead of answering her, Samson decided to show her his tender self and continued his kiss.

When he finally pulled out of her, he realized that he'd guessed right.

"I'm afraid the condom didn't make it." He got rid of the damaged item.

Delilah flinched. "Oh no!"

He put his hand under her chin and made her look at him. "Sweetness, I don't want you to worry about it. I can't get you pregnant, and I guarantee you, I'm completely healthy."

Her next reaction surprised him. "You can't have kids?" He thought he could detect disappointment in her voice, but he had to be mistaken. "Oh." She leaned her head against his chest.

"Are you tired?" He had the sudden urge to change the subject.

"Not particularly. I can't sleep much at the moment. I've been having insomnia ever since I've arrived in San Francisco."

"Insomnia?"

"Yes, it's strange. I've not been able to sleep much at night, and then during the day I'm completely exhausted."

"Have you had that before?" Samson gently stroked her hair.

"No. I'm the kind of person who can sleep anywhere and everywhere. Put me in the back of a car and start driving, and I'll nod off."

"So, what's keeping you up at night then? Too much work?"

Delilah shook her head, before she rested it back on his chest. "No. Work is normal as always. Just some nightmares. Nothing important."

Samson wondered what kind of nightmares a woman like her could be plagued with. "Monsters?"

"Nothing important. Just odd stuff. I could have sworn that I dreamed about this house the night before I met you. But it was probably nothing. I mean, there are so many Victorians in the city, and by night they really all look very similar."

Her hand on his stomach, absentmindedly stroking him, felt right to him. Intimate, personal, good.

"You think you dreamed about this one though? And it was a nightmare? As a man, that doesn't sound like something I want to hear from the woman in my arms. What happened in the nightmare? I hope I wasn't in it."

She gave him a light slap on his arm. "Of course not. It was probably not even your house. It could have been any Victorian."

"So what happened in the Victorian?" He was curious about her dream.

"I wasn't inside. I ran toward it because somebody was following me."

"Like the other night?"

He felt how she held her breath for a few seconds. "Yes. Like the other night." Delilah paused for a moment. "I'm sure it's nothing. It's probably just an unfamiliar bed," she shrugged it off.

He didn't press her. "Well, since this is also an unfamiliar bed, I think I'll just have to keep you entertained then." Samson smiled. "Maybe I can even make you tired enough so you'll be able to sleep."

"I should give you a little break to recover."

He took her hand and led it to his erection. "No need."

She propped her head up on her arm and looked at him. "I don't understand this. How is it possible that you are hard again? It's only been two minutes since you've made love to me."

He threw up his hands. "Believe me, this is new to me too."

Maybe not entirely new. As a vampire, he did have a lot more stamina than a human male. But nevertheless, it was unusual for him. "I just need to be in the same room with you, and I have a hard-on. It's not exactly something I can control." He'd picked up on the fact that she called it making love rather than having sex. Was that what she felt, that he'd made love to her? Was he capable of making love? It would imply more than just the physical aspect of joining their bodies: it would mean emotions were involved.

"I'm not complaining; I'm just surprised." Delilah smiled at him while she gently ran her finger down his cock.

"For all I know, you've put a spell on me." He gazed into her eyes and tried to understand why he reacted to her body the way he did. Why he couldn't get enough of her and wanted her again so soon.

Several hours and lovemaking sessions later, Delilah finally seemed to get sleepy.

"Sweetness, when you wake up in the morning, I won't be here."

"Why not?" She seemed disappointed that he wouldn't wake up with her. And he would have liked to.

"I have meetings all day and have to get going early," Samson lied. "But I'll see you when you get back in the evening. I'll ask Oliver to take care of you tomorrow."

"Take care of me?"

"He's going to be your bodyguard for the day."

"I don't need a bodyguard," she protested and yawned. "That's really overkill."

"You've been attacked twice. I think you can't be careful enough."

"I'm not some kind of celebrity who needs a bodyguard. I can take care of myself." Her voice had taken a harsher tone than he'd heard from her before. Why was she resisting his offer?

"I can't be with you during the day, and I won't be able to concentrate on anything if I can't be sure you're safe. That thug is still out there, and he'll try it again if he gets a chance."

"Samson, you can't just take over my life like that. I was able to take care of myself up until two days ago. I really don't need this."

She seemed adamant about her refusal. There it was again, that control issue she had. As the auditor she wanted to control all aspects of her life. Except maybe sex. There she'd given control over to him, and he'd gobbled it up like a starving man.

But when it came to everything else, it seemed she didn't want to relinquish control to him or anybody else, and arguing with her wouldn't work.

"Please, Delilah. Do it for me."

"Samson, that's really ridiculous. I don't need a bodyguard."

Delilah wasn't going to win this argument, not if he could help it. Either way, Oliver would protect her tomorrow, even if he had to force her to accept it and use mind control to achieve it. But he preferred not to use so drastic a measure.

"What if the shoe was on the other foot?"

She opened her eyes wide. "That's not fair."

"Who says I'm fighting fair? What if I was the one in danger? I should hope that you would want me safe; unless of course, you didn't care about what happened to me."

When Samson looked at her face and noticed her frown, he knew he had won her over.

"Okay, but I do have to go to work."

He greeted her concession with a kiss. "You won't even notice he's there."

"Yeah, right."

Moments later she snuggled into his chest, and her eyelids fell closed. Samson couldn't sleep yet. His body wasn't tired enough despite the physical exercise he'd gotten. He glanced at the half-empty condom box. He'd continued using them despite the fact that one of them had ripped and despite the fact that he'd told her she had nothing to worry about from him.

He would have much rather liked to go *au natural* to get an even more intense feel of her body. Maybe tomorrow night. He knew there had to be a next night. He was nowhere near done with her. Dr. Drake had been wrong when he thought having sex with her would turn him back into his former self. It hadn't. Yes, his erection problems were gone, but now he had a whole different problem on his hands: he was becoming addicted to her.

As he looked at Delilah's sleeping body, he felt the need to capture the image before him. The dark hair fanned out over the pillow, her palm was turned up, the vein pulsating in her wrist, her breasts sitting on her chest, rising with every breath she took.

He pulled out his sketch pad from his bureau and began to draw.

Samson loved drawing ever since he was little boy. He'd had a privileged upbringing in one of the finest households in England. His parents had been patrons of the arts and had encouraged him even as a little boy to follow his passions.

He'd always thought he'd be an artist when he grew up, but unfortunately his father made some unwise investments, and suddenly the family had been penniless. What could a young man with an artistic education do to make money? Nothing. His only chance was to scrape together what he could and get onto a ship to the New World. There were reports that enterprising young men could make a fortune in America, and he'd had nothing to lose.

Leaving his parents behind was heartbreaking, but Samson hoped to return a wealthy man to take care of them the way they'd taken care of him when he was a child. He never thought that the last time he'd see them was when they waved goodbye to him as he boarded the ship.

Without any skills to speak of, he found it hard to find employment until the bored wife of a British officer hired him as a tutor to instruct her children. It wasn't the only thing she expected him to do. Whenever her husband was away she would sneak into Samson's chambers and request his sexual services. As a relatively inexperienced young man, he appreciated the instructions in the carnal arts the woman was willing to provide him with. He was an outstanding student.

With a very healthy sexual appetite, there seemed nothing wrong with what he was doing. Somehow word spread among the bored wives of the area, and offers of employment started flooding in. Suddenly everybody wanted their children instructed in the arts—and their sexual needs met at night.

He'd had no qualms about it, and he'd finally had choices. Until one day, when suddenly there was only one choice left in his life, only one more decision to be made. Her name was Elizabeth …

The day he realized he was in love with her, the rain came and finally cooled the muggy air. Samson opened the door to the stable to get both himself and his horse out of the downpour.

He shook the water out of his hair as he allowed his eyes to adjust to the dim light in the barn. A faint whimper made him spin around. There, huddled in the corner was Elizabeth, the seventeen-year-old beautiful daughter of his latest employer.

"Elizabeth. What are you doing out here in this weather?"

He let go of the horse's reins and walked to her. When she looked up at him, he realized she was crying. Instinctively he knelt down and pulled her into his arms.

"What's wrong?"

"Oh, Samson," she wailed. "I am to be married in a fortnight!"

No! Not Elizabeth; not the woman he wanted for himself.

"Who said that?"

"Father announced it today. He's chosen Fitzwilliam Herman for me. Samson, please help me, I can't marry that man. He's old, he's ugly, he smells. I don't like him."

He stroked her flaxen hair, then put his hand under her chin to make her look at him. Her eyes were puffy, swollen from the tears she must have been shedding for hours.

"Elizabeth, do you trust me?"

She nodded.

"I know this is not like you would have imagined this day. And this is not the right place for it." He glanced around the stable. "But I don't have much of a choice. I can't let you marry Herman. Because I love you."

Her eyes widened.

"And I won't allow it. Please marry me. We'll go away tonight. We'll hide. We'll find a place where we can be together."

Her answer was immediate. "Oh, yes, Samson. Take me away from here."

And then he kissed her. For the first time he kissed the woman he'd secretly been pining after for months. The woman he was hopelessly in love with. Hopelessly, because he knew her parents would never approve of him. All this didn't matter now—action was required. Losing her to another man was not an option.

Her lips were soft and sweet. His Elizabeth was pure, decent—not like the many married women who sought his bed.

"We'll leave tonight. Pack only what we can take on a horse. I'll be waiting for you here at midnight. Be careful," he cautioned her. "Tell no one."

He kissed her again, unable to get enough of her sweet taste.

"I'll be here."

She went to the door of the barn and turned back once more. "I love you."

The hours until midnight seemed longer than they should be. Samson was nervous. What if she'd changed her mind? Going away with him, a penniless man without prospects couldn't be what a rich heiress like her would want.

When the bell of the nearby church chimed out the twelve strokes of midnight, he was ready to go back to his chamber. Elizabeth wouldn't come. She would be sleeping in her warm bed, crying maybe, but she'd stay and do what her parents wanted.

A sound made him turn. She was covered in a dark cloak, a small satchel in her hand. Elizabeth. She was his. Samson pulled her into his embrace and kissed her. Her lips erased all his doubts. Their future was uncertain, but his life was perfect. The woman he loved was prepared to give up everything to be with him.

The horses were saddled and ready. They only rode for an hour before they were attacked. Three men fell upon them, coming out of nowhere. It happened so fast, there was no time for escape.

Samson's horse fell first, its throat ripped open. He hadn't even seen the blow or what had struck it. By the time he freed himself from his horse in order not to be squashed underneath its body, he heard Elizabeth's horrified screams.

What he saw couldn't be happening. Wasn't real. Wasn't possible! One of the men drank from her throat. Her blood. His teeth were lodged in her throat.

Samson fought the other two, but he had no chance. He couldn't get to her, couldn't help her. He'd promised her to keep her safe. He'd failed.

If he couldn't save her, he'd die avenging her. With more ferocity than he ever knew he possessed, he fought, clawed, and bit.

He felt fangs dig into his arm, felt the blood drain from him. Still, he didn't give up. He threw a last look at Elizabeth's dead body, then bit the man's ear off and spit it out. The taste of the attacker's blood in his mouth was metallic. It was the last thing he remembered.

He woke in a shed the next day. How he'd gotten there, he truly didn't know.

To his surprise, the wounds the men had inflicted on him were gone, but when he opened the door and a ray of sunshine touched his arm, the burning sensation made him flinch and pull back.

It was the moment when he knew he'd been condemned to a life as a vampire; nothing else made sense.

One of the bad guys.

Punished for his sins of adultery and debauchery.

Beyond redemption.

Samson finished his drawing. He'd used his drawing skills over the years mostly to convey information to his associates in order to help them apprehend dangerous individuals. His art had gone by the wayside, but drawing Delilah reminded him of what he loved doing. She was the perfect muse. He looked at his sleeping beauty and planted small kisses on her neck and shoulders. His eyes glanced at the clock: the sun would rise in a few minutes.

"I have to go, sweetness," he whispered to her, but she didn't wake. He tucked his drawing pad away on his desk.

Samson collected his bathrobe and dressed, then slowly left his bedroom. Normally he slept in his bed with the shades drawn, but since she was here, he couldn't risk her finding certain things strange when she woke up. For once, he would be hard—if not impossible!—to wake once he was asleep. And if she dared open the blinds to let the sun it, his skin would fry.

He quietly went downstairs. He'd built a safe room in the back of the house behind the garage, where he stayed during emergencies. The room was equipped with everything he needed: enough blood to last him several days, a bed, and communication equipment.

Samson locked the door from the inside and let himself fall onto the bed. He quickly sent a text message to Carl to notify him of where he was, and to Oliver to instruct him to take care of Delilah for the day. He ignored Ricky's message that he needed to speak to him. It could wait. Then his head hit the pillow, and sleep claimed him.

NINE

In steady drops, the blood dripped from her fingers.

Drip, drop.

A small puddle formed on the tile floor. Somebody was watching her, but she was unable to lift her head. Instead she kept staring at her hand.

Drip, drop.

A dark head of hair flitted in her peripheral vision. It bent over her hand. She couldn't see the face, but she heard him inhale sharply. Sniffing her hand?

She tried to pull it back, but felt paralyzed. She saw the pink tongue before she felt it … licking her. Licking the blood off her hand. Tingling pleasantly.

Delilah opened her eyes in a start and let out a few sharp breaths.

Another weird dream.

She pushed it away to make space for more delightful memories.

Snuggling back into the sheets, she soaked in his scent, all male and sexy. Samson was gone as he'd said, but she could still feel his skin on hers, taste him, smell him. She'd never had a night like the last one.

Without regret she'd given control over to him, a complete stranger, and had enjoyed every second of it. In fact, it had been liberating not to have to take charge, but to let herself fall. He'd caught her every time.

She sat up and looked around the room. Dark blinds obstructed the view out the windows, and in addition heavy drapes hung on each side of them. Delilah smiled. Somebody was not a morning person.

She leapt out of bed and pulled up one of the blinds. It was bright outside. She turned her head and checked the antique clock on the mantle: Eleven thirty? How could she have slept till eleven thirty? The fact that she'd had wild and passionate sex with Samson most of the night—at least a half dozen times—probably had something to do with it.

She'd obviously needed the sleep to recover. Just as well that, as an independent contractor, she could pretty much set her own hours. She'd just have to work a little later tonight to make up for it.

In a hurry, Delilah headed for the bathroom and stepped into the shower. Even as she took the soap and lathered her skin, she couldn't stop thinking of the events of the previous night. It all felt so surreal! She'd never met a man who could be so passionate and at the same time so tender—and completely and utterly insatiable. She'd felt his hunger and had developed her own craving for him very quickly.

She'd never laughed so much with a man in bed and had discovered how playful he really was. While she knew exactly what he liked in bed, what turned him on, and what drove him absolutely wild, she still had no idea who he was or what he did. He'd told her that he had business meetings all day, so she assumed he was some sort of corporate manager or director. Not that it mattered. As long as he had no wife coming out of the woodworks, she didn't care what he did.

Delilah knew she shouldn't snoop, but once she'd dried off and wrapped herself into his robe, she figured a little exploration couldn't hurt. If he'd left her alone in his house, surely he didn't have any skeletons in the closet he didn't want her to find. Samson had practically invited her to make herself at home. And that was exactly what she was going to do.

What better way to make oneself at home than to open a few drawers and cupboards? If he didn't want something to be found, it would probably be under lock and key anyway. No harm done then. Having justified her actions sufficiently to herself, she strolled through his bedroom.

His generous walk-in closet was filled with the typical wardrobe a man of means would have, except for his choice of color. Where most man would have gray, navy blue, and brown suits, most of Samson's pants and shirts were black. Delilah ran her hand over the neatly stacked t-shirts. She was sure he looked utterly sexy in black. With a sigh she closed the closet doors.

The bedside tables released no important information. There were novels and books on art. Nothing really revealed anything about him. She glanced at the small wooden bureau in one corner of the room. Writing utensils, old books, and a pad of paper were strewn upon it.

Delilah moved the pad to look at the book covers when a sheet of paper slid out of what she recognized as a drawing pad. Fascinated, she pulled it out completely. It was a drawing of a woman, a naked woman in bed. She blinked—and recognized herself. While she'd slept, he'd drawn her!

The picture was beautiful. She knew she wasn't as beautiful as he'd drawn her. He'd completely glossed over her slightly chubby hips and the extra pounds she carried on her belly. And no way were her thighs this slim. But the woman in the picture was clearly herself, yet he'd drawn her beautiful and perfect. Was this how Samson saw her? Or how he wanted her to be?

A twinge of insecurity hit her. Did he draw all women he slept with? She wasn't naïve enough to think she was the only one. A look through the pad revealed no other pictures. Maybe he discarded them when he was done with a woman. It was better not to think of it.

Delilah placed the drawing back where she'd found it and turned. Her gaze locked on the painting she'd admired the night before. A picture flashed in front of her eyes. A boy with dark hair drawing on a white piece of paper, then lifting it and handing it to an elegant lady he called "Mama." The mirage disappeared as quickly as it had appeared.

Delilah shook her head. She definitely hadn't had enough sleep. But she couldn't dilly dally any longer.

When she was finally dressed, she walked down the stairs. The smell of coffee permeated the house, and she followed the scent into the kitchen. Had he come home? Instinctively she felt guilty for having snooped around his bedroom.

"Samson?" she called out as she entered.

The person standing in front of the sink turned to her. It was the same young man who Samson had sent with the flowers and the invitation to the theater, Oliver.

"Good morning, Miss Sheridan."

She swallowed her disappointment and smiled at him. "Please call me Delilah."

He nodded and gave her a shy smile. "I made coffee for you. Cream, sugar?"

"Just milk, thank you, Oliver." Delilah gratefully took the mug he handed her and sat down at the kitchen island. She sipped the hot coffee and looked at him. He was in his early twenties and seemed to be completely at ease with his role. Was he used to looking after Samson's lovers? The thought of other women having been in her place made her feel uncomfortable.

"How long have you been working for Samson?" She needed to find out whether she was just one of many. Now that she thought of it, he was too smooth in his behavior for last night to be an exception.

"Three years. He's a good boss."

If Oliver had been working for him for that long, he would certainly know about any other women. But how could she find out without being too obvious?

"Carl told me what happened last night outside the theater. You were lucky you were with Mr. Woodford."

"He shouldn't have taken such a risk. The guy had a gun." She still shuddered at the thought of Samson putting himself in danger.

"He can take care of himself. You were never in danger." He seemed certain even though he hadn't been at the scene.

"But he could have gotten hurt." Delilah still had a hard time getting the image out of her mind.

Oliver smiled. "You like him."

Heat suffused her cheeks, and she hid her face in her coffee mug. "He's a very nice man." Instead of milking him for information, Oliver had gotten information out of her. This was obviously not working the way she'd planned it.

"So, do you take care of Mr. Woodford's personal affairs?"

Oliver gave her a strange look, then smiled again. "I'm his personal assistant and driver, and today I'll be your bodyguard."

"Are you also Samson's bodyguard?"

"He doesn't need one. But don't be concerned, I'm fully trained. I'll protect you."

"Do you normally protect women for Samson?" She took another sip from her coffee and tried to look casual while inside, she was nearly bursting with what felt close to dread, anticipating the answer to her question.

"There are no other women in Mr. Woodford's life."

Either he was extremely loyal and secretive, or he was speaking the truth. She tried to read his face, but couldn't tell if he had lied or not.

"He likes you. He wouldn't have asked me to protect you if he didn't."

Delilah didn't know how to answer. She felt embarrassed at how transparent she seemed to be.

"Would you like to eat something? Carl went shopping last night."

Oliver crossed to the fridge and opened it. It was filled from top to bottom with food.

"Maybe just some fruit." She should eat something; she'd barely had any dinner the night before, and it was already lunch time. "And some bread with jam." Suddenly Delilah felt famished.

"Eggs, bacon?"

"I shouldn't. Too many calories." She waved him off. Like she needed another few pounds on her hips.

"I'm sure you'll burn them off in no time." As soon as he said it, she gave him a startled look. Did everybody know what she'd done all night? Obviously Carl knew, and he'd told Oliver.

"I'm sorry, I didn't mean to say that. I just thought you're so slim anyway, you won't put on any weight," he stammered, all of a sudden completely nervous. "You won't tell Mr. Woodford, will you?"

Was he afraid of his boss?

"Why would I? How about those eggs then, and a few strips of bacon, huh?" She smiled at him to put him at ease again.

"Thank you." He gave her a grateful look and started cooking her breakfast. "Sometimes I should just keep my mouth shut."

"No harm done." But maybe now she could find out more about Samson. He owed her. "Tell me a little bit about him."

Oliver hesitated. "Mr. Woodford is a very private man."

"I see." It seemed he would remain tightlipped about his employer.

He served breakfast, and she started eating quietly. The food was just what she needed to get her energy back.

"He's a good man. You'll be good for him; he needs somebody like you."

Her ears perked up. "What do you mean?" Oliver didn't know her. How would he know whether she'd be good for Samson?

"Sorry; I've already said too much." He went back to silently cleaning the counter. Delilah noticed the large cracks in the granite as if somebody had hit it with a hammer.

"What happened there?"

Oliver flinched. "Faulty material. Cracked when there was a little earthquake. I've already called for a replacement."

Half an hour later, Delilah sat in the back of the limousine, with Oliver driving toward the financial district. As they approached the building in which she worked, he turned to her.

"I'll have to figure out where I can park. Which company do you work for?"

"Scanguards. It's on the twentieth floor. I can meet you up there if you need to find a place to park."

Oliver raised his eyebrows, then drove straight into the garage of the building.

"That won't be necessary."

He was let through when he showed the security guard an ID. The guard mumbled something Delilah couldn't understand and pointed toward an area of empty parking spots. He pulled the car into one marked "Scanguards."

When they reached their destined floor and entered the lobby, the receptionist greeted her with a smile.

"Good afternoon, Miss Sheridan."

"Good afternoon, Kathy."

As Oliver followed her, Kathy stopped him. "Excuse me please, who are you here to see?"

Oliver turned. "I'm with Miss Sheridan."

She gave Delilah a look.

"Yes, he's with me."

"Would you please sign in?" Kathy pointed to the guest book with a pen, and Oliver complied.

She smiled at him when he returned her pen after signing. "Go right in."

Delilah walked to the desk the company provided for her. As soon as she reached it, with Oliver following her closely, she caught John's look. He stared through the glass enclosure of his private office, seemingly surprised to see her. He immediately stalked out to meet her.

"I was wondering what had happened." John's tone was accusatory.

"I wasn't feeling well this morning," Delilah lied. "Everything's fine now." She sat down and booted up the computer.

Only now John seemed to take notice of Oliver.

"Can I help you?" His tone was even curter than when he'd spoken to her. She wondered whether he'd gotten up on the wrong side of the bed this morning.

Oliver shook his head. "I'm here with Miss Sheridan." He didn't volunteer any more information.

"Who is this, Delilah?"

She looked up from her desk. "He's here to accompany me."

"Excuse me? We can't just have all kinds of strangers go in and out of the office. I'm afraid your boyfriend will have to stay outside."

Delilah bit her lip. Obviously Samson hadn't thought of this. Oliver couldn't stay by her side all day while she worked. What had he been thinking?

"I'll handle this," Oliver offered.

He pulled out an ID and waved it at John. As soon as he looked at it, John felt the blood drain from his face and gave Oliver a stunned glare.

"Fine," was all he could press out.

So she had called in the cavalry and gotten protection from the top. A bodyguard from Scanguards! And one at the highest-clearance level. It meant he could gain access to anywhere within the company. How had she managed to get this kind of preferential treatment? She was only an auditor. None of the auditors before had ever gotten their own bodyguards assigned. This was not good.

When Delilah hadn't shown up at work first thing in the morning, John had already been licking his chops celebrating, thinking the man he was beholden to had made an attempt on her life after they'd spoken on the phone. Apparently that wasn't the case. How hard was it to get rid of a little auditor?

John knew that now it would be virtually impossible. If she was protected by a Scanguards bodyguard, there was nothing he could do. They were the best-trained bodyguards available in the nation. It was rumored they were even better than the Secret Service. He cringed at the thought of having to tell the man who was controlling his life at present that she'd acquired a bodyguard. He wouldn't be pleased. He'd be furious, and nobody knew what he was capable of.

Unless he already knew.

As John turned back to his office, he heard Delilah's voice behind him.

"Did you get the boxes from the storage facility?"

"Yes," he barked. "They're at the loading dock. I'll have them brought up in a moment." He was running out of time. Once she'd reviewed all transaction documents in the boxes, she would know beyond any doubt that he was the one who was defrauding the company.

Delilah took no notice of John's unfriendly behavior and logged into the desktop computer at her disposal. Not even John's bad mood could faze her today. She felt great. She'd had the best sex of her life, and even the lack of sleep couldn't dampen her euphoric feelings.

She'd noticed a few bruises on her hips when she'd gotten up, but decided they were well worth it. Samson was a passionate man. She realized how much he wanted her sexually, and how difficult it was for him to control his urge to take her every which way he could. When she closed her eyes, she could still feel his hands on her and his unrelenting shaft driving into her. Oh God, yes. Her sex felt deliciously tender this morning: a welcome reminder of the attention it had received at Samson's hands, mouth, and cock.

She'd felt his raw power when he'd blindfolded her, and even though she wasn't normally into kinky stuff, he'd driven her completely wild. None of her former lovers had ever tied her up, nor would she have ever allowed it, but with him, there was something that intrigued her and made her want more. Would he find more sexy games he was willing to teach her?

Delilah looked at her watch. It wasn't even two o'clock yet, and she couldn't wait to get back to him.

***

Samson woke from his deep sleep as soon as the sun set over the Pacific Ocean. He looked at the clock but was in no hurry to get up. For the first time in years he'd dreamed, actually *dreamed*, in his sleep. His dreams had felt like gentle aftershocks of his night with Delilah, reliving the passion he'd experienced with her.

She had made an impression on his sex-starved body. And he wanted her again. Needed her to ease the ache he felt in his groin. Now.

He checked his messages before he went upstairs. Ricky's voicemail sounded more urgent than the night before.

"Samson, we have to talk. As soon as you're up."

As he walked into his bedroom, he dialed Ricky's number.

"What's so urgent? Did you find the guy who attacked us?"

"Thomas is following up on a lead. But there's something else."

"Shoot."

"Not over the phone. We need to talk in person."

Samson looked around his deserted bedroom. Delilah was probably still at work. "Fine. Come over, but make it quick. Delilah should be back soon, and I have plans for tonight." Plans which included her being naked in his arms, maybe involving a few of his best silk ties.

He disconnected the call and threw the phone onto the armchair. In the bathroom he stripped down to his boxers and grabbed his toothbrush.

He could still smell her on his skin. Damn, she had made him hungry for her body. He couldn't believe it himself when he realized he'd taken her more than half a dozen times. He didn't know that he'd had it in him. But whenever he'd thought he was spent, one look at her enticing body and her lovely face, and his cock had sprung back to attention like a Jack-in-the-Box.

Not even with a vampire female had he ever been that active in one night. This human could hold her own. The fire and passion he saw in Delilah rivaled his, if that was even possible.

Samson wondered how long she would hold his interest, how long she would keep him captured like this. Yes, he felt like she had a hold on him, as if some invisible force drew him to her, and he was unable to resist. He dismissed it as a side effect of his long abstinence from sex and figured it would pass. It had to. He couldn't carry on with a mortal.

He wasn't like Amaury who had no scruples about sleeping with humans.

Samson turned when he heard the bedroom door open. That was fast, even for Ricky. He stepped out of the bathroom and broke into a huge smile when he saw his visitor.

"Delilah."

With a few strides he crossed the room and took her into his arms. His mouth was less than an inch away from her tempting lips. "How was your day?"

"Don't ask." She sounded exhausted. He knew just the right remedy for that.

Samson brushed a feather light kiss on her lips. "I missed you." He had, despite the fact that he'd been up only a few minutes.

"Hmh, that's better," Delilah murmured as he sought her lips again. Her hands embraced him and slowly moved from his back further south. He felt her slip them into his boxers, touching his firm ass. Ah, but her hands were soft.

"You're not dressed."

"You noticed that, huh?" He chuckled. "I was just about to take a shower." But why shower alone when she was back? "Care to join me?" Should he just lug her over his shoulder, or would he be acting too much like a caveman? Woman. Sex. It was all he could think of.

Samson didn't wait for an answer, but started to pull down the zipper of her skirt and let it drop to the floor. Her blouse followed seconds later. She didn't show any objection.

"I guess I must have said yes," she smirked, as she stepped out of her shoes.

"That's what I heard."

When he stripped her of her bra and panties, Delilah returned the favor and let his boxers drop to the floor. His hard-on jutted out proudly and pointed straight at her. Samson lifted her up and carried her into the bathroom.

He sat her down before he turned on the water in the shower, but kept his arm around her waist. Her skin was too tempting to let go of.

"I had a hard time this morning doing my hair in here. I couldn't find a mirror."

Samson flinched. Damn, she'd noticed. Since vampires didn't reflect in mirrors, he'd never had a need to have one installed in his bathroom. What else had she noticed?

"Sorry about that. I'm having it replaced. I wasn't planning on an overnight guest." He smiled at her and kissed her quickly before she could find anything else that struck her as odd. His kiss silenced her just the way it was intended to. He pulled her into the shower without releasing her lips.

His hunger for her had just doubled. Had it only been last night that he'd first had sex with her? It seemed that he knew her body much more intimately than that. Every curve was familiar, yet so exciting. He knew he would recognize her touch even if he was blind. The way her hands teased his skin, how her fingers ignited his passion for her, he would always know it was her.

"Why don't you help me get cleaned up?" Without waiting for an answer Samson squeezed a dollop of liquid soap into her hand. As her hands lathered the soap over his skin, he closed his eyes. Never had he felt so relaxed than when he was with her. He breathed in deeply when he felt her hands tending to his shaft and balls. Delilah slowly and deliberately moved her hand up and down, the foam making the movement smooth.

"Good?" His little human vixen was clearly bent on driving him insane and doing an excellent job at it.

"You have no idea." He sighed and allowed himself to be swept away by her touch. His hands sought her out and pressed her against him.

"Rinse me off. I don't want to be all soapy when I slide inside of you." It felt completely natural that he wanted her and let her know what he intended to do. There was no pretense between them.

He saw Delilah smile as she rinsed the soap off his skin. She could get him excited within seconds. Samson lowered his head to her mouth, smothering her with his passionate kiss.

His tongue mated with hers, filling her mouth, just like he wanted to fill the rest of her body. She tasted like a beautiful summer night, like rain after a hot day. Her scent alone drove him to distraction, but coupled with her sweet taste and the softness of her naked skin pressed against his, brought him right back to the night before. There was only one cure for his desire for her. He had to bury himself in her, and he couldn't wait a minute longer.

His cock throbbed almost painfully when he lowered himself a few inches and guided himself in between her thighs so her moist pink petals rested on him. Samson slid back and forth, staying outside her body, letting her ride his hard rod.

"You feel so good." She moaned. Exactly his thought. No. Not good. Amazing! Her soft flesh was warm, her wetness drenching him.

He shifted his angle, and his shaft teased at the entrance of her body. Delilah breathed heavily.

"We should get a condom," she whispered, but her body pressed against his cock. Did she know what she was doing, or was she just as lost in the sensation as he was?

"We should." But instead he eased into her just an inch deep. He would go get a condom from the bedroom if she insisted. "I'll get one." But he didn't move, and her hands held onto his arms. Her muscles tensed around him, as if to pull him closer.

"Samson, don't leave." Her voice was hoarse, but insistent. She pushed toward him, making him penetrate deeper. He was halfway inside her and felt her muscles tantalize him. Hell, he was on fire.

"You want me like this, right now?" Samson waited for her protest, but it didn't come. In slow motion he inched forward, easing himself deeper and deeper into her as he gazed into her eyes. So beautiful, so passionate, and all his.

"I want nothing more."

Her kiss was tender and loving as they rocked to the rhythm of their heartbeats. He pulled up her leg and wrapped it around his hip, thrusting deeper into her. His arms supported her weight. Delilah's lips brought him back into the field of lavender and made him feel the sun on his back, just like the night before. Samson was lost in the sensation as she carried him away.

Her nails dug into his ass as she held onto him, urging him deeper into her. Never had he been with a woman who'd shown such passion, and who he was willing to give everything in his power.

Delilah's moans were like a drug to him, her kisses like a most exquisite wine, and her body ultimate ecstasy. He would never need anything else, only her, like this, right now.

Too late he heard the door to the bedroom open and the heavy steps come toward the bathroom.

"Samson, you're not gonna like this—" Ricky's voice penetrated his bliss.

In lightning speed, Samson spun around to shield Delilah from Ricky's view.

"Get the fuck out, Richard!" he growled low and dark. Even in his own ears he sounded more like an animal than a man. Ricky knew all too well that whenever Samson called him by his full name, he meant business. He did well retreating instantly.

"I'm so sorry, sweetness," Samson whispered to Delilah, making sure his voice was soft again. She was completely still in his arms, obviously shocked at the interruption. He couldn't blame her. "I'm going to have a serious word with him."

Delilah looked up at him, and his eyes were their usual hazel color again, but in the instant when he'd yelled at Ricky, she'd seen them flash red. Like an alarm. Like a stop light. It had shocked her more than Ricky barging in on them. Still thinking of his strange eyes, she went stiff in his arms. This wasn't normal. How could somebody's eye color change like that?

She was glad that Samson didn't look at her now, but again had his cheek pressed against hers, for she wasn't sure she could have hidden her alarmed expression.

"Give me a few minutes. I'll get rid of him. And then I'm all yours."

He kissed her cheek softly and pulled out of her.

"No problem." Suddenly she felt cold. And alone.

Delilah watched him reach for the towel and step out of the shower. She turned away and let the water engulf her, pretending to enjoy the shower. In reality she tried to calm her nerves. When she looked back a few seconds later, Samson had already left the bathroom. She braced herself against the tile wall.

Had she hallucinated? She'd clearly seen the fury in his eyes, and considering the violation of their privacy, she could understand him flaring up at Ricky, but she couldn't understand the red in his eyes. Had he popped a blood vessel? No, impossible. Seconds later, his normal hazel color had returned, and all the red was gone.

She pressed her hand against her sex where she could still feel his pistoning cock. Something wasn't right. Something about Samson was different, and it suddenly scared her.

Samson headed downstairs, having only put on a pair of jeans, no shirt. He found Ricky in the kitchen, leaning against the island and aimed straight for him, grabbing him by the shirt.

"Do you have any idea how much I'd love to rip your head off right now?" The thought that Ricky had seen Delilah's naked body made him furious. Nobody had the right to see her like that—nobody but him.

Ricky leaned back as much as he could to get away from him. "I'm sorry. I didn't realize she was there."

Samson let out a low and dangerous snarl. "You'd better tell me you didn't see her naked."

Ricky lifted his arms in a motion of surrender. "I didn't—I swear."

"If I ever catch you so much as looking at her, our friendship is over, and you can kiss your job goodbye. Is that clear?" He was serious. He had no problem with his friends seeing him naked in the shower. It certainly wasn't a first. But to barge in when he was with Delilah was something he couldn't tolerate. No other man or vampire had a right to look at her like that. Delilah was his. His alone.

His alone?

"Crystal clear."

Samson released him from his grip. Ricky straightened out and cleared his throat.

"You're probably not going to like what I have to say, especially considering how infatuated you are with her—"

Samson's growl interrupted him for a second. He wasn't in the mood to listen to Ricky's observation about his relationship to Delilah. Especially since he didn't know what to make of it himself.

"—but I have to tell you what Carl found."

Samson looked at him with restrained interest. "Go on."

"You had Carl pack her stuff last night."

"Don't tell me things I already know."

Ricky was normally not one to beat about the bush. His hesitancy fed Samson's unease.

"He found some files amongst her things."

"What files?"

"Scanguards' files."

Samson's jaw dropped. "Scanguards?"

Ricky gave a grave nod. "Financial records, asset statements, internal stuff. I don't have a good feeling about it. Why would she have confidential files of Scanguards? Don't you think that's odd? She shows up here two nights ago, and at the same time she has files of your company in her luggage?"

Samson didn't like the sound of it either. It couldn't be a coincidence. There was no reason for anybody to have internal documents of his company. Least of all Delilah. What was she up to?

"What's your theory?"

"She could be a corporate spy," Ricky guessed, but his voice didn't sound very convinced.

"Doing what? Selling our client list to our competitors?"

His friend shrugged his shoulders. "Not much to be gained by that. All our competitors are small fry. Nobody's got the capacity or training to take on our clients."

Samson nodded. "Have there been any operational issues lately that I'm not aware of?"

Another shake of Ricky's head. "Everything's been running smoothly, at least on the vampire side. No idea how the human operation is going, but I haven't seen any alerts come up."

Ricky was in charge of vampire recruitment and training.

"Then it's personal."

"It could be." Ricky avoided his gaze.

"What are you thinking?" Samson wasn't entirely sure if he wanted to know the second possibility.

"What if she's been seeking you out?"

"A slayer?"

"No. There's no sign of that among her things. But I can see all the other signs. She's been wrapping you around her little finger."

Samson wanted to interrupt him and refute his statement, but Ricky held up his hand.

"I can see it just by the way you reacted earlier. She's a human woman. Do you know what human women want from rich men like you?"

Samson stared at his friend. Long and hard. "She wants me for my money ..." His voice trailed off. He felt an uncomfortable stab in his solar plexus. Indigestion? Definitely not this time. Memories of betrayal swept through him. Recent memories. He braced himself against the kitchen island.

The doorbell gave him reprieve. He looked up and gave Ricky a questioning look.

"Amaury's probably forgotten his key again. I'll open up."

As Ricky left the kitchen, Samson was alone with his thoughts. Could it be true? Could Delilah be just another woman after his money? Another one who didn't really care for him? He hoped Ricky's other suggestion was true, that she was a corporate spy. He could handle that, but he couldn't handle a Delilah who was after his money. Not her. Please not her.

Were her kisses all a lie? And when she gave herself so willingly to him, was it all an act to reel him in? The thought stung, much more than he wanted to admit to himself. No wonder she was so willing. The way she'd responded to him in the car and then later in the theater was not normal for a woman who barely knew a man.

He recalled the moment when they were on their way to the bar in the theater and had gotten stuck in the doorway. The way Delilah had pressed her body against his and practically provoked him to touch her intimately now looked like a calculated move on her part. She was playing him the entire time. A veritable Mata Hari!

This was not good news, especially since what had looked like indigestion, if vampires could have indigestion, he now recognized as something much more serious. It was so clear to him now.

At the same time, it was impossible. How could it have happened? All he'd wanted to do was get over his erection problem, and he'd followed Dr. Drake's advice to the letter. He'd done nothing different from what the good doctor had ordered. He'd fucked her, again and again, just like he'd fucked other females before. Vampire females. He'd done nothing different with Delilah, so why was the outcome so different?

Instead of his hunger being sated after a night of sex with her, it had grown. He'd started hungering for her and for her alone. The thought of ever touching another woman suddenly disgusted him. All he wanted was Delilah. And Samson now knew why, even though he didn't understand anything else.

He was falling for her, falling for a mortal.

TEN

Samson remembered the last betrayal all too vividly, a memory he'd banned from his mind. But now it all came back to him in every torrid detail ...

Samson closed the entrance door quietly behind him and listened to any noise from upstairs. He heard the faint sound of Ilona's voice and the trickling of water. She was taking a bath.

For the hundredth time this evening, he'd opened the little box he held in his hand and stared at the enormous diamond ring tucked into the green-velvet cushion. The stunning setting held a three-carat, brilliant round diamond of the highest clarity. The jeweler had assured him it was the best diamond money could buy.

His heart beating as loud as a drum in his ears, Samson moved up the stairs, careful to avoid those steps he knew creaked. He wanted to surprise her. She thought he'd be out on business for the night.

He silently opened the door to his bedroom. Ilona's clothes were carelessly strewn on the bed.

"So he thinks. Uh huh." She was on the phone, probably talking to a girlfriend. "Wait until we're blood-bonded—things will change." Ilona paused. Had she already guessed that he wanted to propose to her? He felt disappointed, deflated. He quietly approached the bathroom door which was ajar.

"And if I have to suck his dick one more time, I'm going to puke!"

Samson stopped cold at the words tearing through him. He couldn't have heard right.

"Sure, that's easy for you to say. You like sucking cock!"

Samson inhaled sharply. He felt as if an ice-cold hand clamped around his heart and squeezed tightly. He fought for air.

"I don't care who sucks his dick when we're blood-bonded, but it sure ain't me. I can't stand his hands all over me ..."

Samson leaned against the wall when he felt nausea overwhelm him. It lasted but a second.

"You know what you have to do once I have access to all his assets." His money. It was all she was after. That's why she was with him: only for his money. Samson felt as if he had been punched in the stomach.

He heard her let out a frustrated huff. *"You know as well as I do that once I'm blood-bonded with Samson, I have to be careful about guarding my mind. He'll be able to read my thoughts. I can't be caught thinking about this anymore, do you understand? That's why you have to do it ...Yes, that part about blood-bonding sucks. Why would anybody want to be able to constantly be in the other person's head?"*

Samson had heard enough. More than enough. With murderous intent, he flung the door open and walked into the bathroom, his steps slow yet determined. Ilona jerked her head around and instantly dropped the phone into the water.

"Samson," she purred and pasted a fake smile on her face—a smile he'd seen a thousand times on her. Only now he recognized it for what it was. Acting. She'd been acting all along. Pretending to be in love with him, when all she wanted was access to his wealth.

With two steps he was by the bathtub. His hand gripped her neck of its own volition. She clawed at him instantly. Water spilled over the rim of the tub onto the marble floor.

"You heartless tramp. I should kill you, right here, right now."

By her throat, he lifted her out of the water as she struggled against his iron grip. No matter. He was stronger, and his fury added to his strength.

Samson glanced at her naked body. His own body showed no reaction to her sensual curves anymore. No hard-on. No desire to touch her. Nothing.

He recognized the flash of fear in her eyes before his own hand opened and dropped her unceremoniously back into the tub. The water splashed around them.

"Get out! I would never blood-bond with someone like you. You're trash, you're nothing. You're lucky you're still alive. But don't count on it staying that way. If you cross my path again, you might find yourself with a stake through the heart."

She'd used him. All she wanted was to blood-bond with him so she'd have a right to what was his. All his wealth, all his power. How could he have been so blind?

After he threw her out of his house and out of his life that night, he'd shut down. He didn't want anybody close to him. He knew it had been a mistake to trust her.

That was when all his problems had started. First his appetite for sex had decreased, and then, when he thought he should indulge in carnal pleasures to distract himself, he was unable to perform. He was unable to get an erection.

Until ...

Until Delilah entered his life. And now? Had she betrayed him too? Was she after his wealth too? The thought made him feel ill.

"You don't look well." Amaury entered the kitchen behind Ricky.

Leaning against the counter, Samson gave him what even he himself knew was a tortured look. "How do you expect me to feel?"

"She can't have gotten under your skin like this, not in one night."

Samson heard disbelief in Amaury's voice. He ignored his friend's remark. "We need to get to the bottom of this, fast."

"I can run a background check on her, see who she really is," Ricky offered.

Samson nodded. "Do that. Amaury, talk to Carl, and find out what else he's noticed amongst her stuff that might be odd. He's been to the place she stayed at, and if it's true what she claims, that she's from New York, the condo probably doesn't belong to her. Find out who it belongs to. Then check with Oliver to find out what she did today. He was with her all day."

Ricky's cell rang, and he answered it instantly.

"Where?" He motioned to Samson and Amaury. "Okay, we'll be there in less than half an hour." He disconnected the call.

"That was Thomas. They've got the guy who attacked you and Delilah."

Samson straightened out, relieved to have something productive to do.

"You and I'll go. Amaury, find out about her what you can. Make it quick. Carl will help you. Ricky, we're taking your car."

Samson headed for the door.

"Hmh, shouldn't you get dressed first?" Ricky wondered.

Samson looked down at himself and realized he only wore his jeans, no shoes, no shirt. "Give me a minute."

He stalked up the stairs and entered his bedroom. Delilah had finished her shower and gotten dressed in a pair of jeans and a plain white t-shirt. It gave her an innocent look. He hesitated when he saw her. Only minutes earlier he had been inside her body and felt no greater joy than being swept away by her kisses, but now he was consumed with doubts. Who was she? What did she want?

"Anything the matter?" Her voice sounded shaky. Did she suspect something? Could she sense his doubts?

"Just a work emergency. I'll have to take care of something." Samson reached into his closet to pull out a black t-shirt. He dressed quickly while she watched him.

"I should be back in a couple of hours, so if you get hungry, you know where the kitchen is."

He was about to storm out the bedroom, when he realized that she probably found his behavior strange. He'd been the hot lover only minutes earlier, unable to get enough of her. If he behaved with such aloofness now, Delilah would become suspicious. It was important to keep her in the belief that everything was okay, that he hadn't caught on to her game yet.

As he approached her, he thought he detected her flinching, but couldn't be certain. He kissed her lightly on the cheek. "Amaury and Carl will probably be around, so don't be surprised if you see them downstairs."

He watched for a reaction on her face which would give away that she found his abrupt departure unusual and noticed her lips curl slightly upwards. It wasn't a smile, merely an acknowledgment she'd heard him.

"Sure, see you later."

As soon as the door closed behind him, Delilah exhaled sharply. He'd seemed normal, maybe a little absentminded, but it sounded like the work emergency he'd mentioned was worrying him. She realized that she truly didn't know him. She'd spend an entire night making love to him, yet she didn't even know what he did for a living, what kind of hobbies he had or what food he liked.

Those were all things normal people discussed on a first date. Had she been crazy to spend their first date entirely in his embrace without asking him the most fundamental questions? It had been such a long time since she'd been on a date that she'd completely forgotten how to act on one. Had Samson taken advantage of that fact? Had he seen her as completely naïve and figured he could just get her into bed quickly?

It still didn't explain the incident in the shower. Oh God, the shower. She'd let him inside her without a condom. What if he wasn't as healthy as he'd said? What if the strange thing she'd seen in his eyes was some weird disease he had? Could he infect her with something?

Then she remembered the condom that had ripped the night before. He could have already infected her with God-knows-what. She clutched her stomach as nausea hit her. Oh God, *no*!

Delilah felt a knot in her throat build, cutting off her air supply. Her chest heaved to compensate, and her skin felt clammy all of a sudden.

She felt so stupid that she'd let herself be lulled in by his tenderness and passion. She'd noticed how smooth he'd been in his seductions as if he had more than enough regular practice. For all she knew, he did this every week, and this week she was his intended victim. Was it wrong that she'd trusted him?

***

"I say, we just kill him now. Let's not waste Samson's time with him," Milo barked and looked at Thomas.

His lover graced him with a displeased look. "Don't be so blood hungry. Samson's made it clear he wants to interrogate the bastard himself, so don't spoil his fun."

They stood in a large and dimly lit warehouse, both dressed in matching black leather gear. The space was packed to the rafters with containers, and the musty smell reminded of worn socks, mold, dust, and sweat. It was eerily quiet except for the faint sound of raindrops falling onto the roof.

"What are you going to do with me?" The voice came from the man they had bound onto a chair.

"Oh, shut up," they answered in unison.

"Hey, do you wanna go and hit the clubs after this? It's still early," Thomas asked.

His lover shook his head. "Sorry, not tonight. I've got to take care of a few errands."

"What's so important that you can't go out with me?"

"Work stuff," Milo answered with a dismissive swipe of his hand. "Some of us here work for people other than Samson, so I can't just hang out with you all night."

"That sucks. Do you want me to get you a job with Scanguards? I could do that, you know."

"No way. I don't want to have to listen to everybody say the only reason I got the job is because my boyfriend put a word in for me with the big boss. Forget it. That's just too humiliating."

"Hey, you two," the man interrupted.

Thomas gave him a venomous look. "Can't you see we're busy right now?"

"If you let me go, I can let you in on a couple of good heists that are going down."

"Not interested." Thomas wasn't one to bargain, and besides, he didn't need money.

"Do we look like we want money?" Milo jumped at the bound man and flashed his fangs. Instantly, he pulled his head back trying to get away, but was restrained by the ropes that bound him. "And if you interrupt our conversation one more time, I'll take a bite out of you," Milo hissed only inches from his face.

As soon as the man recoiled, his facial muscles tensing, Milo returned to Thomas.

"You know that we'll have to wipe his memory clean of this later."

Milo just shrugged his shoulders. "Whatever."

Thomas put his hand on his lover's waist and drew him closer. He lowered his voice so only Milo could hear him. "You know we haven't spent much time together lately. How about a little something now? Samson won't be here for another ten minutes." A quickie would be just up his alley.

But Milo peeled himself out of his embrace. "Not right now. It stinks in here."

"You're blowing me off?"

"Come on, don't start this again. I'm just not in the mood."

Thomas looked at him, suspicion rising in his gut. "If I didn't know any better, I'd say you're seeing somebody else."

"That's bull, and you know it. I wish you'd stop with all that jealous crap."

"Fine." Thomas crossed his arms in front of his chest. He caught a glimpse of the thug staring at them. "What are you looking at?"

The man flinched at his violent outburst, but kept his mouth shut and looked down.

Milo had been kind of distant in the last month, and Thomas figured their relationship was coming to an end. While he was outwardly still the shyer of the two, especially around Samson and the gang, Milo had turned into more of a domineering partner, a role Thomas had traditionally always taken.

They still had sex—and plenty of it—but things were just not quite as passionate as they had been at the beginning of their relationship. Thomas wanted to prolong things, but knew instinctively that eventually their relationship would fizzle out. Nagging thoughts came to the surface again. Milo's secrecy about what he did when they weren't together irked him. He knew his jealousy was probably misplaced; nevertheless, he couldn't rein it in.

Thomas had always been the jealous type. Having become a vampire hadn't changed that. He'd realized his trait over a hundred years ago. Becoming a vampire didn't change your character, it just amplified it. A bad man would be a bad vampire, and a good man would be a good vampire. It was as simple as that.

He didn't regret the choice he'd made when he'd been confronted with it over a century ago, for it finally allowed him to live in an era where he didn't have to hide his sexuality, and for that he was grateful.

In the time in which he'd grown up, men whose homosexuality was discovered were flogged or even killed. Not that he didn't enjoy a good flogging from time to time as long as it was followed by an even better fuck, but that was another matter altogether. Life was better in the twenty-first century.

He eyed his lover from the side. Milo's features seemed delicate even though as a vampire he was nearly indestructible. There was no ounce of fat on his body, and despite his small size he was strong. And incredibly sexy. Glancing at his firm ass, Thomas' leather pants tightened. Whenever he looked at Milo, he got horny.

"Let's have a look at that jerk," Samson's voice boomed through the warehouse.

His coattails flying, Ricky by his side, Samson strode in and marched straight for the captive, planting himself squarely in front of him. The master had arrived, looking every inch the avenging dark angel he could turn into when provoked.

Samson planned on intimidating the thug. It would cut down on the time it took to get all pertinent information out of him. He rarely used torture and found that the suggestion of pain often worked better than pain itself.

"Recognize me?" he asked in a quiet but dangerous voice when he stood in front of the bound man.

A silent nod was the response. "Good. What's your name?"

"Billy."

"Good, Billy. Now that we're on first name terms, let's have a chat. I don't take it lightly to being attacked, but, you know, that comes with the territory, and that's something I can forgive. I can defend myself. But you know what really pisses me off?"

Samson looked at him, daring Billy to answer. The man was smart enough not to open his mouth at the rhetorical question.

"When my woman gets attacked, I have no mercy. Do you understand?" He bent down to Billy, his voice almost a growl. Frightened eyes looked at him. Billy's body started trembling.

"You've put me in a difficult situation, Billy. A man has to protect those he loves no matter what. So, what am I going to do with you?" He tilted his head and flashed his fangs. Samson hadn't bit anybody in years, but his fangs were nevertheless in pristine condition—floss and toothpaste went a long way when it came to dental hygiene for a vampire.

Billy shrieked. "I didn't want to do it."

This was far too easy. The man was clearly not quite the professional criminal Samson had thought him to be.

"But you did. And now you're going to explain to me and my friends here why you were after my woman. This is a small town, but to be attacked by the same guy twice, that's not a coincidence. We both know that."

He let another snarl rip through his clenched jaw and moved his head closer to Billy. He could smell the scent of fear on him—a stench he abhorred.

"I was paid to do it."

Samson straightened. "By whom?"

For a fraction of a second he wondered if Delilah had set all of it up herself. It could have been a ploy to gain his confidence, to sneak into his home and his heart. It would make sense. It would have given her a pretense to gain access to him, awaken his instinct as a protector and then seduce him thoroughly. God, she had seduced him alright, with everything she had: her voice, her body, her touch, her kisses ... her laughter. He had to know the truth, as much as it would pain him to hear the answer.

"Who paid you?"

"My brother-in-law. He wanted her out of the way," Billy suddenly blurted out.

Relief flooded through Samson. It hadn't been her, thank God. "What's his name?"

"John."

Billy started shaking.

"I need a little bit more than that, if you don't mind."

"John Reardon." The name had a familiar ring to it, but Samson couldn't place it.

"And where does he live, this John Reardon?"

Billy gave an address in the Sunset district.

"Why does he want her out of the way?" Samson continued with his questioning. He noticed a sudden widening of Billy's pupils.

"I d—d—don't know." Where did the stutter suddenly come from? At the same time he observed a trembling in the man's legs which travelled up his torso.

Samson searched his eyes. "You're lying."

Billy shook like a leaf, then his eyes started drifting. "Stop!" he screamed. "Make it stop!" His hands balled into fists as he tried to raise them, but came up against the restraints. "No!" A second later his head rolled forward. He'd passed out.

Samson spun around to his friends. "Did any of you do that?" He'd be pissed if someone had used mind control to scare Billy before he could get all necessary information out of him.

Milo and Thomas both lifted their hands in confusion, while Ricky shook his head.

"Scan the vicinity to make sure no other vampires are here and are interfering." Samson looked back at Thomas and Milo. "Then go out to the Sunset and pick up this John Reardon. This one stays here until we've got his brother-in-law. Make sure he stays here; I haven't decided yet what to do with him. Call me when you have his brother-in-law: I want to talk to him personally."

"I'm outta here. I've things to do," Milo protested.

Samson raised an eyebrow, but let it go. Milo didn't work for him. "Ricky, you go with Thomas. I'll take your car back to the house."

Ricky threw the keys in Samson's direction, and he caught them without even looking. As soon as he was in Ricky's car and switched on the engine, he saw Milo exit the building. His cell phone pressed to his ear, he headed for his motorcycle.

ELEVEN

"You said 'Clay Hall'?" Amaury looked at Carl with surprise. They stood facing each other across the kitchen island.

"Yes, down near Taylor, it's a large condo building. I picked up all her stuff. She didn't have much, just some clothes, her computer, and those files."

"That's a strange coincidence," Amaury mumbled, talking to himself. He didn't believe in things happening at random.

"What coincidence?"

"You don't know, do you?"

Carl shook his head, confused. "Know what?"

"That Scanguards owns a couple of condos in Clay Hall. I should know. I bought them for the company."

Amaury's main job working for Samson was to take care of all his real estate investments, both his private ones as well as the company's. He held a real estate license in California and acted as his own broker. Luckily, the medieval rumor that vampires had to be invited into a home was entirely unfounded, which made it possible for a vampire to work as a real estate agent.

"It doesn't have to mean anything. She said she's from New York and on a business trip."

"This'll be easy to check. What was the unit number?"

Carl stared blankly. "Well, it was high up." It looked like he was trying to remember walking down the corridor of the floor he'd been on and finding the right door. "Eight Twelve."

"*Voilà*. It's ours. The only way she could have access to that condo is if she worked for us. Samson said Oliver was with her all day."

Carl nodded in agreement.

"Get him on the phone. Let's see where he took her."

Carl punched in Oliver's number, then put the phone on speaker mode. "Hey Oliver, it's me."

"Carl, this better be important. I'm dead tired," Oliver's sleepy voice came through the phone. Amaury glanced at the clock on the oven. It was barely past nine o'clock. He shook his head in disbelief. Humans!

"Hey Oliver, Amaury here. Sorry about the disturbance. Hope we didn't wake you."

"No problem, Amaury." It sounded like Oliver straightened up. "What can I do for you?"

"You were with Delilah all day?"

"Yes; Mr. Woodford asked me to protect her."

"Where did you take her?"

"Downtown, to Scanguards' offices."

Carl and Amaury looked at each other. Amaury whistled through his teeth. "You wouldn't happen to know what she did there, would you?"

"She worked."

"She worked?"

"Yes, she worked. She's some sort of, I don't know, accountant or auditor, or something like that, I think."

"You sure?"

"Yeah, I'm sure. They knew her and were expecting her. Even had a computer set up for her and all."

"Thanks, Oliver."

Amaury hung up. "I guess that's good news. Still one hell of a coincidence, but at least it doesn't look like she's a corporate spy."

"Still doesn't explain why she's here with him," Carl interjected. Amaury could feel Carl's emotions—the man was protective of his boss and didn't want him to get hurt again, least of all by a woman. "Do you think she knows who he is?"

Before Amaury could answer, the door to the kitchen opened and Samson waltzed in.

"Who're talking about?" he asked.

"You," Amaury answered. "We were wondering whether Delilah knows who you are."

"I wish I knew." It was the truth. It would make him feel a lot better if he knew what she knew about him. Whether it was his money she was after, or whether she was truly here for him. Without an ulterior motive. "Where is she?"

Amaury tipped his head toward the upper floor. "She came down earlier, grabbed a yogurt, and went back upstairs." He paused. "Well, at least we know now who she is."

Expectantly, Samson looked at this friend.

"She's some sort of accounting person for Scanguards."

Samson took a step back. He hadn't expected this. "She works for me?" He was sleeping with one of his employees? Great, at the very least he was setting himself up for a sexual harassment suit.

"Looks like it. Oliver spent the entire day with her at Scanguards' offices downtown, and the condo you picked her up from—it's one of ours."

Samson rubbed his forehead with his palm. "Then it's true. She told me last night she's an auditor."

Amaury grinned. "You guys had time to talk?"

His friend was one to talk! Samson's disapproving look stopped Amaury cold from making any further insinuations. His old friend made it sound like he was a sex-maniac. Of course they had talked, joked actually, teased and laughed, even after Carl had delivered the supply of condoms. As if all he did to entertain a woman was having sex with her!

"She said she's from New York and here on an audit. Have you checked everything out?"

"Not yet, we just only reached our conclusion when you came in."

"Carl, get Gabriel Giles on the phone."

Gabriel was Director of Operations at the head office in New York, and since he was a vampire he'd be reachable, even if it was shortly past midnight on the East Coast.

"You'd better be right." Samson looked at Amaury, a glimmer of hope sprouting in his chest.

Gabriel's voice bellowed through the speaker a few seconds later. "Hey Samson, how you doing?" He sounded more like a Tony Soprano than a vampire. New York could do that to anybody.

"Good to hear your voice, Gabriel. Listen, I don't want to keep you, but I need you to check something out for me. Did you guys send an auditor down to the San Fran office?"

"Let me check." He could be heard typing something on a keyboard. "Sure did. Assignment started Monday. What about it?"

"What's the auditor's name?"

"Delilah Sheridan."

Delilah stopped cold behind the kitchen door she was just about to open when she heard her name coming from a speaker phone. She held her breath. Why were they talking about her?

"Did you do a background check on her?" It was Samson's voice she heard. A background check? On her? What was he trying to find? She held her breath, not wanting to give away that she was on the other side of the door.

"Sure did," the other voice responded. "She's clean. Nothing unusual. Single, no siblings, father is in a home, mother died two years ago. What do you want to know?"

"Does she know who I am?" Samson's voice sounded strangely strained.

While she heard the question, she didn't understand what he meant by it.

"Doubt it," the voice shot back. "We certainly didn't give her any more information than we needed to. You know our policy better than anybody. And since everything is owned by the trust, she couldn't have seen your name in any of the documents."

What documents? What the hell was the man talking about?

She'd heard enough. Samson was checking up on her, for whatever reason. She felt violated. Angrily she pushed the door to the kitchen open. Three sets of eyes instantly landed on her. Three surprised sets of eyes: Samson's, Amaury's, and Carl's. They had all ganged up on her.

"Anything else?" the voice from the speaker continued.

"Thanks, Gabriel." Samson didn't take his eyes off her as he disconnected the call.

Delilah glared at him, unable to speak for a few seconds. None of the guys dared say a word as if waiting for an outburst. She'd give them one.

"You had a background check done on me?" She tried to make her voice sound even in order not to show the pain she felt.

"Delilah, I'm sorry, I can explain." Samson didn't even bother denying her accusation. That confirmed it.

She shook her head. "I'll save you the trouble. I'm leaving." She spun on her heels and stormed out. Taking two stairs at a time, she headed to the second floor. Tears burned in her eyes, but she pushed them back. He wasn't worth it. If he wanted to know something about her, he could have asked her. She would have told him everything, every little detail about her life.

But he hadn't asked. Instead he'd checked up on her behind her back as if she was a criminal. After the wonderful night of passion they'd shared, he had felt the need to check up on her? What had he thought he would find?

***

After locking Billy up in one of the containers, but leaving him with water and a blanket, Ricky and Thomas left the warehouse. They weren't savages. If Samson could treat the man who had attacked him and Delilah with civility, so could they.

"Did you catch what Samson said about her?" Ricky asked.

"You mean the speech about *my woman*?"

"Exactly. Do you think he meant it?"

Thomas shrugged his shoulders. "You tell me. When it comes to you straight guys, I really can't tell when you're into somebody or not. Too much hiding your feelings and crap."

"Trust me, I can't tell any more than you can. But I've never heard him talk like that. I hope she isn't getting under his skin. Something like this can only end badly."

Ricky took the helmet Thomas handed him and swung his leg over the motorcycle to take his place behind him.

"He should have left me my car and taken your motorcycle instead of us cramming onto it."

"What, you're worried because you have to hold onto me?" Thomas laughed. "Since when so homophobic?"

"I'm not; I'm worried about my car. He was ready to kill me today. I hope he's not taking it out on my brand-new ride."

Thomas jerked his head. "Kill you? What did you do to him?"

"I walked in on him while he was shagging Delilah in the shower."

"You can't be serious. That's why he wanted to kill you?" Thomas' reaction was not unusual. Among their kind, sex wasn't necessarily always seen as a private act, unless it happened between a bonded pair. So there was no reason why Samson should get all bent out of shape about being seen fucking Delilah.

"That's what I'm saying. He basically told me to kiss our friendship and my job goodbye if he ever saw me looking at her again."

"Sounds pretty possessive to me."

"Yep."

"Are you thinking what I'm thinking?"

"Yep."

"Oh boy."

Ricky slung his arms around Thomas' waist, and the motorcycle took off. It was still drizzling lightly. Thomas expertly guided them through light traffic. He knew the city like his back pocket and had a keen eye for spotting obstacles in advance, helping him avoid major delays easily.

They drove toward the Sunset district past the forties and fifties era homes, the often unkempt front yards, and the ticky-tacky shops on the way. It wasn't a neighborhood either one of them liked particularly. It was mostly flat and architecturally uninteresting.

The address Billy had given them was a corner home, which looked larger than others on the block and appeared to have been completely renovated. It stuck out like the most expensive house on the block. There was light coming from several of the windows of the home.

Thomas parked his motorcycle around the corner.

"How do you want to play it?"

"Straightforward. We ring the doorbell," Ricky replied.

Their footsteps made virtually no sound as they walked on the pavement. Thomas' nostrils flared as they approached the house. He inhaled. A strangely familiar scent wafted into his nose, but he was distracted instantly when he heard a scream from inside the house.

He and Ricky stared at each other for a fraction of a second then ran to the front door and kicked it in.

The sound was that of a woman, hysterically screaming at the top of her lungs. It came from the back of the house. Then the whining of a toddler mingled with the woman's screams. The sound of the woman was bloodcurdling.

When they reached her, they understood. There was nothing they could do. They'd come too late.

There was no doubt in Thomas's mind that John had been killed by a vampire. He could still sense traces of energy the assailant had left. John's body looked almost peaceful had it not been for the utter horror forever etched into his open eyes. He'd seen his murderer seconds before he'd struck.

John's body lay on the floor of the den. His neck had been snapped. Ignoring the woman's screams, Thomas bent down and closed John's eyelids. There was no need for his wife to continue looking at her dead husband's horrified expression.

They couldn't stay to comfort the woman, but they could wipe her memory. Thomas laid his palm on her forehead. Her screams subsided, and she went still. He not only erased any memory she had of him and Ricky, but also of her husband's eyes. It was better if she didn't know how terrified he'd been in the seconds before his death. Dealing with her grief would be difficult enough.

***

Delilah threw her clothes into her only suitcase, not bothering to fold them. Somebody had moved her things into Samson's bedroom during the day, and now she couldn't get out of it fast enough. She couldn't be with a man who didn't trust her. Hell, he hadn't even made an attempt to get to know her. Instead he'd gone behind her back. She couldn't tolerate that kind of betrayal.

She heard the door open and close behind her and knew Samson had followed her. She had expected as much. She could sense his presence, but she didn't want to acknowledge him. He didn't deserve it.

"I'm sorry, Delilah." His voice was closer than she'd expected. He couldn't be more than a foot away from her. She didn't want him this close. Not now.

"I'll be gone in two minutes, and don't worry: I'm not stealing anything from you." Her voice was icy. She wouldn't give him the satisfaction of knowing just how much he'd hurt her. This wasn't the first time she was disappointed in a man, and it wasn't going to be the last. *He* wasn't going to be the last man in her life. She was more than used to it, used to always dating the wrong guy. Maybe that was why she'd stopped dating altogether. She'd probably make a better choice with a cat or a dog.

"I deserved that." Samson's voice was calm. "Please give me a chance to explain." He probably had a standard speech prepared for occurrences like these. How else could he remain this unmoved?

She felt his hands on her shoulders and pushed them off.

"Okay. I won't touch you." He sounded resigned.

Anger welled up in her. She could feel it boil up from her stomach and travel through her chest. It was too much to hold in.

"How could you? How could you go behind my back like that?" Delilah spun around to face him. "You could have just asked me what you wanted to know." And why was he still so attractive, so sexy, when she needed to be angry at him? In his jeans and black t-shirt he looked as good as he did naked, even though she preferred him naked.

She shouldn't have turned. She should have just walked out without even looking at him.

His biceps flexed, and she was again aware of his strength and physical beauty. The way his hazel eyes searched hers as if he was trying to look into her soul made her knees weak. She had to pull her eyes away from him if she ever wanted to get out of the room.

"It was wrong. But I needed to know who you are."

Standing within inches of touching him only added to her agitated mind.

"I told you who I am. What were you expecting?" She let all her disappointment and pain out in her voice. "After all the things we did

… you couldn't just ask me? No. You had to run a background check on me, like I'm a common criminal."

"Sweetness, don't—"

Samson raised his hand as if he wanted to touch her face, but stopped when she shot back at him, "Don't call me sweetness!"

Delilah had liked it when he'd called her that the night before when they were making love, but not now. She turned and snapped her suitcase shut.

"Delilah, I apologize. I wish I'd trusted my instincts more, but I didn't. When Carl packed your things, he found something and brought it to my attention. I should have gone straight to you and asked you about it, but I … I don't know why I didn't …" His voice trailed off.

His hazel eyes stared into hers, trying to force her to listen to him. "You had files of Scanguards' in your possession."

"So what? I work for them. Carl had no right to go through my stuff."

Samson nodded. "Yes. But he saw them. And I understand now that you had every right to have those files on you. I know that now. Because I now know that you work for me."

Confused, she looked at him. "I don't work for you. I work for Scanguards," she insisted and grabbed her suitcase. "And besides, what's it to you who I work for? I didn't think you were all that interested in what I do." She tried to push past him to get to the door, but he blocked her escape.

"You work for me. I *am* Scanguards. I own it."

Delilah stopped in her tracks, and Samson instantly realized that this was news to her. She hadn't known that he was the owner of Scanguards, that he was worth in excess of a few hundred-million dollars. His heart jumped when the realization settled in, when he understood that his fear had been unfounded. She wasn't after his money, because she'd had no idea how filthy rich he really was.

Samson could see that she was trying to make sense of his words. But then it was like a dark cloud settled over her face. Her jaw dropped, and she glared at him.

"You thought I was after your money? Oh my God! You thought I slept with you because ... Oh my God!"

The pain he saw in her eyes hurt him deep in his chest. If he'd thought telling her who he was would make her understand why he'd acted the way he had, it had backfired. It had actually made it worse. Much worse.

"I've never felt so cheap and dirty in my life. I felt cleaner when you thought I was a stripper. But you thought ... you thought I would ... no, no ..."

She ran for the door, but he leapt in front of her and stopped her. He wanted to take her into his arms and kiss her pain away, apologize with his body for everything he'd done. But he knew she'd push him away. He had hurt her, his lovely mortal, and it pained him more than if he'd been hurt himself. At this point he'd do anything to make her pain go away.

"Please tell me what you want me to do to make it up to you."

She stared at him, her eyes glistening with the tears she was holding back. "You think you can buy me? Haven't you humiliated me enough? Keep your damn money and get out of my way!"

"Please stop for a minute, and listen to me."

"Why? Don't you already know everything you want to know? Isn't that why you assigned me a *bodyguard* today? So you could spy on me? Do you control all your women like that?"

"Delilah, it was for your own safety. I never wanted to hurt you, believe me. But you scared me." He was scared alright, scared of what she could do to his heart. Maybe it was better if he told her upfront what she'd done to him.

"Scared you? How? Because you've been slumming it with a poor little auditor? Yeah, that's downright scary," she bristled full of sarcasm.

"Don't say that. It's the things you make me feel when I'm with you. That's what scares me."

"Stop lying to me." She shot past him and ripped the door open. Her suitcase in her hand, she rushed down the stairs. Samson was right behind her, not willing to let her go.

The entrance door opened a second before she reached it. A sudden blast of cold air entered the foyer and with it Ricky and

Thomas. Ricky stared at Delilah and then at Samson who was only a step behind her.

"I don't think you should let her leave, Samson." He slammed the door shut before she could exit. Samson heard her frustrated sigh as she attempted to get past Ricky.

"I'm not letting her leave."

"Good. 'Cause somebody killed John Reardon. And she might be next."

"John?" Delilah's voice was just a hoarse whisper. She dropped her suitcase to the floor where it made a loud thump.

Samson exchanged surprised looks with his two friends. Did she know him?

Delilah braced herself on the wardrobe. A split-second later Samson was by her side; he wrapped his arms around her and led her into the living room. He wouldn't let her leave, not now, not ever.

Samson gently sat her on the couch and stayed close to her. Keeping his arm around her, he was relieved to feel she didn't push him away.

"Ricky, pour Delilah a brandy, will you?"

His friend complied eagerly and handed him the glass a few moments later. Samson led the brandy to Delilah's lips and made her sip from it as he brushed a strand of hair out of her face.

"Here you go, sweetness." His voice took on a soothing tone while he stroked her arm tenderly. She didn't protest. He knew she hadn't forgiven him yet, but right now she was in shock, and he would do anything to make her feel better. Later, he'd seek her forgiveness. And then there was another hurdle to jump over—but she wasn't ready for that yet.

In the seconds when he'd followed her down the stairs, he'd made up his mind. He wouldn't let her go back to New York. Screw the fact that she was human. She was his. He needed her, and he could make her happy. He knew it deep down in his heart.

He caught Ricky exchanging a look with Thomas who nodded. Neither one of them had ever seen him in such a tender exchange with a woman. Samson planted a soft kiss on the top of Delilah's head, not caring what his friends thought of his behavior.

"Delilah, tell me what you know about this man. He was the one who hired that guy who attacked you."

She suddenly stared at him, her eyes wide in disbelief. "John? John hired that thug?" She looked up at Thomas and Ricky who nodded.

"Yes, it was him. Who was he?" Samson asked again.

"You should know who he is. He works for you."

"For me?"

"He's an accountant at Scanguards," she announced, looking back and forth between Samson and his friends.

TWELVE

Samson sent Ricky and Thomas off to investigate the murder of the accountant. They would also review background checks of John and anybody he worked with at Scanguards. Amaury remained at the house with them.

"I think it's pretty clear that it wasn't John's idea to harm you. He was obviously working for somebody, and this somebody killed him," Samson stated.

"But why would somebody want to harm me? I only met him a week ago, and I don't know anybody else here in San Francisco. I have no enemies," Delilah protested.

"And this person knew we were onto him, don't forget that," Amaury interjected. "And got to John before we could. Isn't that telling us something?"

Samson nodded. "That's right. Whoever it was, he didn't want us to interrogate John and find out who's behind this, or what this is about. Can you think of any reason why he or anybody else would want to hurt you?"

The thought that somebody else was still out there, wanting to hurt the woman he desired so deeply, tore at his heartstrings. If anybody as much as harmed a hair on her head, they'd have to deal with his wrath. It would be ugly.

"I'm only here for the audit, nothing else. I'm used to people not being too happy to see me, but that doesn't mean they want to harm me."

"Then it has to do with the audit. It's your only connection to John and to San Francisco. It's the only explanation. Has the audit produced any results?" Samson was curious.

She shrugged her shoulders. "Nothing unexpected, at least not so far. I've had problems getting to some of the supporting documentation for some of the issues I'm looking into, but I still have till Wednesday, so I'm sure I'll figure out what's wrong." Delilah seemed very confident about her work. "I've always found whatever there was to be found."

"Is that your reputation? Is that why New York hired you?" Samson let his eyes sweep over her small form. Was she some kind of super sleuth? Would she also figure him out soon? How long did he have until she'd discover his secret? How long till she'd run screaming from his house?

"That's all I do. I don't do regular financial audits. I only work on special investigations. If somebody is cooking the books, I'll find it. I've already found a few indications that somebody is defrauding the company. I just have to confirm who is behind it."

There was an air of confidence about her, almost pride. He believed her instantly. If she said she'd find it, she would. Of course, this also meant, he himself had to be extremely careful and quickly come up with a strategy of how to tell her what he was. He had to tell her that he was a vampire, because he wasn't going to let her leave.

"Take all the time you need—I'm extending your contract indefinitely." This would take the time pressure off him. Wednesday was just too early.

"Can you do that?" Delilah looked first at him and then at Amaury. "Can he do that?"

Amaury smirked. "He's the boss. What he says, goes."

"You make me sound like a tyrant." He gave his friend a scolding look. "I assure you, I'm nothing of the kind. But being the boss does have its perks." Samson smiled at her. "You can work out of here. My office is at your disposal. You'll have universal access to all files, not just for the San Francisco branch, but all our branches. Whatever information you need, I can get it for you."

"That won't be necessary. I can work at the downtown office. Besides, I need the box of transaction documents I had John get for me. I'm not done with it yet. It's still at the office."

Samson shook his head. "I'll have somebody bring it here. I'm not letting you out of my sight. If somebody was able to get to John and kill him, they'll try to do the same to you. I can't take that risk." A cold shiver ran down his spine at the thought of anybody harming her.

"Do you always get what you want?" Her voice had an edge to it. He understood why. She was still angry with him for checking up on her background.

"I don't. But this time I will. No discussion. You'll work here. One of us will always be with you." He nodded at Amaury, asking his friend silently to support him. At present, Delilah seemed more inclined to listen to anybody else but himself.

"He's right, Delilah. If somebody thought it so important to get rid of you, they're not going to stop just because we tracked down John and his brother-in-law."

Great, so they were both ganging up on her. Maybe she was still in shock, but her thoughts seemed clear to her. Delilah was still mad as hell at Samson for not trusting her. She was confused about the mixed signals she was getting from him, and she was frightened at the thought of somebody being after her to harm her. If everything had been fine between her and Samson, she would have had no problems with the arrangement, but now, things were different. If he thought that by making her stay at his house, he could get her back into his bed, then he'd get a rude awakening.

She would tell him so right now, so he'd know his place. "Fine. I'll stay here to finish the audit. But I don't date clients."

From his reaction she could see that he hadn't expected her statement. His jaw dropped. It took a few seconds for him to find his composure.

"We'll discuss this later, in private."

The hell they would. The less she was alone with him, the better. Delilah recalled the moment when Ricky had told them about John's death, and how Samson had taken the opportunity to take her into his arms. She hadn't had the strength to protest then, but she felt better now. She wouldn't give him another opportunity to wiggle his way back into her heart, only to let him hurt her again. She had to shut him out. This was just a job, nothing else. And that was exactly how she would treat this from now on.

"I'd better get to work."

"Now?" Samson raised an eyebrow.

"I can't sleep anyway." Delilah knew that with all the things that had happened there was no way in hell she'd be able to close her eyes. "You don't have to stay up with me. Just show me your office and give me access to the files."

Samson's office was larger than Delilah had expected. It was paneled in a rich, dark wood and had one wall of shelves completely stuffed with books from top to bottom. There was a huge desk with several computer screens, a sofa with a couple of armchairs, and a coffee table.

She had expected him to show her the systems and then leave, but instead both he and Amaury stayed and started working with her, assisting her with reviewing files, tracing transactions and making phone calls to New York to verify information. It appeared that even in the middle of the night people worked at Headquarters. With direct access to all files of the company her work would be much easier. Nobody was putting any restrictions on her.

Delilah found it strange that he suddenly trusted her like this. Samson had one of his staff bring the storage box from the office which she'd been working on during the day. Now he and Amaury were pouring over information spread out on the coffee table, while she sat in his comfortable office chair and scrolled through the computer files.

He'd given her his logon and password, and she had free reign. If she had wanted to, she could have gone into all his private files and looked at what he was up to. But she didn't. She wouldn't snoop around. She wouldn't stoop so low and do to him what he'd done to her. This was different from opening a few drawers in his bedroom.

Delilah looked at Samson who had his head buried in the papers, talking quietly to Amaury. His long lashes were as dark as his shaggy hair, which she'd made a mess of the night before, wildly running her hands through it and pulling him closer to her. Even now, despite how much he'd hurt her, she found him more desirable than any man she'd ever met.

As if he felt her gaze on him, he suddenly raised his eyes and looked at her. Caught! He gave her the faintest of smiles, and she felt heat stream into her cheeks. This man could confuse the hell out of her. She quickly turned back to the computer screen. She had to keep a cool head. In a few days her work would be done, especially if she worked through the weekend, and then she was free to leave. All this would just be a distant memory.

The hours ticked by, and to her surprise the two men did not get tired. Knowing that Samson had barely slept the night before when they had—nevermind. And then he'd been in business meetings all day. Well, it was none of her concern anyway. He was a grown up. If he didn't think he needed any sleep, she wasn't going to care. At least tomorrow was the weekend, and nobody would have to get up too early.

She suddenly suppressed a yawn and glanced at the clock.

"Wow, it's almost six o'clock."

Samson and Amaury looked at each other.

"Damn," Amaury exclaimed.

Samson said something to him Delilah couldn't hear, and Amaury nodded.

"I'd better get some sleep. Good night," she said and got up, switching off the computer.

Samson stood and followed her out of the room. " 'Night, Amaury."

" 'Night."

In the hallway, her suitcase was still at the same place she had dropped it earlier. Before she could pick it up, Samson took it and started walking upstairs with it. Tired, she followed him.

"You and Amaury didn't have to stay up with me this long. I could have done this by myself."

"Don't worry about us. We're used to being up late. And besides, it's my company. I have a vested interest in finding out who's trying to pull a fast one on us."

As they reached the top of the stairs, he headed for his bedroom, while she made a move toward the guest room. She stopped when she saw where he was going, still holding onto her suitcase.

"I need my suitcase." Delilah reached out her hand, expecting him to hand it to her.

"That's why I've brought it up with me. Come." He opened the door and turned to wait for her to join him.

"I don't think you understand: when I told you that I don't date clients, it wasn't a joke."

"Then I'm afraid I'm going to have to fire you."

"Don't be ridiculous."

"I'm not. I'm practical." He hovered at the open door.

Delilah crossed her arms in front of her chest, assuming a defensive position. She needed all the strength she could muster. "Even if you fire me, I won't sleep in your room. I'll be in the guestroom." She spun on her heels and walked away.

"I wouldn't do that if I were you." There was no malice in his voice, just a firm determination.

"Watch me." She made her challenge clear. If he really thought he could get her back this easily, he had to be completely loony.

"I would hate to have to beat up Amaury."

"What?" She turned. What did Amaury have to do with this? It made not a lick of sense to her. If his plan was to confuse her, he'd succeeded. She was all ears.

"I would hate to find the two of you together in the guest bedroom. He's staying. So unless you want to start a big fight between two good friends, I suggest you stay with me."

So that was what the two of them had been whispering about in the office. He'd tricked her. "You were planning this, weren't you? You know what? I can sleep on the couch in the living room."

Samson shook his head, and his eyes gazed at her, full of softness and warmth. It wasn't fair.

"I'm still mad at you." She hadn't wanted to say this, but it just came out.

"I know that. You have my word: I won't touch you. I know when I've made a mistake, and I know when to apologize. But would you please give me a chance to explain things to you, so that maybe you can forgive me?" His tone was pleading. "I don't want this to end."

Delilah met his gaze. "What?"

"Us." He stretched out his free hand. "Please talk to me."

Hesitantly she moved toward him, her feet not following her brain, which told her not to fall for his charm again. Seconds later, she was in his bedroom and heard him shut the door behind her. She was alone with him. She needed to be whipped, severely. Had she not just five minutes ago promised herself to stay away from him?

Samson switched on the fireplace and sat down in front of it, looking into the flames. "I never wanted to hurt you."

"Well, you did." She wouldn't make this easy for him. If he wanted her forgiveness, he'd have to work for it. Hard. Just looking so darn irresistible wasn't going to get him out of this quagmire.

Sure, tell your body that! Oh, shut up!

"And I'm very sorry about it. I know I can't take it back, but I would like you to see my side of it, too. You showed up at my house, completely unexpected and so enticing. And then you instantly wrapped me around your little finger—"

"Did not," Delilah protested, but inwardly had to smile. He really thought she'd wrapped him around her finger? No man had ever said that of her. She wasn't a temptress. Never had been, never would be. She wouldn't even know where to start.

He smiled at her. "Did too. And you so willingly shared my bed. Believe me, no man is that lucky."

Delilah looked at him. Did he actually mean that? Had he looked in the mirror lately? Guys like him *did* get this lucky. All the time.

"That's not a good enough reason for going behind my back."

"No, but fear of another betrayal is. What's that saying? 'Once burned, twice shy'?"

"Betrayal?" Now she was curious.

"There was a woman." Samson looked at her to check for her reaction. Should he tell her the whole story, all of it? It would help her understand why he'd been so afraid. Why thinking she would betray him had sent him into such a tailspin.

"The redhead."

He was stunned. How had she guessed?

"You looked so tense, so full of rage when you spoke to her."

He stretched out his hand to motion her to sit with him. Delilah obliged him and took a seat on the floor pillows next to him. He wanted to feel her close when he told her what had happened. Not even his friends knew the details he was willing to share with her. All they knew was that he'd discovered that she'd been after his money. He'd never told anybody about the horrible things he'd overheard her say on the phone.

"I was introduced to her by a mutual acquaintance. Ilona was new in town. We started dating, and she made me believe that she cared for me. I was at a point in my life where I didn't want to be alone anymore."

"Did you love her?" Delilah's voice was low, almost as if she hadn't wanted to ask that question. No woman wanted to hear a man confess that he loved somebody else. Even he knew that much.

"I believed so at the time. Everybody told me what a great couple we were, so I figured if everybody saw it, it had to be true. The night I was planning to propose to her, I surprised her. She hadn't expected me. I overheard her on the phone, talking to one of her friends. The things she said ..."

Samson felt her soft hand on his forearm, stroking him gently. It felt so good to have Delilah's warm hand caress him. He didn't dare touch her for fear she'd stop. Her fingers were comforting and soothing.

"She said, she hated being touched by me, that she couldn't stand making love to me, and that once she'd be bl ... married to me, she didn't care who saw to my sexual needs, but it wasn't going to be her. That she'd throw up if she had to kiss me again." Even now he couldn't repeat her exact words.

Delilah looked at him, her eyes wide in shock.

"All she wanted was my money." And once she had it, she would have had somebody get rid of him. He couldn't prove it, but he suspected it.

"But weren't you going to have a prenup? Everybody in California has one."

He shook his head. "That's not how it works with me. No prenup. The woman I marry one day will have equal rights to everything I own. She will be my partner, in life and in business. Once I commit myself to somebody, it'll be without reservations." A blood-bond was more than a marriage. A blood-bond was marriage without prenup, without divorce. It truly was till death do us part. He would have to explain it to her, one day, one day soon.

"Oh."

"But that's not all. After I broke it off with her, I couldn't trust another woman. I didn't want to see anybody, nobody interested me."

"That's normal after a breakup like that," she said softly, compassion clearly written in her lovely face.

Samson shook his head. "It's not normal for a man to suddenly have no sexual appetite anymore. And it's *definitely* not normal to have no erection for nine months."

Her mouth fell open at his frank admission.

"It's true." He nodded, watching her.

"Your friends know all this?"

"Only the basics, I never told them what actually happened and what she said. You're the only person who knows."

He'd confided in her and her alone. He felt her move closer to him.

"So your friends tried to help you and got you a stripper ..." Delilah let the sentence hang in the air.

"And instead, you showed up, and suddenly everything sprung back to life. I couldn't believe what was happening at first, but when I kissed you for the first time, and you were struggling to fight me off, I got so turned on ... Suddenly everything that had been dormant for so long woke up."

Her cheeks colored a gorgeous shade of pink.

"Can you imagine how scared I was when Carl found those files in your luggage, and I thought our meeting wasn't a coincidence? That you'd been playing me? That you didn't want me, but my money? I'd just started feeling something again, and just then, I thought you'd been ..." It was painful to talk about it even now. "Please forgive me. I should have talked to you immediately and asked you about the files. I could have spared us this."

Delilah put her finger onto his lips. "Shh." How could she continue to be mad at him when he'd opened up to her like that? What man would admit that he'd had erection problems, especially to a woman he wanted to get into bed? This couldn't be some cheap trick. She looked into his eyes, searching for a sign that she was mistaken, that he couldn't be trusted, but there was none. Nobody would stoop this low to get what he wanted, would he? No. His voice, his face, everything felt and sounded honest, open. He'd told her everything.

But there was still another question. She didn't want to ask it, but she had to. She owed it to herself. At least then she'd know where she stood.

"I'm sorry, but I have to ask. Does this mean that you just want sex? I mean, it's ok," she added hastily. She didn't want to sound like a prude or too needy. "If that's all you want. I can understand, given the circumstances. I mean, what man wouldn't want to catch up, right? Nine months is a long time for a man. And we're both consenting adults. I mean, this is just a fling. Anyway, I don't even live here, I have to go back to New York ..." She was babbling. She knew there was no future in this. At least she knew now that the reason he wanted her was because he was starved for sex. Fair enough. They were adults. She could deal with it, couldn't she? Couldn't she?

Samson's hand went to her face, his thumb stroking her jaw. His gaze moved from her trembling lips to her eyes. She shivered, but she wasn't cold.

"I want more."

"More sex?" Her voice shaky, she avoided his gaze.

"More of everything. More of you, not just sex. This isn't about sex anymore. And I'll prove it to you. Tonight—"

"It's already day."

"Today, all I want is having you sleep in my arms. No sex: I just want to be close to you. You don't even have to be naked. In fact, it's probably better if you're not. I don't expect you to forgive me immediately; I know you're still mad at me, but I need to have you close. I need to feel you breathe beside me, I need your warmth. Please."

As much as Samson hungered for her body and to be inside of her, he owed her this much. He needed to prove to her that he didn't just want her for sexual gratification, that he respected her decisions. If he could hold off his sexual urges for the day to prove to her that he needed her for something other than sex, he had a chance at making her his for good. It was worth the sacrifice. *She* was worth the sacrifice.

"You want me just here with you? You won't kiss me?"

He looked at her lips, slightly parted and moist. Of course he wanted to kiss her, but how could he stop after that? He pulled Delilah into his arms and pressed her head against his chest, smoothing his palm over her hair. "I promised you when you came in here tonight that I wouldn't touch you. I'm gonna stick to it."

"You're touching me now."

"You know what I meant, so don't split hairs with me." He chuckled softly, knowing that if she teased him, she couldn't be quite as mad anymore.

Samson let her change in the bathroom while he stripped down to his boxers in the bedroom. He used the spare bathroom down the hall to get ready for bed, figuring as a woman she'd be in his on-suite bathroom for longer than he cared to stay up. The sun had come up already, and he needed to get some sleep. He felt his body tiring fast and his energy draining quickly.

He lay down in bed, pulling the covers over him. It only took a couple of minutes until he heard the bathroom door open and saw her. If he had been tired before, suddenly all of that was wiped away. Was she planning to seduce him?

Delilah wore the sexiest baby-doll nightdress he'd ever seen—the only one he'd ever seen—the fabric of which was far too thin to leave anything to the imagination. Not that he had to imagine anything in the first place. He had a mental photograph of every inch of her body safely locked away in his memory bank.

She slipped underneath the covers and right into his arms, molding her pliable body to his. Samson was sure she noticed the hungry look with which he devoured her. He hoped that sleep would claim him soon so he could keep his promise, but knew instinctively that it wouldn't come fast enough.

"You said you wanted me to sleep in your arms, right?"

"Yes, but I also said, you should not be naked." His hands went around her, pressing her closer to him. He could feel every muscle in her body.

"I'm not naked."

"That's debatable." She felt naked to him. His response was automatic. Blood surged to his loins as if somebody had opened the gates to a dam. Hoover Dam, for all he knew.

She moved her head close to his, tempting him with her sweet scent. "Don't I get a goodnight kiss?"

"Better not." He could barely speak now, trying to hold back the urge to take her. Images of her glistening skin against his flooded his mind. Their bodies moving in synch, his hard cock impaling her, pumping hard, slamming into her. He felt pearls of sweat building on his brow, heat surging through his body as he tried to fight against his nature.

"Don't you find me attractive anymore?"

She knew exactly what she was doing, even more so when he felt her hand run down his chest, to his stomach, to his boxers. He was unable to stop her, not because he didn't have the physical strength, but because all rational thought flew right out of his head. When her hand wrapped around his erection, he knew he'd lost the battle, but he made one more attempt at keeping his promise.

"You should stop. I made a promise." It was difficult for him to speak. All his brain could think about was her soft palm moving up and down his cock.

"I didn't, which means I can touch you all I want." He couldn't believe his ears. The reason he had promised her not to touch her was so he could gain her trust back and earn her forgiveness, and what did she do? She shamelessly seduced him.

"You can't be serious. You're mad at me, remember?"

Delilah looked up at him and shook her head. "Not anymore. If I was still mad at you, I wouldn't be in your bed right now. And I wouldn't be touching you the way I am." Her hand squeezed tighter around his hard shaft as she moved along his steely length. "So, would you please stop playing hard to get and kiss me?"

"Hard to get? I don't think I've ever been called that." He suddenly felt her shift, and within seconds she was on top of him, straddling him. With one swift move, she lifted her nightgown over her head and threw it off the bed. His eyes took her in, all of her gorgeous nakedness, her silken skin, her curves. He stared at her round twin globes that would fit perfectly into his palms.

Slowly Samson took her face into both hands and pulled her down to him. "I would have kept to my word, but you leave me no choice." He captured her mouth, devouring her. He was starved, starved for her taste. For a second he pulled back. "And I want you to know, no more sex: from now on, we make love." It was important to him to make that distinction. He was done with mindless sex. He wanted a different kind of intimacy with her. All he wanted now was to show her what he felt for her, to win her heart and her trust so that soon he could tell her the last of his secrets and reveal his true identity.

Samson's lips went back to kiss her, and if Delilah had ever had any doubts about him, he just kissed them away. This man had opened up to her like no other man ever had, and even though she had circumvented his efforts to keep to his promise of not touching her, she had seen the sincerity in him in trying to keep his promise. It was all she needed to know. There was no need to waste the night—or rather the day—without touching. There was only one place she wanted him right now, and it was inside of her, captured between her thighs. For how ever long she could keep him there.

His kiss was more tender than it had ever been before. She could feel his hunger and need beneath it, just barely kept in check, ready to break to the surface. But still, he overwhelmed her with his tenderness, with the intimate caress his tongue unleashed on her mouth. His fingers framed her face, softly stroking her skin and teasing her sensitive neck as if he couldn't bear to let go of her face.

There was longing and promise in his kiss, as if he'd opened his heart and invited her in. And there was something else she hadn't felt before: the feeling that he needed her, not to satisfy his carnal need, but to fulfill his emotional need. She responded to him with her own brand of passion and need. Her head filled with images of bliss, of the two of them dancing in the sun, in a sea of flowers.

Samson pulled back and suddenly gave her a short break to
breathe. "I can't get enough of you. Don't leave on Wednesday."

"But, I have to go back when the audit is done." Her protest was
weak. She didn't want to leave, but she couldn't just stay either. She
had a life in New York, well, she had an apartment. "I have no reason
to ..." A rented apartment. Really just a place where she kept her
belongings. A tiny place, something her German ancestors would call
a *Wohnklo*, a tiny studio with an equally tiny bathroom.

"I can give you a hundred reasons to stay." He took her upper lip
between his and sucked gently. "That's one." His tongue swept over
her lips. "Here's another. We'll talk about it tonight. But right now ..."

He flipped her masterfully and brought her underneath him, gazing
into her eyes for a long moment.

Samson took what was his, and Delilah surrendered to his mouth,
his tongue, his hands, and his body. His lovemaking was more tender
than he thought he'd ever be capable of. There was no rush to join his
body with hers. They would have plenty of time to explore each other.

This time all he wanted was to feel her, experience her body's
heat, feel her heart beat against his lips with an excited rhythm. Under
his hands and his mouth, he felt her come alive and open up.

Delilah arched toward him every time his hands stroked from her
neck down to her navel. Like Magellan, he circled her breasts and
sailed South, only to detour before reaching the South Pole. He
navigated the small channel between her breasts like the Bosphorus,
not being able to decide whether to lavish his attention first on Europe
or on Asia. Both looked equally enticing.

What perfect mountains with rock-hard peaks. His tongue lapped
at her engorged tips teasing a strangled moan from her throat.

"Sweetness, I haven't even started yet."

Her breath caught. "Oh, mercy."

Mercy wasn't what he had in mind. No, he was headed for the lush
canopy further South which sheltered a treasure beneath—one he was
determined to reacquaint himself with.

His searching fingers found the hooded nub and brushed over it.
Delilah's pelvis bucked toward him instantly, pushing his hand onto

her moist petals. Unable to resist, he slipped his finger into her welcoming sheath.

"I want you now."

Samson had never heard her voice with such a husky undertone.

"You have me." He underscored his statement by plunging his finger deep into her. She had no idea how she owned him – body and soul. He would tell her, soon.

The urging of her body became more intense, her hips moving in synch with his hand, riding him, like he knew she wanted to do with his cock. And she could ride him whenever she wanted to: he would never be able to deny her.

With slow movements, Samson eased himself above her, centering his aching cock. And inch by inch he descended until he was deeply lodged inside her. Every thrust made their joining deeper, connected their bodies more until they moved as one.

They weren't only connected by his erection impaling her, but also by their legs entangled, their arms intertwined, their lips merged. Her body fitted perfectly to his, as if someone in heaven had molded her for him.

Samson had never felt closer to any woman than to Delilah at that moment. He could feel as her excitement built, as her pelvis started grinding against him more urgently. He responded in kind, moving in the rhythm she demanded. He realized how it filled him with joy, knowing he could pleasure her.

Samson held himself right at the edge, denying his release until he could be sure she was close. Her urgency took over, demanding he'd thrust harder and deeper, and he complied all too willingly despite the strength it cost him to hold back his own climax.

"Don't stop." Her wish was his command.

"Not a chance."

Her heels around his backside dug in deeper, and her fingernails on his back would have drawn blood if he'd had the fragile skin of a human. Then her orgasm hit him—as if her body was about to shatter into a million pieces. And like a row of dominos it reached him, taking him with her, igniting his own release, making him spread his seed in her.

But it wasn't over. He kept moving inside her, rocking back and forth, kissing her lips, holding her until he felt the last of her spasms subside.

As he locked eyes with her, he couldn't speak. And didn't want to break the magical moment of complete and utter bliss. He rolled to the side, taking her with him, unable to release her from his embrace, unwilling to leave her body.

When he finally spoke, his voice echoed in his ears: hoarse, colored by passion and desire, and something else he hadn't felt in a long time—affection.

"I can give you a million reasons not to leave."

And he would draw on every single one to convince her to stay.

THIRTEEN

It happened frequently that Amaury spent time in a bed which wasn't his, but generally for other reasons than on this occasion. By the time he and Samson had looked up from their work helping Delilah, it was too close to sunrise to risk him going home. As much as he hated to intrude on the two lovers, he had no choice but to stay in the guest room.

Which, unfortunately, shared a wall with the master bedroom.

His sensitive hearing picked up more than he wanted to know or be part of, so he fashioned some makeshift earplugs out of cotton balls he found in the bathroom. It helped somewhat. At least he couldn't hear their voices anymore. It was another matter for the barrage of their emotions that hit him. They made it virtually impossible for Amaury to switch off. It appeared make-up sex was going well.

In all his years as a vampire he'd never met a woman who had stirred him the way Delilah affected Samson. Amaury was quite a bit older than his friend, by almost two hundred years, and he'd tried them all. How he had survived that long, he really wasn't quite sure, especially since he'd made enough enemies amongst humans and vampires alike.

He'd lived through difficult times in the fifteen and sixteen hundreds in his native France, before he'd felt it was time to get a fresh start on a new continent where his reputation as a scoundrel and philanderer didn't precede him. Plus, he'd gone through every woman aged from fifteen to fifty, and he was slowly but surely running out of willing bedmates. He was more prolific than Don Juan or Casanova, even though his name didn't quite make it into the history books. Just as well – he didn't need any publicity.

The guest room was comfortable enough, but his own personal nightmares woke him too early, an hour before sunset. The nightmares were familiar and hadn't changed much in the last few hundred years. Despite working with Dr. Drake on the guilt that plagued him, he couldn't rid himself of the images which tormented his sleep every night.

There was no need to stay in bed if he couldn't get back to sleep. A quick shower was refreshing, and so was the blood he found in the fridge in the pantry, the combination of which was no secret to him. He'd stayed at Samson's often enough to be familiar with all supply cabinets, and for now he didn't have enough time to go out hunting for a fresh meal. How Samson could live off the packaged stuff was beyond him.

Amaury preferred the warm and tasty red liquid pouring straight out of a breathing human. Preferably a female with whom he could satisfy two desires at once—two birds with one stone. And frankly, his carnal desires would need some major soothing soon. He rarely went a night without it.

Amaury wasn't in a relationship with any particular female. Instead he took whatever he could get from whichever willing female was available. Thanks to his good looks, there were always sufficient females interested in a roll in the hay with him. Well, these days, it wasn't in the hay anymore, since he actually preferred a soft mattress with high-thread-count Egyptian cotton. Mainstreaming *did* have its luxuries.

He poured over the newspaper Oliver had brought in earlier in the day. There was no sign of him in the house now; instead, Carl would be reporting to duty soon after sunset.

Minutes after delving into the paper, he heard steps on the stairs. It wasn't Samson's heavy footsteps, but Delilah's much lighter ones which approached. She appeared in the kitchen seconds later, a warm glow about her.

"Morning," she greeted him with a smile.

"Evening, Delilah. Samson up yet?"

"No. I let him sleep. He seemed exhausted."

He grinned. "No surprise."

The house had practically shaken like an earthquake, with the epicenter right in the master bedroom. Or maybe it was just Amaury's sensitivity to emotions, his special gift—and painful as hell—which had made him feel like San Francisco was in for another big one.

Delilah's resulting blush would shame a ripe tomato. She would get used to it. If he had read their emotions correctly last night, she would become a permanent fixture in this household.

"I'm starving. Shall I make you a sandwich while I'm at it?" Delilah opened the fridge and started taking out some bread, cold cuts, and salad items.

"No, thanks; solid foods after I've just gotten up don't quite agree with me." It wasn't a lie. Solid foods didn't agree with him, but not just for breakfast. Not that he wouldn't have liked eating a juicy steak if he could. As a Frenchman the loss of good food after he'd turned into a vampire had hit him the hardest.

Delilah went about washing some tomatoes. "You know, I've found something in the transactions last night."

"Go on." Amaury had a more than basic understanding of accounting and was a good partner to bounce ideas off.

"So, imagine you want to get past the internal controls to move valuable assets out of the company—what would you do?"

He shrugged his shoulders. "I'm not sure what you're getting at. You can't just move assets out of the company without signoff from higher sources than this John was. I'm sure you know that as well as I do."

"Agreed, but John had signing authority for other things. Like if he wanted to scrap an old computer, he'd sign off on it, and it went to a vendor who recycled old electronics," she explained as she buttered a slice of bread.

"Sure, but you'd have to scrap a lot of little things to make a dent in it. And besides, whatever you scrap probably has very little value left anyway, so what's the point? I don't see how you can move a large amount of assets out of the company like that. You'd be busy for years," Amaury rebuked her idea.

"That's what I thought at first, too. But what if the true value of the asset isn't just scrap value, but much more?"

"How?"

"Depreciation."

"Depreciation?" Amaury didn't quite understand. Of course he was familiar with the concept of depreciating an asset over its useful life to reflect an accurate value on the books and claim the expense on the profit-and-loss account of the company. But that's where his knowledge ended.

"Yes. John was authorized to scrap old assets below a value of $2,500 without getting any other signoff from HQ. He accelerated depreciation to reduce the value of these assets to below the threshold he could sign for, thus eluding internal controls."

This sounded promising, he had to admit. "And then?"

"Then he would transfer the asset to somebody outside the company, who in turn sold it for what it was truly worth. He'd give the scrap value back to the company and keep the difference for himself." She bit into her sandwich and chewed.

"But how much money could he really have stolen like that? What if it amounts to fifty- or a hundred-thousand dollars? That's peanuts. Not enough reason to send somebody after you to kill you. You saw yourself from the records we looked through yesterday that this has only been going on for about a year."

"But this doesn't change the fact that he was clearly defrauding the company. The transaction documents point to him. His signature was all over them. He initiated and then authorized the transactions. Yes, it wasn't exactly the most sophisticated fraud, and it certainly isn't new either, but maybe that kind of money meant more than peanuts to him. And maybe he wasn't trying to kill me; maybe he was only trying to scare me away?"

"What for? The next auditor would just come along and continue where you left off. It would just be a temporary fix at best."

"Temporary? Hmm." She clearly gave it a thought.

"Maybe he had something else up his sleeve."

She knit her brow. "You mean a better fraud?"

"Why not? At some point criminals get greedy. Trust me, I've seen plenty of greed in my life." Amaury wasn't exaggerating. He'd seen more than his fair share of greed in his long life.

"Greed. Hmm. It reminds me of something my teacher used to say to us in class. If you want to embezzle, you have to embezzle big. Get what you want in one big strike and get the hell out. Long-time embezzling schemes never work."

"Interesting teacher. What kind of school did you go to?" Amaury gave her an amused smile.

"He was my accounting teacher in college. Believe it or not, accountants and auditors need to actually learn how to perpetrate a fraud in order to spot one in the books."

"Like a security specialist who has to have broken into a few safes, huh?"

"Exactly. So, is that how Scanguards trains its people?"

Delilah had finished her sandwich and was putting the remaining food back into the fridge.

He gave her a sideways glance. She probably had no idea how close her question cut to the truth. Not only did Scanguards employ a majority of vampires, some less tame than others, a large number of their human employees were reformed criminals.

"I'm afraid I can't disclose our methods of how—"

She interrupted him. "Amaury, that was a rhetorical question."

He let out a nervous laugh and changed the subject. "You know what surprises me about John? He goes through this complicated setup to steal a little money, when it would have probably been so much easier to get at Scanguards' liquid assets. You're familiar with our balance sheet. We have very little in fixed assets, many of the buildings we operate out of are rented, the vehicles are generally leased. But we run a very heavy cash position. So why not get at the cash? Wouldn't that have been easier?"

Delilah pursed her lips. "Your internal controls around cash are pretty solid. Any cash transfers go through a double-approval process. I've read the procedure manual on it. He couldn't have done it on his own."

She placed the dishes into the sink and started cleaning them.

"I think we're overlooking something. Let's examine the facts. You audit the company. John gets nervous because he has been embezzling from us. He hires his brother-in-law to kill or ..."

"... or scare me away ..."

"... or scare you away. And just when we catch onto him, he is murdered. It wasn't his brother-in-law, since we'd already apprehended him. It wasn't a random killing. It was deliberate. So, what would John have told us if we had gotten to him earlier? Would he have confessed that he embezzled from us? Maybe. But that would only hurt himself."

"Somebody clearly didn't want us to confront him. John knew that person, and knew what he did, or knew what he'd let him do."

"That's right, because John helped him with it. There's no other reason for somebody to want you dead than thinking that you'll uncover what they did, and it has to be bigger than accelerated depreciation and selling off small assets. Much bigger."

Delilah turned around to look at him, interest shimmering in her eyes. Seemingly unaware that she held a sharp knife in her hand, she made an animated gesture. As the blade slipped out of her hand, she made an attempt to grip it, but only caught the sharp end between her fingers. It effortlessly cut into the soft flesh of her fingers before it landed on the floor. Blood immediately ran down her hand.

"Damn!"

"Oh shit!" Amaury exclaimed. That was all he needed – the scent of fresh blood on a virtually empty stomach. "Let me help you bandage it." The faster he sealed her wound, the better for all of them.

He pulled open a drawer and grabbed a clean napkin. "Let me see."

She held her good hand against her stomach. "Oh, God, I can't look."

"It's just a little blood," he assured her and couldn't help but notice that she'd gone white.

Amaury took her hand to look how deep the wound was, as he held the napkin underneath it to stop the blood from dripping on the floor. He held his breath in order not to become overpowered by the utterly enticing smell.

***

Samson scented the blood as soon as he stepped out of his bedroom, freshly showered and dressed. There was no doubt whose blood it was and where it came from. His nostrils flared, and his body tensed.

Delilah!

He knew Amaury's love for warm blood better than anybody and cursed himself for having let him stay while Delilah was with him.

As he flew down the stairs and burst into the kitchen, he was battle ready—to save his woman from his best friend. If Amaury had bitten her, he'd kill him. Fury shot through him as his eyes focused on the scene in the kitchen: Amaury bent over Delilah's bleeding hand.

Without thinking Samson lunged at his best friend, and with a loud thud they both crashed onto the hard kitchen floor.

"*Noooooooo!*" Samson's scream echoed in the kitchen. He flashed his fangs and snarled, pinning Amaury underneath him as he pummeled him with his fists. His friend's arms came up in defense, trying to shield his face.

"Stop!" But Amaury's voice was drowned out by Samson's fierce roar. Samson's fist connected with his friend's jaw once more. Deflecting his next hit, Amaury held him at bay.

"Samson!" Delilah's voice finally penetrated his head.

"I didn't do anything," Amaury hissed.

"Samson! What's going on?"

He jerked his head and instantly knew he shouldn't have turned toward her when he saw her reaction him. In his daze he'd forgotten about everything. He hadn't realized what she'd see: his vampire side.

Delilah shrieked, eyes wide, mouth open, her hand holding onto the counter as she backed away from them.

"Oh my God!" Her chest heaved as if she couldn't get enough air. "Oh my God, what are you?" It wasn't really a question. It was more of a statement.

He was so screwed.

***

Samson's eyes were red. Blinking freaking red!

They looked the same way as that time in the shower, when Ricky had interrupted them. She hadn't seen wrong, as much as she'd wanted to explain it away. But she couldn't explain it away, not anymore, not when she looked at his mouth from which two teeth were protruding now.

No, not teeth.

Fangs!

Pointy, sharp fangs like those of an animal. Like a Sabertooth tiger.

She couldn't think it, no, because to think it made it real. It couldn't be real. It didn't exist. He didn't exist, not like that.

Was this one of her strange dreams again? When would she wake up from this nightmare? When? Delilah gripped the counter behind her harder to counterbalance her buckling knees and felt the pain in her fingers where she'd cut herself. No, this wasn't a nightmare, this was reality. Bizarre reality.

She watched Samson get up, releasing Amaury from his grip, slowly moving toward her.

"No!" Her breath caught in her chest.

Need air. Need air now.

"Delilah, everything's ok." His voice was as soothing as it had been the night before.

"Get away from me." She backed away further until she hit the wall behind her. There was nowhere else to go. She'd managed to back herself into a corner. And he was coming toward her, slowly, but steadily. *Oh, Jesus Christ!* Her throat dried up. Her vocal cords froze. She had to face facts now. She couldn't deny it any longer.

She'd made love to a vampire, over and over again.

Dracula. A vampire.

Samson was a vampire, a vampire whose mouth had devoured her, whose fangs had been so close to her jugular—he could have killed her with one bite.

"I'm not going to hurt you."

She let out a hysterical laugh. "No, you're just going to bite me. That's what you want, isn't it? Oh God, how could I have been so stupid?" Really, how could she have been such a fool? Why had she not seen this coming? She felt like one of those stupid heroines in a B-grade horror movie, running up the stairs in her nightie with the killer hot on her heels.

Delilah frantically looked around for anything she could use as a weapon.

"Amaury, would you give us a moment alone," Samson requested.

"Do you think that's such a smart idea?" Amaury rubbed his jaw.

"I want Amaury to stay," Delilah said quickly, hoping that at least he could provide some protection against Samson.

Samson gave her a surprised look. "So you think having two vampires in the room is safer than one?"

That's when it hit her. She drew in her breath. They were both dangerous, they were both vampires. Amaury didn't show any fangs, and now that she stared at Samson again, his had retracted too. His eyes were their usual hazel color. Had she hallucinated? Was she even awake?

"Samson, I wasn't attacking her. I was helping her bandage the wound."

They exchanged looks until Samson finally nodded. "I'm sorry I misjudged you, but I couldn't take the risk of anybody hurting her. The situation—"

"I'm not as bloodthirsty as you think, and I would never touch your woman." Amaury sounded a tad hurt. A vampire hurt by somebody else's words?

Get real! You're seriously losing it.

Delilah slowly moved along the wall while the two vampires had their chatty conversation. She barely listened as she slid along the wall toward the kitchen door. Just a few more steps and she would reach the door.

"Where're you off to, Delilah?"

She stopped in her tracks. So much for her escape. She bit her lip.

"Let's bandage your hand first, before the scent of blood drives one of us over the edge." His voice seemed calm, but it could be a trick. For all she knew he'd suck her dry as soon as he saw the blood drip from her fingers.

Samson took a few steps toward her, and she pressed herself harder against the wall. But there was nowhere else to go. He was only inches away from her now.

"Please, I'm sorry you had to find out like this. I was planning to tell you—"

"When? Before or after you bit me?" She shouldn't show him her fear. It made her even more vulnerable, but she had no idea how to hide it. And animals like him would pounce as soon as they smelled fear, wouldn't they? Would he? Would he attack her when he realized that she was scared shitless?

She could feel his breath on her face. It reminded her of the way he'd kissed her, how he'd made love to her, how he'd touched her. How could he be the same man? No, he wasn't a man, he was a vampire.

Wake up and smell the blood!

"I'll never hurt you, sweetness. I was trying to protect you. I smelled the blood and thought Amaury had attacked you." Did he have to look so deadly sexy while he was only inches away from her? It wasn't fair.

She felt his hand reach for hers and tried to pull back, but he held on.

"Amaury, Band Aids are in the top drawer next to the stove."

Seconds later, his friend handed him the box of bandage strips. Samson lifted her hand to his mouth. Delilah shrieked. He was going to drink her blood. She knew it! It was just like in her nightmare.

He acknowledged her frightened look. "I'll lick your wound. My saliva will seal it, and it'll stop bleeding. Trust me."

Trust him? Was he kidding?

There was no way she would trust him, but he held her hand in an iron grip, and she couldn't free herself. Helplessly, Delilah watched as his tongue licked gently over the cuts, lapping up the blood. She felt a warm tingling feeling on her fingers and noticed that the blood flow stopped instantly. Samson placed the Band Aids over the sealed cuts. When he closed his mouth, she saw him swallow and inhale sharply.

His eyes suddenly locked with hers. "Oh God, even your blood tastes of lavender."

She watched him lower his mouth, but couldn't stop him. His lips brushed hers lightly before he took her mouth and captured her. That was when she knew with absolute certainty that she wasn't dreaming. She knew his touch, his taste, his scent. He was real, and he was a vampire.

She couldn't stop her body from reacting to him in the same way she'd reacted to him the night before and allowed his tongue to enter and caress her.

But this wasn't like the night before—he wasn't the same. He was a vampire, not the man she thought he was. She had to get away from him.

Samson was too engrossed in kissing her that the kick to his groin hit him like a train. He instantly let go of her and doubled over. Hell, nobody had ever kicked him in the groin. Right where it hurt most. Nausea overwhelmed him. As a vampire he could take pain, but even for him this was right up there with getting fingernails pulled out of their sockets.

When he looked up he caught a glimpse of Delilah as she ran out of the kitchen. Unable to run after her just yet as he still fought nausea, he gave his friend a command. "Bring her back."

By the time Amaury came back with her, Samson had recovered from the pain and was able to stand upright again. Amaury held her, too tight for Samson's liking. A pang of jealousy hit him. This was not good.

"Sweetness, you have to stop hitting me. I'm sure we can find another way for you to show your affection." He had to hand it to her. She had a lot of spunk, and taming her would be fun, if exhausting, and at times probably painful.

"I'm not your sweetness!"

Ah, that was more like it. He didn't like the fearful look she'd displayed earlier. He much preferred her being a fighter. Something he could work with.

"Can Amaury let go of you now, or are you going to bolt again?"

Delilah shook off Amaury's arm as Samson nodded to him. She immediately crossed her arms in front of her chest. Definitely ready for battle. Not that she'd win. Ever. But he'd let her try.

"Can we talk now?"

Delilah didn't answer and instead, pressed her lips together even tighter. He knew exactly how he could get those lips to open up, but it was probably better to not try it while she was still pissed at him. He didn't fancy another kick in the balls.

"Shall I leave you guys alone?"

He nodded to his friend. "Thanks. Make yourself comfortable in the living room. This will take a while."

Once they were alone, he looked at her. Her expression hadn't changed. He could see the tension in her body and face, the fierce determination not to let anything get to her. She wasn't ready to listen to him, he knew that. But he had to try anyway.

"Delilah, I'm still the same man."

She shook her head without saying a word. Ah, the Silent Treatment. A woman's prerogative.

"What we have together—"

"We have nothing together," she interrupted him. "You lied to me." At least she was talking now. It was a start.

"I wanted to tell you. But this isn't exactly the easiest thing to explain. What should I have said? 'Hey honey, let me take you to dinner, and oh, by the way, I'm a vampire, so just order anything you want while I drink a glass of blood.' "

"You never had the intention of telling me. All you wanted was a little sex toy."

"That's not true, and you know it. I told you last night—"

She interrupted him. "Lies. That's what you told me. I even fell for your cute story about your erection problem. Is that what you tell all the others?"

Delilah uncrossed her arms and fisted her hands at her waist.

"There's only you. And what I told you last night is true."

"Bullshit. Is that why the redhead dumped you? She found out you were a vampire?"

"First of all, she's a vampire too, and second, I left her." He stared at her shocked face. She obviously hadn't expected to hear that Ilona was a vampire, but she caught herself quickly.

"So what, you ran out of vampire women and had to fuck a human?"

"It wasn't about sex, at least not after the first night."

"Liar."

"You're repeating yourself."

"Because you keep dishing up the same stories."

"Because they are true. I admit, the first night was all about sex, but after that, damn it, it wasn't. I wanted you, and not just for physical pleasure. You can't tell me you didn't feel that when we made love."

Delilah had felt it, but it had to be an illusion. He'd tricked her. She'd slept with a vampire, she'd let him inside her, not just her body, but her heart. People like him shouldn't even exist. Something was so wrong in this world.

"You're a vampire. You're a vampire."

As if by saying it, it would go away, but it didn't. He was a vampire, and he stood in his kitchen looking at her, making her feel like she'd hit her head and was coming out of a daze. But she hadn't hit her head. He was real.

"I slept with a vampire." She dropped her arms to her sides and let her shoulders slump.

Samson nodded. "And you liked it just as much as I did."

"No."

She had to deny it to keep her sanity. What would happen to her world if she suddenly had to admit that she liked, no, *loved* sleeping with a vampire? Everything around her would crumble. Creatures like him shouldn't—couldn't!—exist. Vampires were myth, folklore—stories to tell around a campfire to scare people. They only lived in the movies, never in real life. Every child knew that! Just as everybody knew there was no Easter Bunny. This couldn't happen. None of this could be true. Denial was the only way to go.

"I have to go. I have to go back to New York now."

He slowly shook his head and came closer. "No. You're not leaving." With his knuckles, he stroked her cheek softly. "I need you."

"You're a vampire."

"Don't you think I know that? It doesn't change how I feel about you."

"Get away from me." She used all her strength to reject him, when her body was trying to lean into him. He still had the same power over her he'd had ever since she'd met him. She still wanted him, wanted to lick every bit of his skin with her tongue. She wanted to have his hard body pressed against hers and feel him impale her, when what she should want was to impale *him*—with a wooden stake right through the heart! If he even had a heart.

"Don't touch me!" At her outburst, he instantly pulled his hand back as if she'd slapped him. She could see the anger well up in him, his eyes suddenly flickering red. It looked as if it took all his strength to control himself.

"Amaury! Get in here." Samson's voice was sharp. She flinched. Would he lash out at her? Hit her? Bite her?

His friend appeared instantly.

"Watch her," Samson ordered and bolted from the kitchen.

Her eyes followed him before she looked back at Amaury who casually leaned against the kitchen island as if nothing had happened.

"He wanted to kill me, didn't he?"

Amaury nodded. "Yes, and he will—between the sheets, over and over again." He grinned devilishly.

She gave him an undignified look.

"Hey, don't blame me; I'm just reading his emotions."

Reading his emotions? What the hell was Amaury talking about? Her look must have been utterly confused, because he threw up his hands.

"Special gift. Pain in the butt." Then he winked. "And don't worry, I'm not going to tell him what you feel. He'll have to coax that out of you all by himself."

She listened to the footsteps above her. Samson was pacing.

"Don't worry about him. He'll cool off. So, to get back to our conversation before we were so rudely interrupted. Have you—"

"You want to talk about the audit like nothing has happened?"

"Sure, we still have to solve that issue. Just because you now know that we're vampires doesn't change the fact that somebody is messing with Samson's company and wants to harm you."

Delilah shook her head. "What *are* you guys? How can you think of business right now? Shouldn't you be biting me and drinking my blood by now?"

"Thanks for offering, but Samson would so kick my ass if I did that, and, yeah, most likely turn me into dust. So, no thanks. You're safe from me."

"I wasn't offering ..." Was she truly safe from Amaury? He looked too relaxed, leaning against the kitchen counter, to seem ready to attack her.

"I know that. Anyway, while Samson and you had your lover's quarrel, I was thinking. Have you looked into what else John might have done besides those depreciation entries?"

If he wanted to talk about the audit, fine. At least it would bring some normalcy back into her shattered life. "What do you mean?"

"What other transactions has he authorized? What information has he accessed? I think we have to look at everything he did."

Delilah had an idea. "Does the computer system track which logon has accessed certain files?"

"Sure does." Amaury nodded, obviously understanding what she was thinking about.

"Then let's see what he's been up to."

FOURTEEN

Eventually his antique rugs would show the wear and tear from his heavy footsteps, but Samson didn't care. He'd screwed up. He wasn't angry with Delilah, but rather with himself for not handling the situation right. Since he'd betrayed her trust before when he'd looked into her background and had gotten caught red-handed, she was obviously not cutting him any more slack.

He couldn't really blame her. Having to accept that she'd slept with a vampire—and liked it—was probably too much to swallow in one big gulp. But he had to get her to accept the fact. And not just that, he had to get her to embrace it, to embrace him, because he knew he couldn't give her up. When he'd smelled her blood he'd already realized that he was lost, but when he had tasted it, tasted her, he had known there was only one acceptable resolution to their situation: a blood-bond.

Even though Dr. Drake had not helped him resolve any issues before, he'd been right about one thing. A vampire could sense a bond with the person he was meant to blood-bond with, even before the ritual was performed.

Samson sensed this special bond with Delilah. He couldn't describe the feeling; he just knew that it was right. Almost … *instinctual* … was the word that came to mind. Whenever he looked into her eyes, he lost himself in them and knew she had to sense it too. There'd been such understanding in her eyes the night before that he was certain he wasn't wrong.

But even if he tried to explain all this to her, he figured she wouldn't listen to him. Not right now. But maybe she would listen to a professional. He had to try.

Amaury and Delilah weren't in the kitchen any longer. Samson listened and could hear faint voices coming from his office. What were they up to? He found her sitting in his chair behind the desk with his friend hovering over her as they both stared into the computer screen.

Even though he knew Amaury would never make a pass at his woman, Samson didn't like how close his body was to hers. His stomach tightened uncomfortably. Would he always be this jealous when another male was close to her? Was this what it meant to love somebody?

He stopped at the open door without making a sound.

"I'm not sure why he would access this file," Amaury said.

"Wouldn't this be part of his job?"

"Not really."

"Can you check what other coded transactions he submitted?"

"Sure. Won't be easy, though. I should probably get Thomas to help us: he's the IT expert, not I."

Delilah, sweetness.

She looked up as if she'd heard his voice, even though he hadn't spoken. Her eyes met his. Yes, she sensed the connection too, probably without realizing what it was.

"What are you guys working on?" Samson stepped into the office.

"We're looking into what files John accessed recently," Amaury answered. Delilah had gone quiet at the sight of him entering the room.

Samson raised an eyebrow. "Good idea, Amaury."

"It wasn't mine; it was Delilah's."

Samson looked at her with approval. "Even better. Check it out. But I need to steal Delilah from you for now. We have to talk." He looked at her, but she made no move to get up.

"We have nothing to talk about. I'll finish the audit, and then I'm leaving. The sooner, the better." She had that hard, unyielding tone in her voice again.

"We have plenty to talk about. It's time we resolved our relationship issues." He walked around the desk as Amaury backed away from her.

Delilah glared at him, defiance in her eyes. "We have no relationship issues, because we have no relationship. I'm not dating a vampire."

"Trust me; there's a lot more you're going to do with this vampire than dating. Let's go. Dr. Drake's expecting us." He took her arm and pulled her out of her chair. She tried to shake him off, but he held her with a firm grip.

"Oh my God—you're trying to have me turned into a vampire! What is he, some evil surgeon making vampires out of people?" she screamed at him, panic clearly written all over her face.

"Delilah, I'd never turn you into a vampire! How could you think that of me? Do you really think I'd wish this on anybody I care about?" Samson was disgusted at the thought. "Dr. Drake is my psychiatrist."

Delilah gasped as she tried to digest his words. "You have a shrink?" Since when did vampires lie on a couch? A coffin would be more like it. This was just too bizarre. First of all, vampires shouldn't exist at all. They were just folklore, myth, or whatever people might call them. And secondly, vampires wouldn't live regular lives like humans—with visits to the *shrink*!

"Yes, I do, even though I'm sure he prefers to be called psychiatrist." A tiny smile crept onto his lips.

"He's a good doctor, even though his methods might be a bit unorthodox," Amaury noted behind her.

"You're seeing him, too?" She couldn't hide her shock. They were both *muy loco*.

"Hey, we all have our issues. It's not easy living as a vampire." Amaury threw up his arms.

"What kind of parallel universe did I land in? You guys are nuts, right?" She was trapped in a house with two crazy ... vampire wannabes.

"I assure you, I'm perfectly sane, not that I can say the same for my friend here." Samson gave a smirk.

Okay, perhaps only one crazy vampire wannabe then. Yeah, right!

Instead of a reply, Amaury merely shook his head and rolled his eyes.

"Let's go. We don't want to be late for our couple's therapy session."

Samson pulled her out of the room and led her downstairs to the garage. To her surprise, he didn't have Carl drive them. He opened the passenger door of a silver-and-black Audi sports car, an R8. The car looked like it belonged on a race track, not a street of San Francisco.

Samson got into the driver's seat after he'd closed the passenger door behind her like the perfect gentleman. As he shot out of the garage seconds later, she gave him a sideways glance.

She couldn't make sense out of what she'd learned. If he was a vampire, why did he not bite her? Wasn't that what all vampires did? Shouldn't both he and Amaury be hanging on her neck, drinking her blood?

And for that matter, why in hell wasn't he cold? Vampires were dead, right? Or undead—either way he shouldn't have a normal body temperature, should he? Sometimes, he was downright *hot*— She shook her head to disperse the images of Samson over her, behind her, beside her, his shaft impaling, thrusting— Damn it! Enough along *that* line of reasoning. Anyway, it was only one question among about a million she had at the moment.

The thought that Samson operated a security company didn't make any sense either. Shouldn't he, as a vampire, attack people rather than protect them? And why was he not living in a cave with bats? Okay, so maybe that was Batman. Wrong superhero.

No, not superhero. Monster. Right, he was a monster.

And, hell*ooo*—since when did monsters look so damn gorgeous and sexy? When he'd dragged her behind him down the stairs into the garage she'd been unable to tear her eyes away from his butt. And more than anything, she wanted to dig her hands into him, maybe even bite him a little. Would he like that?

Stop!

No more thoughts like that. At least she knew for sure now that she wasn't afraid of him. He seemed to make no attempt to attack her. He'd even sounded disgusted when she'd accused him of wanting to turn her into a vampire. As if that was the furthest thought from his mind.

Delilah looked at her hand. The Band-Aids were still on her fingers, but she knew the cuts had sealed when he'd licked her with his tongue. The tingling sensation she'd felt had shot through her entire body, not just her hand. Just remembering it created goose bumps on her arms.

Samson turned on the heating system. "It'll get warm in a second. Sorry, I should have brought a sweater for you."

His concern for her was evident. His hand brushed hers lightly before he put it back on the steering wheel. The moment was so brief she could have dreamed it, but the lingering pleasant tingling on her skin told her she hadn't. His touch was as real as he was.

Her instincts had been correct in the shower when she'd seen his eyes flash red. And she now understood why there was no mirror in the bathroom. If it was true that vampires didn't reflect in mirrors then there was no need for him to have one. No wonder he hadn't been able to be with her during the day. If he was a real vampire, he couldn't be outside in sunlight without turning into ash.

When he and Amaury had stayed up with her all night, they hadn't become tired. It was all so clear now. Even when he'd sent Carl out to buy some food for her, she'd bet that there hadn't been one single edible item in the fridge before. The little signs had been there, but she hadn't seen them or hadn't wanted to see them. Even his tremendous strength when he'd kicked the gun out of the thug's hand was probably because he was a vampire.

And whenever he'd carried her, it had seemed that he'd had to expense no strength at all, as if she was light like a feather, which she knew she definitely wasn't. There were these few persistent pounds around her waist she could never quite get rid off.

I can't get you pregnant.

Delilah suddenly remembered his words when he'd realized that the condom had ripped. So it was true: as a vampire Samson couldn't father children. Why wasn't she relieved about this? Shouldn't she be glad that at least she wouldn't already be pregnant and carry the spawn of a vampire? Strangely the thought of it filled her with regret rather than relief.

She suddenly remembered the strange dreams she'd had. The house she'd seen in her dreams was Samson's, she was certain now. And the bite on her neck she'd dreamed of? Was this a warning of what was to come? Would he bite her one night in her sleep and drain her? If she was smart, she'd heed the warning.

When the car stopped at a red light, she was wondering why she didn't make a run for it. She could easily open the car door and jump out. He wouldn't know what hit him. She was fast and would be able to get away. It would be easy. She eyed the door handle and stretched out her hand.

"Please. Don't run away." Samson's voice wasn't a command, it was a plea. She met his gaze and noticed his eyes shimmer golden, the same way he'd looked when he'd made love to her in the morning. Delilah put her hand back into her lap and averted her eyes. He shouldn't look at her that way. It was confusing as hell. She wished he'd flash his fangs again, so she'd have the courage to run, but when he looked at her that way, things didn't make sense. Nothing made sense. Would it ever again?

When he finally parked the car outside an Edwardian home, she knew they had reached their destination. He didn't lead her through the main door, but instead showed her to a side door which led to the basement of the building. She hesitated at the door.

"Nobody will hurt you," he whispered behind her. "I give you my word." The word of a vampire. She had to be crazy to believe him, after all the lies she'd caught him in.

The blond bimbo at the receptionist's desk barely gave her a second look and instead looked straight at Samson.

"He's just finishing up with his last patient. It'll be a couple of minutes."

She pointed at the couch. Delilah made no move to sit, and Samson remained at her side. She looked around the waiting room. There were several comfortable chairs, a coffee table with newspapers … Did she see right? *SF Vampire Chronicle* one of the papers said. They had their own newspaper? She gave Samson a curious look and noticed that he'd been watching her.

"We do read, you know."

Smartass!

She turned away from him and continued her perusal of the room, not in the mood to engage in any conversation. Her gaze stopped at the vending machine. She suddenly felt thirsty. Maybe she could get a bottle of water or some juice. When she took a step toward the vending machine, she felt Samson's hand on her arm. She gave him an annoyed look, but he only shook his head slowly.

"I'll get you something to drink when we get home," he announced.

"I want some now." She knew she sounded like a spoiled child, but she didn't care.

"I don't think you'll like what they offer."

Delilah looked back at the vending machine and focused on the bottles behind the glass. Bottles, small plastic bottles with red juice. Tomato juice?

She took a step closer. Oh, no. This couldn't possibly be what it looked like! The labels on the bottles said simply *A, B, AB* and *0*.

Her stomach dropped. Blood. Blood in a vending machine!

She shot Samson a stunned look. He simply shrugged his shoulders.

Before she could say anything, the door opened, and a man stepped out. He seemed to recognize Samson and gave him a brief smile.

"How are you, Samson?" They shook hands. "You won't mention this ..." He gestured toward the doctor's office.

Samson shook his head. "Goes without saying. Good to see you, G."

As soon as the man, who looked strangely familiar to her, passed by her, he suddenly stopped and inhaled deeply. He turned back to Samson and grinned.

"A mortal? You, of all people?" He looked her up and down, making an appreciative sound. Instantly Samson put a protective arm around her waist and pulled her closer. "Not to worry, old friend. I know better than to touch what's yours. But if you would like me to do the honors, I'd be more than happy to ..."

Samson nodded but didn't release her. "I might just take you up on it."

The man left, and finally she realized where she'd seen him before. "Was that the—"

"The mayor of San Francisco, yes."

She gave him a questioning look. "Is he also...?"

Samson nodded. "Yes, he is."

"What did he mean by doing the honors?"

"I'll tell you later."

"Dr. Drake will see you now," the bimbo interrupted them. "Go right in."

"Tell me now."

"Later."

Delilah wasn't sure what she expected of Dr. Drake's office, but it certainly wasn't the coffin-couch. If Samson hadn't shoved her through the door and blocked her exist, she would have turned on her heels and made a run for it.

She was still digesting the news that the mayor of San Francisco was a vampire. The fact that Samson had immediately possessively pulled her toward him when he had shown her more than a passing interest, hadn't escaped her either. She'd virtually felt his jealousy physically, and a shudder had gone through her at the intensity of it. She hadn't felt it wise to pull away from him at that moment, but had let it happen instead.

At least Samson didn't seem to want to hurt her physically. Neither did he want to share her. Better the vampire you know …

And if she was truly honest with herself, she would admit that she had felt comforted by his touch, but she wasn't ready to be honest with herself. Neither would she want to be honest with the shrink, if he was even a real doctor. Delilah looked at the man. He seemed ordinary and human, even though she was sure he wasn't. She saw him inhale sharply. No, definitely not human. Did they all have to sniff at her like dogs?

"Ah, the human woman, I suppose? Delilah?"

She was surprised he knew her name. How much had Samson already told him?

"Yes, this is Delilah." There was something in Samson's voice she hadn't heard before. Pride?

Samson led her to an armchair and had her sit down while he leaned against a filing cabinet close to her.

The doctor sniffed again, then raised his eyebrows. "How can I help you this time?"

"That question would imply that you helped me last time," Samson replied sarcastically.

The doctor didn't seem to be insulted. "I know my advice obviously worked. I can still smell you on her. In fact she's positively reeking of you."

"Doc, I'd appreciate it if you kept comments like those to yourself. Delilah and I are here because we need some help with our relationship."

"Relationship?" the shrink asked.

"We have no relationship!" Delilah protested. It was better to set things straight immediately.

"Ah, I think I see where the problem lies." The doctor caught on quickly.

"No, you don't. You told me to just go and sleep with her, and everything would be okay again."

"Well, did you have an erection? Were you able to perform?"

Delilah felt embarrassed at the frank exchange and felt heat rise into her cheeks. So it was true. He'd seen the shrink to get over his erection problem. At least he hadn't lied about that.

"Yes."

"Then, I don't see where the problem is."

"The problem is that I can't get enough of her. Every time I look at her, I want more. Whenever I touch her, I can't stop. When I'm away from her, I miss her. When another man looks at her, I could kill him. Do you get the picture?"

"You can't sue me for that. I told you to sleep with her, once, and then move on." The doctor threw up his hands.

"Oh shut up, you quack!" she interrupted. "What kind of doctor tells his patient to sleep with somebody? Where did you study medicine? In a whorehouse?" If he had actually studied medicine. She doubted it.

Drake wanted to protest, but she continued. "What? Am I getting too close to the truth? Don't bother answering, 'cause I don't care what you have to say. You couldn't prescribe him some Viagra instead? No, you had to tell him to sleep with a human."

"Viagra doesn't work on vampires," Samson interjected.

"I can see why you like her." The doctor gave Samson a knowing look. "She's a lot like you."

"I'm not like him at all!"

"Case in point. Just as stubborn and insolent. It doesn't surprise me at all that you two are drawn to each other."

"I'm not drawn to him. I don't want a relationship with a vampire. Damn it, he dragged me here."

The doctor shook his head. "That's what your head's telling you, but your body speaks louder. How did you get here?"

"What's that got to do with it?" Defiantly Delilah crossed her arms over her chest. If he was trying to trick her into something, she'd be on her guard.

"How did you get here?"

"In my car," Samson replied in her stead.

"Willingly then."

"No."

"You bound her?" Did they have to talk about her like she wasn't even in the room?

Samson shook his head. "Delilah had plenty of opportunities to get out."

"Yet you didn't—because you don't want to get away. Not from him and not from this relationship."

"That's not true!" she yelled at him.

"Just because you're getting louder, doesn't make it true. Who are you trying to convince? Me? Samson? Or maybe yourself?"

Delilah didn't answer. She hated it when people found her buttons and pushed them.

"Let's get back to the beginning then. When you had sex with each other, I assume, you didn't know Samson wasn't human?"

"You've got that right." No way in hell would she have slept with him had she known. Right?

"Well, did you feel that something was wrong when you had sex with him?"

"Wrong? No, nothing felt wrong." Their lovemaking was perfect.

"It was perfect," Samson said quietly.

She looked at him, not knowing whether to answer back or not.

"I've never felt anything better in my life." It was as if he plucked the thoughts right out of her head.

Her cheeks heated at Samson's admission, and she turned away. It wasn't fair that he made her feel so warm inside.

"So you had sex, and then? What happened?" The doctor leaned forward.

"We had sex again, and again. Shall I go on?" Samson smirked.

Was he actually enjoying this session?

The doctor waved him off. "I think I get the picture."

"You're leaving something important out," she sniped. "Namely that you checked up on my background because you didn't trust me. You thought I was after your damn money. Looks like I should have checked up on *you* instead!"

"I explained to you why I did it, and I apologized for it."

"And then you turned around and continued lying to me about what you are!"

"What did you expect me to do? For the first time in my life I meet a woman who makes me feel things I've never felt before, who takes me to another place when she kisses me, who makes me feel the sun on my skin ... and then I'm supposed to tell her the one thing that will make her run away from me? So I hoped that if I made you love me first, then maybe I had a chance that you'd stay with me once I told you. I needed more time. I was going to tell you." Samson's voice was pleading, urging her to listen to him. She didn't know how to respond.

"Tell me about the sun on your skin," the shrink demanded. "I'm curious."

Samson looked at her when he answered the question. "When you kiss me, you transport me to a meadow of lavender. I can feel the sun shine on my skin, but it doesn't burn, my skin doesn't blister. I feel the warmth, and I can smell the scent of lavender in the air as if I was actually there, walking on soft grass."

With every word Delilah recognized what he was describing. It was an actual place, a place she knew, a place she'd been to. There was no explanation how he could know about it. It wasn't possible.

"How did you find out about this place?" She had to know if the background check had revealed it, as impossible as this seemed. Nobody knew what the meadow represented for her. It was all she had left from her childhood. The only good memories she had left of her baby brother, before the unthinkable had happened.

She doubted that even her parents ever knew what the place meant to her. A place where she felt at peace with the world. Happy.

Samson gave her an incredulous look. "You mean the place exists?"

"Of course it does! How did you find out? The background check on me?"

He shook his head. "No. I told you, when you kiss me, you take me there. I feel it. It's as if you teleport me to it. I can feel it with all my senses. I can smell it, I can touch it, I can hear the sounds, see the sun. All of it."

"It's not possible. You're lying."

The shrink interrupted. "Tell us about the place. What's its significance?"

"I don't share this memory with anybody. It's private." She lowered her eyes.

Samson moved closer to her and crouched in front of her chair, looking up at her. "You've shared it with me before. You've taken me there before. Doesn't that mean you wanted to show it to me?"

She shook her head. This was too close. If she let him too close, he'd hurt her.

"Don't shut me out, please."

"What do you want from me?" Delilah shot up from her chair. "Can't you find another sex toy to play with?"

"I'm not playing with you. And this is not about sex."

"This is not about sex?" the doctor interrupted.

"What makes you think this was about sex?" Samson gave his shrink a frustrated look. "Has anybody here been listening to a single word I've said? What the hell do I pay you for? Do I have to spell this out? This is about me wanting to blood-bond with Delilah."

FIFTEEN

Ilona paced the full length of her eighth-floor condo, holding her cell phone pressed to her ear. Without interest she glanced out the floor-to-ceiling windows with the city lights sparkling just below. Tonight she wasn't in the mood to admire the stunning view.

"No, you're listening now. I've had it, you incompetent fool!" Her voice bristled as she let out a frustrated huff. "If we'd done it my way in the first place, we wouldn't be in this predicament. But, no, you thought you could handle it better. Don't you dare interrupt me." She paused briefly, but the caller on the other end had finally started to listen to her and didn't let out a single peep.

"Good. Here's what you do, and I really don't care how, as long as you do it tonight. I want her gone. Not only is she going to figure out what we're trying to do to his company, but now he's even made her his lover. Do you know how that stings? Do you?"

There was no reply. "I'm talking to you." She was furious. No wonder everything was falling apart if she had to rely on family.

"I thought you didn't want me to say anything anymore," her brother finally said on the other end.

Did they really have any DNA in common? It was hard to believe.

"Idiot! I can't believe I'm related to you."

"Hey, I'm not as stupid as you make me out to be. I got you all the inside information you wanted. Don't forget that. At least I can keep my mouth shut, not like you."

"Don't you dare bring that up again!" Her own failure still stung, even after nine months. She'd been so close! She'd virtually been able to taste victory.

Her brother flared up. "Oh, yes I will. If you had just continued to suck his dick until you were blood-bonded to him, all his money would have been yours, and you could have just let me kill him, but no, my big sister can't swallow, can she?"

"Maybe you should have sucked his dick instead!"

"I'm not his type. So don't make this sound like I'm the one who screwed up. You got yourself into this situation. Do you have any idea about the things I have to go through to fix this for you? No, you think it's so easy."

Ilona stomped her foot, not that her brother would know, but she needed an outlet for her frustration. Too long she'd worked on this, and finally the prize was within her reach again. Just another few days and all of Samson's money would be hers.

"Oh, stop whining. Once all this is over, you'll be swimming in money. Are you nearly done with the upload?"

"I'm working on the encryptions. A few hours more work and then I can start authorizing. We're almost there."

Ilona let out a sigh of relief. "Good. But we still have to take care of her. We can't risk her finding what we're doing and stopping us just before we reach the finish line."

"I'll get rid of her. Just as well he's made her his lover. Samson will be so devastated; he won't even notice what's happening to his company. It plays right into our hands."

What was her brother talking about? "Devastated? He's just fucking her."

"Just fucking her? Dream on. He's in love with her, calls her 'his woman.' Looks like he's finally over you. Took him long enough. I'll call you when it's done."

"Wait," she tried to stop him, but he'd already disconnected the call.

Samson was in love with that little bitch? She didn't give a hoot one way or the other about Samson's love life, but to be replaced by a human? Now, that hurt. Bastard!

Ilona tossed her phone onto the couch and kicked off her stilettos. On the way to her bedroom she shrugged off her dress and let it fall to the floor. Her staff would clean up later. She had more important things to do.

***

Amaury dialed Thomas' cell phone and was connected instantly.

"I need your expertise."

"What about?" Thomas sounded distracted. In the background he could hear somebody else.

"I need you to go through some files for me. You're better at IT than I am."

It was true. Thomas was the resident IT expert on anything to do with Scanguards. Whatever was needed, Thomas knew how to do it.

"Now? I'm in the middle of something."

Amaury rolled his eyes. "Stop fucking Milo and get your ass in gear. I've found something that makes me think John Reardon was involved in something bigger than just siphoning off a few grand. He uploaded encrypted files to headquarters, and I need to know what's in them."

"You don't need me for that. I know you're capable of cracking the encryption yourself," Thomas pushed back.

"I know I am. It's just taking me longer than it will take you. So, do it."

Thomas was clearly hesitating, until he finally conceded. "Fine. I'll get on it. What's the location for the files?"

Amaury informed him of the server location and the code by which to identify John's files.

"We'll split the work. I'll start on the bottom and work my way up. You'll take the top. Call me when you find something," Amaury instructed him and finished the call.

It was a good thing Amaury had seniority over Thomas. When push came to shove, Amaury normally won the argument. It also helped that he was Samson's closest and oldest friend.

He'd spent the last hour going through a history of what John had worked on in the last month, specifically which files he'd accessed. Delilah's suggestion to look at everything accessed under his login had proven successful. John had been all over the place, sticking his nose into files he'd had no business viewing in his position, files other staff should have worked on, not he.

Carl stuck his head into the office. "Amaury, is Mr. Woodford with you?"

He shook his head. "You can call him Samson, you know. I know he's offered it often enough."

"I'd rather not."

"He's out with Delilah. What do you need?"

"I've remembered something that's been bothering me." Carl shifted from one foot to the other.

Amaury pointed at the chair opposite the desk, silently asking Carl to take a seat.

"It has to do with Miss Ilona."

"Ilona?" Amaury couldn't suppress his surprise. Nobody had mentioned her name in Samson's household in over nine months. Just as well he wasn't home. And hopefully wouldn't be in the next five minutes. If he heard her name uttered in his house, there would be no telling how he'd react.

"She spent a lot of time here. I know she never liked me, so I stayed out of her way as much as I could. I didn't want to upset Mr. Woodford, and after she left there wasn't really any good time to mention it. Mr. Woodford was so unapproachable for a long time."

Amaury remembered well. His friend had been withdrawn and preferred his own company to that of his friends. He'd built up a lot of anger, and the anger had turned to depression until he'd finally returned to what seemed his normal self. Except for the fact that he'd shunned the company of women after that.

"And then I just forgot about it, figured it wasn't really important."

"Carl, you're waffling." Amaury was eager to get back to analyzing the encrypted files.

"Sorry, Amaury. It's just, I don't even know whether it's important."

Amaury gave him an unmistakable look. Either talk or get out of the room.

"Miss Ilona. I saw her at his computer one day when he was out. I'm not sure whether she was able to log in or not, but when she saw me she pretended she was looking for a pen and some paper. Later that same night, Mr. Woodford threw her out. When I saw Miss Delilah sit at the computer last night, I remembered it again."

"I didn't realize you came back to the house last night."

"You were all so engrossed in your work, you didn't hear me. I didn't want to disturb."

Amaury nodded. It was true; they'd been so absorbed that they'd forgotten the time and missed sunrise.

"Don't mention anything about Ilona to Samson. It'll only upset him. I think we should keep it to ourselves. I'll make some inquiries and see what I can find out."

Carl got up. "Thank you, Amaury. I'm sure it's nothing. It was just odd. Especially given that he never lets others touch his computers, except for you, and now Miss Delilah."

Amaury smiled. "I think we all should get prepared for a lot more he's going to let Delilah do."

"You think she'll become mistress here?"

"Mistress? I guess that's as good a description as any. She sure has him in the palm of her hand. Not that she has any idea." Amaury shook his head and smiled. How a woman could be so oblivious to the effect she had on a man, was beyond him.

"It will not be easy to hide who we are if she stays."

He gave Carl a surprised stare then slapped his hand on his forehead. "Oh, that's right. You don't know yet."

"Don't know what?"

"She found out a couple of hours ago."

Now it was Carl who had a stunned look on his face. "And she's still with him?"

A loud thud told them that somebody had slammed the door shut. Seconds later the door was opened again and slammed a second time.

"We're not done talking!" they heard Samson's furious voice.

"Oh yes, we are. I'm not marrying a vampire!" Delilah shouted back.

Carl and Amaury exchanged smiles. "A hundred bucks says she won't marry him," Carl suggested.

Amaury shook his head. "You have to learn a lot more about women. Not only will she marry him, she'll blood-bond with him."

He stretched out his hand to seal the bet, and Carl took it. "And you have to learn more about Mr. Woodford. There's nothing more that he likes than his peace and quiet at home. By the sounds of this, she's not going to give him that."

Amaury laughed out loud. Carl might have been spending more time with Samson in the last eighteen years than he had, but Amaury was the one who truly knew his friend best. And peace and quiet was not what Samson liked best at home. Not by a long shot.

There was one thing his friend craved more than anything else in his life, something he had never had since he was a vampire, despite the friendships he'd formed: family. But Carl couldn't know that. His friend had never verbalized his deepest wish, but Amaury had always felt it.

Another door slammed, and he knew Delilah had entered Samson's bedroom.

***

For the second time in as many days Delilah swung her suitcase onto the bed and threw in the few items she'd taken out earlier. She tried to avoid looking at the tangled sheets on the bed, evidence of their night of passion.

How could this have happened? She was in the house of a vampire. She'd had sex with him, mind-blowing sex, and he'd dragged her to the shrink where he'd announced that he wanted to marry her. And not only that. Blood-bond with her, whatever that meant. She hadn't waited for an explanation.

Not that a girl didn't like to get a proposal once in a while, but by a vampire? At the shrink's office? It couldn't get any stranger. Had Samson really thought she'd be jumping at the idea?

She couldn't reconcile the man she'd made love to with the vampire who'd licked her blood off her hand. They were two different people. One she knew she was falling in love with, the other she didn't even know.

The pain in her chest knowing she had to leave him felt unbearable. But she had to do it, and do it now. This man had lied to her at every turn. She would never be certain of what the truth was.

"Don't shut me out," Samson's voice came from behind her.

She hadn't heard him come in.

"Delilah, please talk to me." His voice teased at her neck.

She shook her head.

"What are you afraid of? I know you're not scared of me. I can feel it." Samson touched her hand with his and intertwined his fingers with hers.

His touch was the last strain her psyche could take.

"Please, let me go. I can't be with you."

"I can't let you leave. I'm connected to you. And you're connected to me. Can't you feel it? I've never felt this close to anybody. I can sense things about you ... the lavender meadow ... it's like I'm in your head ..."

"No, please."

"There is more. I can feel the sadness, but I don't understand it. It's there when you think about the meadow. It's as if there is pain associated with it. Delilah, let me in ..."

How could he know about the pain, when she herself had tried to bury it deep in her memories?

"I can't."

"Sweetness, I need to understand you. I need to know."

"You can't know. Nobody can ever know what it was like. What I did!"

"I'm here for you. Please, tell me what's causing you this pain. I can feel it here." He pressed his hand to his heart.

She couldn't explain why he knew anything about her past, but she herself had had strange visions which were all related to him.

"The meadow," she started, "it's located near a small village in France."

She looked at his face, but didn't see him. All she saw was the meadow and herself as an eight year old girl ...

Delilah cradled her little baby brother in her arms.

"Careful," her mother cautioned. "He's fragile. Hold his head up with your arm."

"I can do it, Mom, don't worry. I'm a big girl. See?" She showed her mother that she knew how to hold little Peter. "He's so tiny. Was I so tiny, too?" With big eyes she looked up at her mother, who gave her a warm smile.

"Just as small. And just as cute as he is." Her mother kissed her on the top of her head.

"Well, there are my two favorite girls!" Her father's voice suddenly echoed from the path leading to the lavender meadow as he approached them.

Almost every afternoon when he was done with teaching he'd find them lounging in the meadow, enjoying the long summer days. They would spend their afternoons laughing, playing games and chatting, the perfect family. A loving mother, father, and a little baby brother. It was all she'd ever wanted.

Delilah's childhood was perfect. She didn't mind the fact that they lived in a country whose language she barely spoke, and that she had to make new friends at school. All her difficulties were forgotten when her bother was born. He made their little family perfect.

He was like a little doll she'd play with all day long. And she never got bored of him. She loved her brother, more than all her toys together.

Her parents trusted her with him. One night at the end of the summer, her parents wanted to celebrate their anniversary by eating out at a local restaurant. It was only one block from their house, so they left Delilah in charge of her brother.

It would be an early dinner, and they wouldn't stay out longer than an hour. Peter was asleep when they left. He'd been fed and bathed and was a happy little boy when he was put to bed. Delilah was to call the old lady who lived downstairs from them should her brother awaken, and she in turn would fetch them from the restaurant.

All went quiet after her parents left for the restaurant. Delilah played with her dolls. She checked on him to make sure he was covered by his blanket. And that's when she noticed something.

Peter was too quiet. She couldn't hear anything. He just lay there in the crib surrounded by silence. She shook him.

"Peter, wake up." He didn't wake like he normally would when he heard voices. She shook him again, but he didn't respond. Maybe he was just really fast asleep. Maybe he was so tired he couldn't hear her.

But he wasn't tired, and he wasn't asleep. Fear froze her to the place where she stood, looking down at his quiet body. No breath, no movement came from him. And Delilah just stood there, in shock, unable to move, unable to make a decision. She wasn't prepared. She only stood there.

Delilah hadn't moved from the place by the crib when her parents returned twenty minutes later. She barely heard her mother's screams when her father lifted Peter's lifeless body out of his tiny bed.

He was gone, because she had hesitated. It was her fault. She was in charge of him, and she let her parents down and destroyed the family.

After Peter's death, they moved back to the States. Her parents never blamed her openly, but she knew it was her fault. She never saw her mother laugh again. And her father, he tried everything to cope with the loss and to help his wife as best he could, but the loss of his son was too much for him too, and it seemed like all joy had left him.

Delilah blinked the tears away when she felt Samson's strong arms wrap around her.

"You were eight years old."

"It doesn't change anything. I froze. I didn't do anything, when I could have saved him."

He shook his head. "No, sweetness. It should have never been your responsibility."

"But it was." His embrace felt good, but she knew it was only temporary. She wanted to soak up as much as she could, before she had to leave him.

"Shh. Think of the meadow. Think of how happy you were back then. I was there with you."

She looked up. "But how? It's not possible."

"Every time you kiss me, you take me there. Because that's where you were happy, and that's what you wanted to show me. A place to be happy. Take me there now, Delilah."

Samson put his hand under her chin and nudged her head up. His lips met hers for a gentle touch, then a deeper connection, before she abruptly pulled away from him.

"I can't. I can't stay with you."

"But why?"

"I don't know you. You've been lying to me so many times. It's not a basis for a relationship."

"I've apologized for that, and I've explained why I did it."

Delilah shook her head and shrugged off his hand. "You want forever from me. I can't give you forever. I don't even know how I'll feel tomorrow or a week from today."

"I know it's hard to accept what I am, but you know that I will never hurt you—"

"That's not the point. You want me to make a decision which will affect the rest of my life. I've only known you for three days. How can you want a lifetime commitment from me after such a short time? How can you even be sure?"

She saw a smile form around his lips. His face was soft and gentle. "I feel the bond between us. I know you're the one. It's something I've never felt—not with Ilona or anybody before her. I know we're meant to be together. To be blood-bonded."

"You talk about this with such certainty. I don't have that. And blood-bond? I don't even know what it means. I know nothing about your life. How can you make me choose between my old life and a new one when I don't even know what I'm choosing?" Delilah felt confused. Nothing made sense. What Samson wanted from her was too all-consuming. It was something she couldn't control.

"A blood-bond is a unique connection between two people who love each other. It'll tie us together for eternity. We'll belong to each other. Everything that's mine will be yours."

"I don't want your money. I want nothing. I don't know what I want. Don't you understand? This is too much, too soon ..." She felt tears build up in her eyes. "How can you even be sure that you love me? You know nothing about me."

Samson shook his head. "I know everything about you." He put his hand to where his heart was. "I can feel you inside me. When you're in pain, I can feel your pain. When you're happy, I take part in your happiness."

"It's not possible. You just want me because you were starved for sex, needed it like a drug to fix your 'condition.' What you feel now will vanish, and then? What are you going to do then? Discard me? No, I can't do this."

"Delilah, what I feel for you is true. It won't go away. So what if we've only known each other for three days? Have you never heard of love at first sight? I fell in love with you the moment you fell into my arms when I opened the door. I just didn't know then. When I'm with you, my world is perfect. The things you make me feel ... I've never been a tender man, but with you, I yearn to be tender and loving. You bring the best out in me. You soothe me, you warm my heart. I know I've made mistakes, but I'll start all over again for you. I'll give you anything in the world you desire. I'll do anything to make you happy."

His words touched her. She couldn't deny it. But she wasn't ready to make a decision like this, a decision she couldn't reverse. Forever was too foreign a concept.

"Samson, I can't—"

A loud knock at the door interrupted them.

"Samson!" It was Amaury.

"Not now!" was Samson's reply. "Please, Delilah, stay with me. Be mine. Let me be yours."

"We have a traitor in our midst!" Amaury's voice was insistent.

Samson yanked the door open.

"I think it's Thomas; he's behind it."

Samson's face froze. "Oh, God, no."

He looked back over his shoulder. "We'll talk later, Delilah. You are my life now, whether you want it or not."

Delilah gave no indication whether she believed him, but Samson couldn't wait any longer. The unshed tears in her eyes made his heart constrict, and more than anything he wanted to hold her, but he had to take care of this problem now. Thomas, of all people. He didn't want to believe it.

He rushed down to his office, flanked by Amaury.

"Show me."

Amaury pulled up the transaction screens and explained what was happening. "Here, see, Thomas is logged on as we speak, and he's authorizing all of John Reardon's encrypted transactions."

The screen was littered with pop-up windows showing approval notices.

"What are they?" Samson scanned the screen.

"Wire transfers. He's wiring all our cash to offshore accounts."

"All?"

"Yes, all he can get his hands on. Millions. If we don't stop him, you'll have to shut down the company tomorrow—we wouldn't be able to even make next week's payroll."

The news was devastating. Thomas, his friend of almost a hundred years was betraying him, stealing from him. And not only that, he was the one who'd tried to harm Delilah. No matter how long his friendship with him had lasted, there was only one thing to do now.

"Let's go," he ordered Amaury. "Carl?" he called out into the hallway as they rushed out. Carl appeared out of nowhere.

"Yes, Sir?"

"Protect Delilah."

"Yes, Sir."

They jumped into Amaury's Porsche which was parked on the street and raced toward Thomas' house. Samson pulled out his cell phone and instructed Ricky to meet them there and bring two of his men. They needed all the help they could get. A vampire out of control was a dangerous animal. They had to be prepared for everything.

"Doesn't this thing go any faster?" Samson couldn't contain his impatience.

"I'm going as fast as I can without killing anybody. I'm just as angry as you are," Amaury confessed.

"I know." Samson looked out the window, recalling what Delilah had told him.

"Do you love her?" Amaury's question was unexpected.

Samson gave him a sideways glance. "More than my life. But she doesn't understand what that means. She's resisting. I don't think she's forgiven me for hiding things from her."

"Does she know that you'd never hurt her?"

He nodded. "And I told her I'll give her anything she'll ever want. I explained to her that she'll have a right to everything that's mine."

Amaury shook his head. "Sometimes you're so dense, it's not even funny."

What the hell was his friend talking about? "I'm not dense."

"Sure you are. A woman like Delilah doesn't want money or worldly goods. She wants a man who will always be true to her. Somebody who'll never lie to her, somebody she can always rely on."

"But I've told her I love her. I told her, I'll never hurt her. I even apologized for lying to her. I've done everything I can." Samson felt exhausted.

"Words. It's all words. She doesn't trust your words. She only trusts your actions. You'll have to show her what you feel. You have to do something for her that'll prove that you mean what you say."

"But do what?"

"How would I know? You've spent the last few days with her. You know what's important to her. You feel the bond with her—"

"You know that?"

"You forget that I can sense your emotions. I know you feel the bond with her. Use the bond to find a way to convince her. Give her want she wants, truly wants in her heart, and she'll be yours."

His friend's words made sense. Samson closed his eyes and opened his heart to reach out to her. Too much pain clouded her heart. She had to let go of it before she could recognize what else her heart was hiding. He had to help her with this journey. He suddenly knew what he needed to do, and he hoped it was the right thing.

Samson dialed Gabriel Giles' number in New York. His call was answered almost immediately.

"Gabriel, I need your help on something."

***

Thomas lived in a home built into a hillside below Twin Peaks. It afforded the most stunning views of San Francisco. The house was modern, with floor-to-ceiling windows overlooking the city and a hidden cave carved into the mountain behind. This was where Thomas' bedroom was, shielded from any daylight.

Ricky arrived at the same time as Samson and Amaury and was accompanied by two other vampires in Samson's employ. This situation needed to be handled delicately, and Samson was pleased to see Ricky had chosen two of his most loyal and discreet employees. While Samson didn't know many of his human employees, he knew virtually every vampire on staff. Ricky was in charge of vampire recruitment at Scanguards and selected every vampire personally.

They all nodded to each other. Ricky's normally cheerful face was overshadowed by solemnity. It mirrored Amaury's. Nobody looked forward to what they had to do. They were a tight-knit group; finding out that one of them was a traitor hit all of them equally hard.

"Amaury, can you sense him?" Samson asked his friend.

Amaury looked at the house and closed his eyes. "Yes, he's here."

"Let's go," Samson ordered.

"Wait!" Amaury's voice was a command, stopping the four other vampires in their tracks. "Something is wrong. His emotions don't make sense."

"What do you mean?" Samson inquired.

"Too many emotions all at once. All jumbled."

"Could it be that he's not alone?" Ricky interjected.

Amaury shook his head. "I can only sense him."

"We have to go now." Samson pulled out a wooden stake from his pocket. What he had to do was painful, but there was no other resolution. Thomas had been his friend for many years; at least he would make it quick. No torture, no pain for Thomas. He owed him that much.

Samson caught his friends' looks as they glanced at the stake, and shuddered inwardly. But he couldn't show weakness now. This betrayal warranted the highest punishment.

The two vampires Ricky had brought were positioned outside the house to prevent Thomas from escaping.

Ricky opened the door with his spare key—a security measure they'd put into place years ago, making sure the four friends could gain access to each other's homes in emergencies. Quiet and darkness greeted them as they entered.

Samson's eyes adjusted to the dim light and quickly scanned the interior. The great room they found themselves in was empty as was the adjacent kitchen and bar area. A wall with a door separated the house into two parts: the open and public area, and the private and dark quarters behind.

Samson made a sign to Amaury and Ricky, indicating he was going in first. The corridor was even darker than the front of the house, but just as empty and quiet. He inched forward, his feet making virtually no sound.

Behind him, Ricky and Amaury were as quiet as he was. A small sliver of light came from beneath the door Samson knew to be Thomas' bedroom. They stopped in front of it.

Samson knew that even though the three of them had been quiet, Thomas would have heard them. A vampire's hearing was sensitive, and Thomas would have picked up any or all of the noises they had made. It was strange that he hadn't made a move yet, unless, of course, he had set a trap for them.

Samson braced himself when he turned the knob and swung the door open. Within a split second he'd entered the room and surveyed the scene. Ricky and Amaury did the same, positioning themselves so the three of them formed a triangle at the outer edges of the bedroom. In this formation they could attack.

Only, there was nobody to attack. The room was empty. No Thomas.

"Amaury?" Samson's question was as clear as if he'd spoken it.

"I can still sense him. He's in the house." Amaury closed his eyes again, concentrating. "Downstairs in the garage."

The house had a garage as well as other caves reaching into the hill.

"He should have been alerted to our presence by now," Ricky claimed.

Samson nodded. "I don't like it."

They stalked downstairs and made their way through the garage which was filled with various motorcycles and a sports car. Nothing out of the ordinary.

"Behind this door. I can feel him."

Samson was about to put his hand on the door knob when Amaury jerked him back.

"No!"

Samson gave him a questioning look.

"Thomas is in pain."

"In pain?"

"Silver."

All of them stared at the door knob, and now Samson noticed it. The knob was covered with silver foil. He shrugged off his jacket and wrapped it around his hand before testing the knob. He could feel the effect of the silver even through the thick cloth, but it was muted.

Silver was the only metal capable of burning a vampire's skin. It served as the only way to restrain a vampire.

Samson nodded to his friends, then jerked the door open. Before them was the dungeon. Samson had always suspected Thomas of having a room where he unleashed some of his baser fantasies, but he had never expected it to be quite like an exhibit as could be seen at the Folsom Street Fair. Flogging galore. Not for the faint of heart.

Samson rushed into the dimly lit room, Ricky and Amaury on his heels. The source of Thomas' pain was evident instantly. He was restrained against a wall, held in place by silver chains. Chains he would be unable to break. His skin was covered in painful sores where the silver touched him.

Relief flooded through Samson instantly. Thomas hadn't betrayed him. Somebody had overpowered him.

"Thomas!"

Thomas' head lifted an inch, but he appeared too weak to look at them.

"Ricky, Amaury," Samson ordered with a shrug of his head toward the chains.

Ricky and Amaury did like Samson and took off their jackets, wrapping them around their hands to work on releasing the chains.

When the last chain fell free, Samson caught Thomas' injured body in his arms and placed him on the chaise in the corner.

"Ricky, get him some blood. Upstairs."

He stroked a hand over Thomas' burned face and heard him wince.

"Who did this to you?" Samson's voice was low.

Thomas' lips moved. "Milo."

"Amaury, find him."

Thomas' hand instantly gripped Amaury's to hold him back.

"No."

Samson looked at Thomas, not understanding.

"He's dangerous."

Ricky arrived with the blood. "Drink." He led a bottle of blood to Thomas' lips and let him gulp it down. Seconds ticked away. Amaury's impatience showed.

"Milo stole my password. He's going to ruin you," Thomas pressed out. "I'm sorry Samson; I didn't see it coming." Genuine regret flooded Thomas' eyes.

"None of us did. We'll get him, don't worry." Samson's voice was calmer now. Knowing that he didn't have to kill his friend Thomas had eased his pain.

"I can reverse it. Get me upstairs to my computer. I can do it."

Samson and Amaury helped him up. "Can you stand?"

Thomas nodded. "I'm better. But you have to hurry. Milo will get away, and so will Ilona."

"Ilona?" Samson stopped in his tracks.

"Yes. She's his sister. He's doing this for her. She's been after your money all along."

So she hadn't given up after he'd dumped her. He should have known.

"How did you find out?"

"Just a hunch that Milo was hiding something from me. And then, when Ricky and I went to find John … When we got to his house …" he hesitated and looked straight at Ricky. "I know I should have said something right then, but that's when John's wife screamed and we ran inside."

"What happened?" Samson asked.

"I picked up a familiar scent. It was faint, but I thought I recognized it. Now I know for sure. It was Milo. He killed the accountant."

Samson swallowed hard. "I remember that he was in a hurry to leave the warehouse. It should have tipped me off, but I wasn't thinking straight."

"None of us noticed … and of all people, I should have caught onto him much earlier. I spent the most time with him. I should have seen it," Thomas blamed himself.

Ricky waved him off. "He deceived you. It's not your fault."

Amaury nodded in agreement. "If anything, I should have picked up on his emotions. I should have figured it out."

"Stop, everybody," Samson said. "What's done is done." He looked at Amaury. "Milo would have guarded his emotions from you. He knew about your gift. As for deceiving a lover—we've all been on the receiving end of it at one point or another. You're not to blame, Thomas. I'm just glad he didn't kill you." He put his hand on Thomas' shoulder and squeezed it in assurance. "What happened then?"

"I guess it's a good thing I'm the jealous kind." He gave a bitter laugh. "I managed to put a chip into his cell phone yesterday to record his conversations. I was just playing them back when Amaury called me to help him with the encrypted files—"

"I thought I'd heard Milo's voice in the background."

Thomas nodded. "I recognized Ilona's voice when he spoke to her. They are brother and sister. I never saw the resemblance, but now that I know, I can see similarities, gestures they have in common." He cast Samson a hunted look. "You're lucky that you never blood-bonded with her. If you had, you'd be dead now."

The realization hit Samson hard. "Dead? Killed by a blood-bonded mate?"

"No. Killed by her brother. She would have been unable to keep her murderous thoughts veiled once you were blood-bonded. You would have sensed it. But if she had arranged everything with Milo beforehand, you would have remained in the dark about her intentions," Amaury explained in Thomas' stead.

"All this for money?" Samson shook his head.

"You sound surprised," Amaury noted.

"I shouldn't be."

"Ilona will stop at nothing to get what she wants. That's why Milo infiltrated our group. It all makes sense now, even the timing." Thomas looked into the round. "Just after you dumped her, Milo showed up. First he gained my trust, and then he tried to figure out how to get at your money. Took him long enough. So he figures out who to blackmail to get at the books from one side, then steals my logon and password to finish it off. No wonder he didn't want us to talk to the accountant."

"Do you know where he is now?"

Thomas shook his head. "No, but we can try to trace the chip. If he's still got his cell phone on him, I'll find him."

They reached Thomas' office upstairs, and Thomas let himself fall into his chair. His hands instantly flew over the keyboard as various screens popped up.

"He's somewhere in the vicinity of Ilona's place. They are probably on their way to pack up and leave the city. You have to go, now."

"You think you can reverse the transactions?"

"Yes, trust me. The transactions are on a time-delay loop. It's a little program I put in place a couple of weeks ago for extra security. We'll get all your money back. They won't get away with this. You just make sure you catch the two before they can hurt anybody else."

Samson put his hand on Thomas' shoulder and squeezed.

A minute later they were outside.

"Ricky, call backup. We need a dozen guards to close in on them. It will take us too long to get to her place from here. They'll be gone by then."

Ricky instantly dialed on his cell and gave orders to his subordinates.

Samson's cell vibrated in his pocket.

"Carl?"

"Miss Delilah is gone."

Samson's throat constricted and his heart froze as all the strength flowed out of his body.

SIXTEEN

The Chinese New Years Parade was in full swing, and the masses of people watching the festivities squeezed through the narrow streets of Chinatown. The colorful dragon which was carried on sticks by even more colorful young Chinese men wound its way through the festive streets. Lanterns and lights hung from each shop and each restaurant on the way.

Delilah had tricked Carl. She'd sent him on a fool's errand to the drugstore—pretending to have stomach cramps—and had been surprised at how easily he'd bought her lies. She knew that Samson would probably punish him for leaving her alone, but she couldn't allow herself to feel sorry for him now. She needed to get away.

A future with Samson was impossible, and the faster she put a stop to all this, the better for all involved. The last day and night had severely tried her belief in reality. Suddenly she'd been confronted with a world in which vampires not only existed but pretended to live lives similar to humans.

And in the last few days she'd also had to realize that all walls she'd built around herself had started crumbling. She'd never told anybody about the pain she'd carried around with her for so long, and she still couldn't understand why she'd told Samson. Of all people, he didn't deserve her trust.

He'd lied to her, again and again. And he would continue lying to her. In his eyes she'd seen his desperation to have her, consume her. What other lies would he dish up, just so she'd stay? She barely knew him, and the idea of spending eternity with him was too foreign, too much, too soon. While she was with him, she knew she couldn't think straight. He'd make sure of that by seducing her over and over again. And Delilah knew she would be unable to resist him.

But she couldn't make an important decision like that, a decision that meant being with a vampire forever, while she was in his arms, when her brain was utter mush.

It was pure luck that Amaury had interrupted them, and she took it as a sign that she had to escape. It was now or never. She finally had to think with her head and squash the little voice coming from her heart—the voice which kept on insisting that she was making a big mistake.

Delilah knew she couldn't make it to the airport for the last flight out, since it was too late already, but she would hide in a small hotel, somewhere where he wouldn't find her. She'd give a wrong name, pay cash. And tomorrow morning, she'd be on the first flight to New York. She was pretty confident that she'd considered every precaution she had to take, because if anything, Samson was resourceful and would try anything to find her.

Delilah had forgotten about the parade. The crowds made it difficult for her to get through the streets, but there'd been no taxi. She had to make it down toward Union Square where she hoped she had a better chance of finding transportation.

Her suitcase felt heavier and heavier as she rolled it behind her. She had taken everything that was hers, not wanting to give herself an excuse to go back. She was weak enough in her resolve as is.

The music and the noise of the crowd drowned out some of her thoughts as she tried to push her way through the sidewalk. Every few seconds she got bumped by somebody or felt another foot on hers. Her toes were already bleeding, she was sure.

Under other circumstances she might have enjoyed the colorful parade, sampled some of the exotic foods, and even bought a trinket or two, but a sightseeing tour of San Francisco was the last thing on her mind.

Different languages whirled past her ears as she inched forward through the crowd. Young and old faces passed her, men and women, children and seniors, Caucasians and Asians. It took more than fifteen minutes just to advance one block.

Delilah was relieved when she finally made it through the maddening crowd and found herself in a quieter alley. She would be able to cut through the worst of the crowd from here and find her way to Union Square down the hill.

The sound of the wheels of her suitcase on the cobblestone street echoed through the alley. In the background the music mixed with it and then the sound of cars and motorbikes.

Another faint sound made her spin around, but she saw nothing. She was still too jumpy. It would settle, soon. Her imagination was just playing tricks on her.

Delilah turned into the next street which was wider than the alley she'd come from. To the left was a dead end, so she turned right. The street was lined with apartment houses three stories high, and their entrances were blocked with iron gates, their piercing spikes accusingly stretched toward heaven. She walked along the sidewalk and lost herself in her thoughts again.

She had to convince herself that she was doing the right thing by leaving him.

Too late Delilah heard the sound behind her, the engine of a motorcycle. She twisted her head and saw it heading straight for her. She was unable to make out the dark figure riding it.

Her feet picked up speed, and instinctively she let go of her suitcase. She ran, but the motorcycle gained on her, the sound of its engine growing louder as it approached. Louder and more menacing with every second. She could never outrun it. Frantically she looked to both sides to find a hiding place where the motorcycle couldn't follow her.

Out of the corner of her eye she noticed a movement, but it was too quick for her to register what it was.

"Delilah!"

The bellow echoed through the street and bounced off the buildings. A bellow of somebody clearly horrified. Before she could turn, she felt arms push her out of the way, slamming her onto the asphalt. She fell hard. The impact made her ribs hurt, and she groaned loudly.

The lights of the motorcycle blinded her for a second as she whipped her head around, just in time to see the bike hit the person who'd pushed her out of the way. She saw the figure flung into the air as if it were a ragdoll, then crash down. The downward fall was broken by the spikes of the iron gate.

The body hung there, impaled.

The motorcycle skidded, a figure tumbling to the ground, rolling, then getting up, obviously uninjured. The engine suddenly cut out, and it was quiet.

Delilah's side hurt as she tried to move, but she had to. The biker was heading for her after briefly glancing at the figure impaled on the gate.

Delilah stumbled to her feet. It was too dark for her to make out who the person on the gate was, but she knew nevertheless. She'd heard him scream her name in a voice that was all too familiar. He had pushed her out of the way and saved her life, if only for a few minutes.

But she didn't want to acknowledge who he was. Because if she did, her whole world would collapse. The person who'd pushed her out of the way of the motorcycle, trying to save her, was now impaled on the gate, seemingly lifeless.

Delilah tried to move, but her feet froze firmly in place when the biker came toward her, as if somebody was keeping her in place by invisible strings. She tried to lift one foot in front of the other, but couldn't. Nothing would move. She was paralyzed.

Something caught her attention and made her snap her head to her right. That's when she saw them: several men in dark clothes rushing toward the scene. That's when she realized she had no chance. It was over. They were coming for her. They would kill her, just the way the motorcyclist had killed her rescuer.

Delilah looked back at the biker who suddenly turned away from her and sprinted in the opposite direction, away from the men. What?

"Delilah?" she heard another familiar voice. A second later, Amaury stood next to her. "Are you okay?"

She nodded, dazed. Suddenly her muscles moved again, and she almost collapsed. Amaury caught her.

"Samson?" Her head tilted to the direction of the iron gate. She didn't want to hear the answer. She watched in horror as two of the men brought him down from the spikes and laid him on the ground. A slight movement caught her eye. Had he moved by himself?

"Samson!"

Delilah tried to run toward the man they'd laid on the pavement. Samson. A strong hand pulled her back.

"No," Amaury said. "You don't want to see him like that."

She yanked her arm out of his grip. "He's hurt because of me!"

She ran to him, dropped down next to him. Samson's body lay slack on the ground, blood pumping from several large wounds. So much blood! But to her surprise, she didn't feel the usual queasiness in her stomach that normally befell her when she saw blood.

Delilah looked at his face. It was smeared with blood. But his eyes were open.

"Samson." She stoked his cheek. Her eyes filled with tears at pain displayed on his face. She'd never seen anybody in this much agony, this much physical pain.

In the background she heard Amaury give commands, but all she saw was Samson, the man from whom she'd tried to run away. Why? She couldn't remember.

"Somebody help him! We need to get him to a doctor," Delilah called out to Amaury. Cold fear gripped her as he gave her a grave look.

"A donor is on the way."

She didn't understand. "A donor?"

Samson tried to speak, but his voice was a mere gurgle. Delilah bent closer to him, trying to soothe him. But she didn't know what to do. She had no first-aid skills, and even if she did, would they even work on a vampire? She was helpless.

"Don't try to speak. We'll get you help. Everything will be alright, please, just hold on," she encouraged him, knowing her words were a lie, ringing hollow in her ears.

Samson moved his head from side to side.

"No!" she screamed, understanding what he meant. "Amaury, tell me what to do!"

Amaury was at her side. "His injuries are too extensive. He knows it. I'm sorry, but he'll die if he doesn't get human blood immediately."

"Then get an ambulance, and get him a transfusion." She suddenly remembered the vending machine at Dr. Drake's practice. "Can't you get some bottled blood somewhere?"

"Bottled blood won't work, not this time. His injuries are too grave. He needs blood coming directly from a human's vein. He needs the life force of a human to help him regenerate."

"I'll give him mine." Without hesitation Delilah pushed the sleeve of her sweater up

"No …" Samson's voice was weak, but determined. His eyes cast a pleading look into Amaury's direction.

"He won't let you," Amaury explained.

Delilah gave him a surprised look then shook her head. For once she didn't give a damn what anybody did or did not want her to do. She would not sit by idly and let him die.

"I don't care. He'll take my blood."

"I can't let you do that, Delilah. Samson forbids it."

Tears flowed from her eyes and ran down her cheeks as she looked back at Samson. "I won't let you die."

It looked as if he tried a smile, but his face distorted in pain instead.

She put her wrist to his mouth. "Bite!" she ordered with fierce determination.

But he didn't bite. Instead, he turned his head away from her wrist.

"You stubborn vampire! Fine, you won't bite, I'll have one of your friends bite me, and then I'm going to force-feed you my blood. Do you understand?" Anger colored her voice, and she saw something flicker in Samson's eyes. Disbelief?

"Amaury, bite my wrist," she commanded, stretching her wrist toward Amaury.

He shook his head. "I can't."

She gave him a sharp look. "Somebody else then? You!" she shouted at one of the men who'd helped take Samson off the gate. "You're a vampire—bite me, damn it, so I can feed Samson."

The vampire hesitated and looked between her, Samson and Amaury.

Suddenly Delilah felt a hand on her other arm and turned. Samson's hand had gripped her.

"… don't want … hurt you," he pressed out, his voice barely audible.

Now he had decided he didn't want to hurt her? What about when he'd lied to her? The man's timing sucked. Major. She'd have to have a word with him about that, but later.

"You will only hurt me if you leave me. Don't leave me, please."

She placed her wrist at his mouth again, but he made no move. That's when she lost it. Anger rolled over her. "Bite me, damn it, or I'll kick you in the balls so hard you'll scream into the next century! Do you understand?"

A second later she felt the sharp pain of her skin breaking and liquid dripping. A fraction of a second later the pain was gone, and Samson's fangs were firmly lodged in her wrist. She felt him suck, his eyes closed.

With her free hand she smoothed his hair back from his bloodstained face. "Take what you need, my love."

Delilah felt more than heard his sigh. She dropped her head to his, and placed a kiss on his forehead. "I'm here, Samson, I'm here."

Amaury helped her lift Samson's head into her lap so it was easier for her to feed him.

"Thank you."

Amaury shook his head. "Samson is a very lucky man to have you."

The commotion behind her made her turn her head.

Two vampires brought the struggling biker with them. The helmet was gone now, and revealed was a head of long auburn hair. She'd seen the woman before, at the theater.

Ilona Hampstead, Samson's ex-girlfriend.

Ilona tried to escape the hold of the two vampires, but despite her struggles, she couldn't. They were stronger than she was. Her expression was furious.

The woman stared right at Delilah, watching how she let Samson drink her blood.

"What, you think he's going to be yours just because you let him have your blood? Dream on, sister!" Her voice was laced with venom.

Delilah returned her vile look with a killer stare of her own. "Bitch! I'll deal with you later!"

She wanted to wring the woman's neck for hurting Samson, for nearly killing him. Delilah looked down at him as he suckled from her wrist and saw how Samson's eyes flew open in shock.

"Everything will be fine, my love; they've got her. She can't hurt you anymore," she whispered to him. His eyes fell shut again, and then he let go of her wrist. She looked at Amaury, alarmed.

"It's fine. He'll take however much his body can process at a time. He'll need more, later. We'll have a donor by then," Amaury assured her.

She shook her head. "No. I won't allow it."

"How cute," Ilona spat out.

Delilah ignored her. "He'll only drink from me, nobody else."

"But it's too dangerous. He needs too much blood," Amaury warned her.

She lifted her hand in protest. "Only from me."

Then she gave Ilona another look and took off her jacket. She rolled it up and rested Samson's head on it, before she got to her feet, still wobbly. Her ribs hurt, and she put her hand to her side to support her movements.

Amaury offered his arm to steady her, and Delilah gladly took it.

"What are we going to do with her?" Delilah asked him.

"We?" Amaury gave her a stunned look.

"Yes, 'we.' And don't even think about excluding me. I have every right—"

"You're not going to have a little mortal tell you want to do, are you?" Ilona taunted Amaury as she struggled in the grip of the two vampires holding her. "Wimp!"

Amaury gave her a nonchalant smile. "You should know that I'm not susceptible to your insults, Ilona."

"You're gonna screw her too once Samson discards her? Or maybe even before?"

"I think you should shut up while you have a tongue," Amaury warned her. Delilah shot him a surprised look.

"Oh, yeah, bitch. That's what he does, the high-and-mighty Amaury. He fucks Samson's castoffs."

"As if you hadn't asked for it," he retorted.

Ilona let out a bitter laugh. "I wonder whether your friend knows about it. Maybe somebody should tell him."

Delilah's look bounced between the two. Clearly they knew each other more intimately than anybody would have guessed. Had Amaury somehow been involved in Ilona's and Samson's breakup? Had he betrayed his best friend?

"It's not working, Ilona. You can't finagle your way out of this one. So, where is Milo?"

"Milo?" Delilah echoed.

Amaury gave her a sideways glance. "We've just found out that Milo is Ilona's brother and is behind the entire scheme to rob millions from Samson's company. He deceived Thomas and got access to his password."

Delilah stared at him in shock. "Milo masterminded this?"

Ilona blew out an annoyed huff. "That idiot couldn't plan anything. He couldn't even execute what I told him to; otherwise, you little bitch, you'd be pushing up daisies by now. But no, he had to give the job to some idiot human who screwed it up every time. I should have done it myself in the first place," she ranted.

"Shoulda, coulda, woulda," Delilah replied sarcastically.

Ilona snarled at her. "You think you can have him and all his money? Think again. He's just playing with you: Samson never loved anybody but himself. He's a selfish man and an even more selfish lover. He'll grow tired of you, and then he'll dump you."

"Just because you couldn't give him what he needs doesn't mean I can't. And as for being selfish, why don't you look in the mirror sometime—you'll see who's selfish. Oh, sorry, I forgot: you can't look in the mirror, can you? Then I guess you don't really know *how* ugly you actually are, so I'll just give you the skinny—you're a fucking hag."

Ilona hissed and struggled to free herself from her two guards, murder in her eyes. "Let me just get my fangs into you, bitch—I'll show you how ugly I can *really* be!"

"Enough! Where's Milo?" Amaury gave the two vampires a nod to increase their hold, twisting Ilona's arms back to an unnatural and painful position. She winced.

"I don't know where the idiot is."

"Fine, then we have no more need for you."

Delilah looked at Amaury. "You're not letting her go, are you?"

"Letting her go? No. We're killing her."

Amaury pulled a wooden stake out of his jacket pocket. Delilah stared at the stake then back at Ilona, whose eyes had grown wide. She knew what was coming. Yes, she would die, but Delilah wanted to be the one to deliver the final blow. It was her man Ilona had nearly killed, so it would be only right for her to punish the woman.

Delilah made a grab for the stake in Amaury's hand, but he stopped her.

"No, it'll be my pleasure. Samson is the best thing that ever happened in my life. Anybody who wants to hurt him had better defeat me first."

Delilah had to concede. Amaury's determination was palpable.

"Thanks for the great sex, but as I said before, it's all meaningless. See you in hell."

Ilona's eyes widened as if she couldn't believe he'd actually do it. Her lips opened, but no words came out. Amaury raised his arm and slammed the stake into her heart. For a split-second disbelief spread over Ilona's face. A second later she was dust. The air picked up the tiny kernels of dust and carried them away.

When Amaury turned back to Delilah, he gave her a long look. "Without emotions, it's all meaningless."

Amaury organized Samson's transport back to the house while more vampires were dispatched to hunt down Milo.

Carl expected them when they returned and had already prepared Samson's bedroom, placing clean sheets on the bed. Carl and Amaury helped cut the torn clothes off Samson's body and clean his wounds before they placed him onto the bed and put a single white sheet over his body.

"He'll need fresh blood every couple of hours," Amaury advised. "You can change your mind, you know. He wouldn't expect you to do this. In fact, he'd want me to dissuade you from continuing this."

Delilah shook her head. "He's hurt because of me. I'll give him what he needs."

She'd changed into a t-shirt and leggings and sat next to him on his bed.

Amaury nodded. "Carl, we'll have to mix Delilah some strengthening tonic so her blood regenerates faster. We should have everything we need in the kitchen."

Samson stirred.

"He needs you now."

Amaury and Carl left the bedroom, and Delilah leaned down to Samson, placing her wrist at his mouth. Without opening his eyes his fangs sank into her skin.

"Yes, drink, my love. We're home now."

She cradled his head in her lap as she fed him. Already she could see that some of the wounds had started closing. The blood flow had stopped, and the blood was clotting, creating a crust over the wounds. The healing process had started.

The sucking sensation on her wrist wasn't painful; on the contrary, it filled her with peace.

When Samson finally let go of her wrist, his lips moved. "Delilah," he whispered, but drifted back into unconsciousness instantly.

Delilah held him while she watched every movement of his body. This time she had not hesitated when action had been required of her. This time she hadn't stood by to let somebody she loved die. She had acted. She had surprised herself at how strong she'd been there on that street. The courage she'd felt when being confronted with Ilona had been new to her, but knowing that all the vampires that had surrounded her were on her side, had helped.

Amaury came back to the bedroom, bringing her a disgusting-looking concoction of vile-smelling liquid.

"What's this?"

"You don't want to know. But it will help you sustain the blood loss."

Delilah believed him. How had her world changed like this? She was lying in bed with a vampire who she would give as much blood as he needed and willingly drank the vilest liquid her lips had ever touched, trusting the vampire who handed it to her.

"I'll keep you company." Amaury pulled the armchair closer to the bed before sitting down. "He'll need about twenty-four hours to recuperate."

"But he'll pull through, won't he?"

"With your help, he will."

Amaury rested his head against the high backrest of the chair.

"Tell me what happened," Delilah wanted to know.

Amaury nodded. "Samson told you about Ilona, about their breakup?"

"Yes. He told me about her. But he didn't mention that you and she …" Delilah cleared her throat.

"He didn't know." His look when he met her eyes was sincere. "Listen, there's no need for him to know. I didn't betray him. She came to me after he'd thrown her out of his life. Hey, I'm not proud of it, but I'm not exactly choosy when it comes to women."

"You killed her as if you felt nothing for her." The thought made her shudder. What did it take for a lover to be so cold? When she looked into his eyes, she recognized pain.

"Sex is just sex for me. Nothing else. It's something I need, and I pretty much don't care who provides it. I don't mean to shock you, but that's who I am. It doesn't change where my loyalties lie." His gaze drifted to Samson, and she understood. "Without Samson, I wouldn't be here today. He saved my life numerous times. He's a good man."

She nodded and stroked Samson's cheek. "And he's mine." She looked back at Amaury just in time to catch his warm smile. "What was Ilona's plan?"

He sighed. "She wanted to be mistress to a multimillion-dollar fortune. She wanted what is his. If Samson had blood-bonded with her, Milo would have killed him. And all the money would have been Ilona's."

"Oh my God, she wanted him dead?" Cold fear gripped her.

"That's what greed does to people. Living off his fortune wasn't enough for her."

"What do you mean?"

"When a vampire blood-bonds, his mate has a right to everything that's his. They will become joint owners. It obviously wasn't enough for her. She wanted it all. When Samson broke it off with her, her dream went up in smoke. So she had to figure out something else."

Delilah shook her head, trying to shake off the images in her mind. "What was she planning?"

"First she had her brother, Milo, infiltrate us. We had no idea. She was new in town herself, and suddenly Milo showed up and … well, it wasn't that hard for him to seduce Thomas, I guess. He's a big softy at heart, and frankly, even in San Francisco, there aren't that many gay vampires. So his choices were always a little limited.

"Milo figured out enough about the internal workings of Scanguards to know that just stealing Thomas' password wasn't enough. So he dug around in the records, and must have found out about John's little depreciation fraud and used it to blackmail him. It was easy enough. You were on the right track, you know, with your audit. You would have found it eventually."

He gave her an approving look.

"You did half the work," she conceded.

"Only after you showed me which way to go. Ilona was smart. Carl told me earlier today that he saw her at Samson's computer once, possibly trying to get into the system, but he'd never given her his logon or password. So she obviously had the idea before."

"Are you sure? He gave it to me, and he's known me a lot less time than he knew her."

"Not even I know his password, and I'm his closest friend. He trusts you like he's never trusted anybody else. I don't think he *ever* trusted Ilona, even though he was prepared to marry her. I guess the loneliness was finally getting to him. He always wanted a family."

Amaury smiled softly, his look drifting to Samson on the bed.

"Once Milo had John's password, he was able to upload encrypted wire transfers. He then just had to go back in with Thomas' password and authorize them."

"Thomas must be devastated."

"Milo overpowered him earlier tonight and chained him with silver."

"With silver?"

"It's the only metal we can't break or bend. Vampires can't escape silver chains. And it burns our skin. We were lucky to get to Thomas in time. He was in a lot of pain, but he'll be fine. Personally, I'm surprised Milo didn't kill him. Maybe there were some feelings involved after all …"

"I feel sorry for Thomas to be tricked like this by his lover. Do you think John knew what Milo was up to?"

"Probably not," Amaury guessed. "And even if he had an inclination, he probably just ignored it, figuring the less he knew the better. John was really a pawn in this game. Not quite an innocent, but he certainly didn't deserve to die."

"What's going to happen to his family? He had a wife and children." Delilah could only imagine the pain his wife was experiencing.

"Samson will take care of them. We have a large charity fund which helps the families of those employees who die in the line of duty. It happens, you know, with some of our bodyguards. And even though John didn't die in the line of duty, Samson will do right by him."

"And the man who attacked us?"

"I've sent two of our men to release him. They have instructions to erase his memory of anything related to Samson, you, or any other vampire. There is no need to punish him any further. John's wife will need all the support she can get."

"Others in your situation wouldn't be this kind."

"You mean because we're vampires?" There was no accusation in Amaury's voice.

"Even humans would be crueler. I certainly didn't expect this kind of consideration from vampires—no offense."

Amaury shook his head. "It has nothing to do with being a vampire or not. There are good and bad among us, just like there are good and bad among humans. Turning into a vampire doesn't make you bad. And being human doesn't make you good."

"And you and Samson, you are good."

"We're no saints, but we try to be as good as we can. It's a constant struggle, but we win more often than we lose."

Delilah smiled at him. "How did Samson find me in time?"

"Your scent. He could have tracked you through the entire city. He knew your scent so well, and then of course, he licked your blood from your hand—that only intensified it. When Carl told him you were gone, and we knew Milo and Ilona were loose in the city … I've never seen him so panicked in his life. He was ready to kill somebody."

"I'm sorry." She truly was.

"Next time you're planning to leave him, give me a heads-up, will you? So I can get out of the line of fire."

She wouldn't leave him again. If he still wanted her, she'd be his. She planted a kiss on Samson's forehead and ran her hand through his hair.

"That won't be necessary, Amaury." She smiled at him and saw that he understood.

"He'll be glad to hear that when he wakes up. Why don't you sleep a little? I'll watch over him and make sure he feeds when he needs to."

"Thank you, Amaury; you're a great friend."

Her eyelids were heavy, and within minutes she was out, sinking back into the pillows as she kept Samson's head cradled in her lap.

SEVENTEEN

"Delilah, wake up," Amaury's voice came through her dreams. She tried to ignore it, but it wouldn't stop. "Delilah."

She opened her eyes and looked at Amaury holding a glass of the same horrible liquid he'd made her drink twice already. She had no idea what was in it and had no intention of ever finding out. For all she knew, it would be toadstool—or just the toad.

"Again?" She'd practically gagged the last time she drank it.

"Sorry, but you need it. He's been taking a lot of blood from you." She drank, trying to ignore the awful taste.

Then Delilah followed Amaury's look, resting on Samson beside her. He looked better. His wounds had closed, and new skin was growing over them.

"How much longer?"

"Soon. In the meantime, you're needed downstairs in his office. There's somebody who wants to talk to you."

She gave him a questioning look. "Who?"

"You'll see."

Her gaze drifted back to Samson, not wanting to leave him. "What if he wakes up while I'm gone?"

"I'll be here. I'll call you immediately."

Reluctantly she got out of bed. She felt dizzy when she suddenly stood. Her body swayed, and Amaury instantly grabbed her. A low growl came from the bed.

Both she and Amaury turned their heads to look at Samson. He was seemingly still asleep, but his fangs were showing. Amaury instantly let go of Delilah's arm. Samson's fangs retreated, and his lips closed.

"He can sense you even in his sleep. He doesn't like you being touched by another man."

"But, you were just trying to help me," Delilah protested.

"A vampire who's found his mate is very possessive."

Delilah smiled at Samson. Even in his sleep he was trying to protect her. "I'll be back in a short while, my love."

She saw a content smile form around Samson's lips as if he could hear her.

Carl expected her in Samson's office.

"Please take a seat here, in front of the computer, Miss Delilah."

"Carl."

He looked at her questioningly.

"I'm sorry. Did I get you in trouble with Samson? I'll talk to him when he's better. I don't want you to be punished for letting me escape," she said ruefully.

"It doesn't matter what happens to me, as long as Mr. Woodford will be alright."

"What will he do to you?"

"I was ordered to protect you, and I failed. All that's important is that he got to you in time."

"But it was my fault. I tricked you."

He gave a faint smile. "No matter, Miss. I shouldn't have let you trick me. If I may say so, for a human, you're very smart."

"And if I may say, for a vampire you're very kind."

He nodded. "Mr. Woodford has arranged a teleconference for you."

Carl pointed to the computer screen. She sat in the chair he held out for her.

"A teleconference. What for?"

Carl switched on the monitor. A picture of what looked like a hospital room came into view. He adjusted the small camera on the top of the monitor and pointed it directly at Delilah.

"There's somebody Mr. Woodford wants you to talk to."

"Are we connected?" a voice came through the speaker, and a second later, a tall man stepped into view.

"Yes, we can hear and see you clearly, Gabriel," Carl replied. "Miss Delilah, this is Gabriel Giles. He runs Scanguards' headquarters in New York. Gabriel is one of us."

"A ...?" She perused the man on the monitor. His long hair was swept back in a ponytail and his otherwise handsome face showed an ugly scar from his ear to his chin. Yes, somehow she would guess he was one of them.

Gabriel nodded. "Yes, Miss Sheridan, I'm a vampire. It's a pleasure making your acquaintance. I hope that I'll have the opportunity to meet you in person at some later time. Samson speaks very highly of you." Delilah recognized his voice as that of the man on the speakerphone.

"Thank you. Did you want to talk about the audit with me?"

"No. Everything has been settled regarding the audit. We're aware what Milo and his sister Ilona were trying to do, and we're working on reversing all their actions. No. This is of a much more personal matter." He cleared his throat. "Samson has asked me to see your father."

"My father?" Delilah gasped. Were they intending to hurt him? She pushed the thought away instantly. After her conversation with Amaury she had no reason to believe that anybody would want to hurt her or her family. "What are you trying to do to him?"

"Don't be alarmed, Miss Sheridan. You have my and Samson's word that your father is safe. We understand that he's in the later stages of Alzheimer's and doesn't recognize you anymore. But there's something you need to talk to him about, something you've been carrying with you for over twenty years. You need closure, and only your father can give you that."

Delilah shook her head. She understood what he alluded to, but it didn't matter. "There'll never be closure. You said it yourself. My father doesn't recognize me anymore. He doesn't have any memories of what happened."

"That's not entirely true. He still has memories, they are just locked away."

"Mr. Giles, I'm sorry that you're wasting your time, but I can't talk to my father anymore."

"Please, hear me out. I can unlock his memories long enough to allow you to talk to him as if he was healthy again. It'll give you the opportunity to say what you need to say to him."

"That's impossible."

"It's not. Some of us have special gifts. This is mine. I'm happy to use it for this purpose. But you'll only have a few minutes, before his mind will cloud again, so use the time wisely. Just tell him."

Delilah swallowed hard. The camera tilted away from Gabriel to a chair. She recognized her father instantly. His stare was blank, his shoulders slumped. Tears formed in her eyes, seeing him like this. Nothing would bring him back. She could never ask him for forgiveness.

Gabriel stepped behind her father and held his hands several inches above the old man's head. Gabriel's eyes closed. A few seconds later her father's eyes suddenly took on life, and he looked straight at the camera.

"Delilah!" her father exclaimed. "Sweetheart, it's so nice to see you."

"Daddy?" Her voice broke. He'd recognized her. After so many years, he finally knew her again.

"What's wrong sweetheart? Why are you crying? Did somebody hurt you?" His voice was full of concern.

"No, Daddy, I'm just happy to see you."

"So am I, so am I." He gave her a ravishing smile, reminding her of how he'd always looked at her when she was a young child. "It's been a while. Your mother and I miss you. You're working too much, you know that?"

Delilah blinked. He didn't know that her mother was dead. He had no memory of it. It made sense. Her mother had died when he'd already been afflicted with Alzheimer's. There was no need for her to bring it up now. She didn't want to cause him any undue pain.

"I know, Daddy. I'll come and visit you and Mom the next free weekend I get. How is that?" she lied, unable to bring herself to tell him the truth.

"That sounds like a plan."

Delilah cleared her throat. She was at a loss of how to approach him. Too many years she'd carried her guilt with her, and now that she had the opportunity to talk to her father about it, she was at a loss for words. There was no right way to start this conversation.

"Do you sometimes still think of our time in France?"

He smiled. "Many times, sweetheart."

"Me too. I think of it a lot."

"You were such a young child then, I'm surprised you remember much." His voice was soft, but also laced with pain.

"I remember all of it from back then."

He raised his hand to stop her. "Many things are best forgotten."

"But how can I forget?"

"Only think of the good things, don't dwell on the bad."

She shook her head, too choked up to speak.

"Have I ever told you what a joy you were to your mother and me? I can still hear your laughter when I would push you on the swing, and you would demand to go higher and higher. You were such an adventurous little girl. So brave. Always so brave." He gave her a big smile.

"I'm not always that."

"In my eyes, you are."

"Oh, Daddy, I'm so sorry!" Tears started forming in her eyes.

He furrowed his brows. "Sorry for what? What's wrong, sweetheart?"

"Peter," she pressed out. "I should have done something. I ..." A single tear rolled down her cheek, leaving a hot trail on her skin.

"Peter?" His voice sounded surprised. "But, sweetheart, you couldn't have prevented his death, neither could your mother or I. Peter died of Sudden Infant Death Syndrome. Even if we'd been there that night, we couldn't have done anything. We always blamed ourselves for leaving you in charge of him. I'll never forget the horror on your face that night. I wish we could have spared you this. You should have never seen him die. We were so worried for you."

"But, Mom was so sad all the time. I thought you blamed me."

"Blamed you? Oh God, Delilah, no." He sat forward in his chair, wringing his hands. "We blamed ourselves. If we hadn't had you, your mother and I would have never made it through this dark time. You were the only light we had. You were our only sunshine, but we felt so guilty that you had those nightmares, seeing him dead in his crib over and over again. We didn't know what to do, so we never spoke about it. We always thought time would heal all wounds, and children forget. In hindsight, we should have gotten you professional help, but we just didn't know what to do. I'm so sorry we failed you. Please forgive us." Her father's eyes filled with tears.

Delilah's eyes finally released the tears she'd built up over all those years. "Oh, Daddy. There's nothing to forgive. I love you."

"I love you, too, my sweetheart, and so does your mother. Promise me something."

"Anything," she agreed without hesitation.

"Stop dwelling on the past, and think about the future. Your future."

"I promise."

"Goodbye, Delilah," he said, and his eyes went blank again.

Delilah slumped in her chair and gave her sobs free reign. Her father loved her and didn't blame her for Peter's death. She was free, finally free of the guilt she'd carried for so long.

Strong arms lifted her up and carried her to the couch. She opened her tearstained eyes and looked at the man who carried her.

"Samson!"

"Don't cry, sweetness," he whispered and sat down on the couch, keeping her in his lap. He wore a long robe and looked as vibrant as ever.

"I'm so sorry, Samson; I put you in so much danger." Her tears flowed freely.

"You saved my life."

He brought her head close to his and lowered his lips to hers, kissing her softly.

"I thought I'd lost you," she said.

Samson shook his head and chuckled. "I'm pretty hard to kill, even though this time it was close, too close. Without your blood—"

She put a finger on his lips. "Shh. I owed you."

His face took on a stern look. "You felt obligated? That's why you saved me?" His shoulders sagged, as if all energy had left his body.

"I couldn't let you die. I put you in this situation. If I hadn't run off, you would have never been injured."

"I see."

So she'd done it out of guilt? That was all she felt? Samson felt his heart contract painfully. She'd saved him, only to kill him by leaving him again. He felt her blood run through his veins, sensed the very essence of her, yet at the same time he listened to her words. Words he didn't want to hear. She'd saved him because she owed him.

Abruptly he removed her from his lap and sat her on the couch while he rose.

"I'm sorry that you feel this way. You don't owe me anything. I'll ask Carl to make arrangements for you to return to New York."

He'd barely pressed out the word when he stalked out of the room and ran up the stairs. Seconds later he slammed the door to his bedroom shut. Delilah didn't love him. He'd completely misread her. She'd only given him her blood because she'd put him in danger in the first place, not because she couldn't live without him.

How noble of her!

A bitter taste spread in his mouth. He had to get her out of his life now, before she ripped his heart out and fed it to the lions. Everything that reminded him of her would have to go. He yanked open his desk and pulled out his drawing pad.

The drawings he'd made of Delilah during their first night fluttered to the floor. Samson bent down and stroked his hands over them, as if touching her instead. He yearned for those moments again when he had her in his arms.

"They are beautiful," Delilah's soft voice whispered behind him.

How had she been able to sneak in without him hearing her? He had to attribute it to his recovering state.

"You drew these of me." Not a question, just a simple statement.

He didn't turn. "You were asleep. I wanted to capture your beauty." It seemed so long ago now. "If you want to pack, I'll leave you to it." He took the pictures and rose to turn away, but felt her hand on his arm.

"Please look at me," she begged, her voice soft and gentle.

Samson complied and turned.

"If you think I give my blood to anybody and then just walk away, you're wrong. Do you really want to know why I didn't let you die? Do you?" She paused. "Because for once, I wanted something that's just for me, and I didn't care about the consequences. When you were laying there dying, the only thing I could think of was myself. Call me selfish, but I couldn't imagine living a life without you. That's why I gave you my blood, because I wanted you. And I still do."

Samson's jaw dropped, his fingers released the drawings, scattering them on the floor once more.

"You want me? No matter what?"

Delilah nodded. "I love you, and if that means you'll have to turn me into a vampire so I can be with you, so be it."

"Turn you …? No!" He pulled her into his arms. "No. I love you too much to do this to you."

He sank his lips onto hers, claiming her. This wasn't the gentle kiss he'd bestowed on her in his office, but the possessive kiss of a vampire claiming his mate. Delilah was his.

"Blood-bond with me." He looked deep into her eyes.

"Please explain it to me again. Last time I wasn't in the right mind to listen."

"It means you'll be mine forever, and I'll be yours."

"Forever? But I'll grow old and you won't."

Samson smiled. "No, you won't. Once we're blood-bonded, you'll draw on my essence. You'll remain human, but you won't age as long as I'm alive. I'll only drink from your blood, and you will drink from mine. You'll be able to sense me because my blood will run in your veins. We'll be connected. You'll always know what I feel and I'll know what you feel."

"But I will still be human?"

"Yes; you'll still go out in the sun. You'll still eat real food. But you'll be my wife, my mate for life, and I'll never let you go. There's no turning back once you've decided. We'll become part of each other, one incomplete without the other, two halves of one whole."

Her eyes locked with his. There was no hesitation in her response. She brushed her hair aside and exposed her neck to him. "Bite me, then."

A second later, the bedroom filled with his laughter. It was like a release to him. In her own quirky way she had accepted. "Sweetness, there's a little more to this ritual than just a bite. And believe me, you're going to enjoy every second of it."

The entrance door slammed loudly. Samson's ears perked up. Several men had entered his house. All of them vampires. He could sense them clearly.

"We have visitors."

He quickly pulled on a pair of jeans and slipped into a t-shirt, before he took Delilah's hand in his, intertwining his fingers with hers.

The commotion in the living room grew louder. When Samson and Delilah reached the foyer, they already knew who was assembled: Ricky, Amaury, Carl, and Milo, the latter restrained by two strong vampire guards.

"So you found him." Samson entered the room, nodding to his friends. He looked at Milo, who had a disgusted sneer on his face.

"Your sister said hi before she went to hell," Samson greeted him.

Milo snarled at Delilah. "Bitch!"

"If you're talking about your sister, I must agree. Otherwise, you'd better hold your tongue, or I'll cut it out."

"Go ahead. Since you're going to kill me anyway, get it over with." Milo's voice was cold and impassive.

"I'm not going to kill you," Samson said slowly, watching Milo as he exhaled sharply, letting him experience a brief moment of relief. "I'm going to have Thomas do it. He'd be annoyed with me if I deprived him of this."

He reveled in the shock on Milo's face. For a short moment he'd obviously thought he'd get away unscathed.

"It was all my sister's doing. She was behind it. She forced me to do it," Milo whined. "You've already killed her. So you've had your revenge."

The front door opened, then closed again.

"I'll make sure you'll get all the money back. I have access to the accounts in the Caymans—I'll wire it all back."

"That won't be necessary," Thomas' voice came from the hallway. He came into sight an instant later. "I've reversed all transactions. Samson, the money is safely back in your account."

"Thank you, Thomas."

"How?" Milo sounded confused.

Thomas approached him, stopping inches from him. "You might have fooled me about your feelings for me, but when it comes to IT, you can't hold a candle to me. I reversed every one of your transactions."

"Thomas," Samson addressed him.

For the first time, Thomas looked straight at him. "Yes, Samson?"

"What do you want to do with him?"

"I?"

"Yes, he betrayed you. You'll be his judge. Amaury took care of Ilona. And thanks to Delilah's insistence to feed me her blood, I survived Ilona's attack, so I have no further need for revenge. But you may take yours."

Thomas gave Delilah an admiring look. "I can't imagine anybody more worthy to be Samson's mate than you. He is truly lucky."

Samson caught the shy smile curling around her lips and squeezed her hand in agreement. "I know I am, and even more so since Delilah has agreed to blood-bond with me."

Suddenly everybody was talking over each other. The excitement in the air was palpable.

"See, I told you so."

"Who would have thought?"

"You owe me a hundred bucks, Carl!"

"Congratulations!"

"I'm so happy for you two!"

"What hundred bucks?"

"We had a bet."

"When's the happy event?"

"Oh, damn, just kill me now, before I puke!" Milo shouted and shut everybody up.

"It looks like somebody doesn't share our joy for your union, Samson," Ricky said pointedly.

"Luckily I don't give a rat's ass about what Milo thinks." He caught himself and looked at Delilah. "Sorry, sweetness, I shouldn't curse in front of you."

She gave a hearty laugh. "You're funny, you know that? Do you really think a curse word or two can shock me after all I've been through in the last few days? If I can get married to a vampire, I think I can deal with a few cuss words."

"Oh cute," Milo said sarcastically.

"Shut up, you prick!" Delilah snapped at him.

The room broke out in laughter, all except for Milo. Samson wrapped her into his arms and pulled her face up to his. "I can see already, that we're going to have lots of fun in our lives together."

He restrained himself from devouring her right in front of his friends. What was between them was private. Soon he would be alone with her, and she would become his forever. The thought warmed his heart like never before.

"Have you made a decision, Thomas?"

Thomas nodded and addressed his lover.

"You gained my trust under false pretenses. You betrayed me, you stole from me, and you tricked me. You almost killed me, and you killed innocent humans. And your actions threatened those people who are dearest to me. You're scum, vermin. I regret the day I set eyes on you. The world would be a better one without the likes of you. But I'm not a killer, and you're not going to turn me into one. You're not welcome here anymore. I'll send word to every coven in the United States: if anybody shelters you, I'll come after them and then after you. If you ever set foot in this country again, I *will* destroy you."

Milo appeared shocked at Thomas' verdict. "You won't kill me?"

Thomas addressed the two guards. "Accompany him out of town, and make sure he leaves the country."

The two guards looked at Samson for approval, and he nodded. A few seconds later they led Milo out of the house.

Samson placed his hand on Thomas' shoulder. "It was a wise decision. I commend you for it."

Thomas shook his head. "It was a coward's decision." He turned, and Samson saw the anguish in his face. "I couldn't kill him because I still love him."

Thomas left the house a minute later. Samson understood his need to grieve and come to terms with his decision on his own. Making him stay to celebrate Samson's own happiness would have been cruel.

"He'll be alright," Amaury said once the door had shut behind Thomas. "Give him some time."

"Carl, how about some drinks to celebrate Samson and Delilah's impending union?" Ricky suggested.

"Champagne?" Carl asked.

"You know we don't drink champagne, Carl." Ricky laughed.

"Yes, but I don't think it's polite in mixed company to gulp down glasses of blood." Carl threw a cautious look into Delilah's direction.

"Carl, when you say mixed company, do you mean women and men, or do you mean humans and vampires?" Delilah asked and smiled.

"I meant humans and vampires."

"Bring the blood, Carl, and a glass of champagne for me. I'm not a shrinking violet, and I don't want you to treat me like one. I'm not going to faint at the sight of blood. Not anymore anyway."

Carl straightened.

"You heard the mistress of the house." Samson grinned. Delilah would fit perfectly into his life.

"Yes, sir."

EIGHTEEN

When Delilah stepped out of the bathroom, her cheeks were rosy, and the glow of the many candles Samson had lit in the bedroom shimmered golden on her skin. He'd never seen a more beautiful sight. She had donned a robe, wearing nothing underneath, just like he'd asked her to.

Finally they were alone in his house, his friends having departed only minutes earlier. He stood waiting for her in front of the fireplace, equally only dressed in a robe, nude underneath it. His cock stirred violently at the sight of her and at the thought of what they were about to do. He'd never imagined how it would feel, but now that he did, he was certain that he'd never felt anything even close to the love he felt for her.

"Thank you for making it possible for me to talk to my father."

"I'll always do everything in my power to make you happy. Whatever it takes." He stretched out his arms.

Delilah came to him, slowly but steadily, and he folded her into his embrace.

"Are you ready for the rest of your life to begin?"

"With you by my side, I'm ready for anything." Her voice was like music to his ears.

He stroked the pale skin of her neck and felt her artery throb underneath his fingers. Her eyelids fluttered. "Will it hurt?"

"You'll feel no pain, only pleasure. We'll bond at the height of ecstasy, when our bodies are joined. You'll drink my blood, and I'll drink yours. We'll be truly one, one body, one soul. You'll sense everything I sense, and I'll feel everything you feel. There'll be no secrets between us. Do you want this?"

Samson had to give her one more opportunity to change her mind, because once they were blood-bonded, they were joined forever. He knew it was what he wanted. The certainty he felt was intoxicating and frightening at the same time. If she refused him now, it would break his heart.

Her green eyes sparkled when she looked at him. "Samson, I've been sensing strange things the last few days. I sensed things about you that I couldn't possibly know. Like the fact that you painted that picture." She tilted her head toward the painting over the mantle. "When I look at it, I see a little boy showing his mother a drawing."

"Those are my memories, sweetness."

"But we haven't blood-bonded yet. How is it possible?"

He smiled. "Those who are truly meant for each other already have a bond between them. That's why you can already sense me, and that's why I knew about the meadow. We're already connected."

"Care to make it official?" Delilah whispered, her lips plump and red.

In slow motion his lips descended on hers until finally they locked together in a kiss of pure love. He'd never kissed any other woman like he kissed her. Capturing her lips with his, he poured his heart into her as he invaded the caverns of her mouth with his tongue. He wasn't there to plunder, but to share. Her tongue met his, offering him what he knew he could never take: her trust. It was for her to give.

Their mouths fused in a passionate surrender to each other, neither one being the conqueror nor the conquered. Partners, equals in love. Both with equal strength and equal weakness for each other, both powerful and powerless at the same time.

Samson felt images invading his mind again, images of lavender, the meadow, the sun. She opened up to him to take him to a place of utter happiness, a place without a care in the world, a place where he was just man, not beast.

Never breaking their kiss, he lifted her into his arms and carried her to his bed, no, to their bed. He laid her onto the crisp sheets and covered her with his body. The only things between them were their thin robes, barely providing any barrier to their passion.

With eager hands Delilah pulled at his robe until it gave way and opened so she could feel his skin under her fingers. Never in her wildest dreams had she thought she could love a man without reservations the way she loved Samson. Excitement pulsed in her veins as she felt his hands unwrap her from her robe.

Finally Samson's naked skin connected with hers. She virtually felt the sizzle the connection created, the thrills it sent through her body, the anticipation is created in her brain. His erection pressed against her thigh, not asking for entry yet, but reminding her of his purpose. To take her, to possess her, to share himself with her.

His hands roamed her body liberally, without rush, but with determination. She returned his ministrations with the same fervor he showed. No square inch of his body would escape her touch. Not her fingers, nor her mouth or tongue.

Where hours earlier he'd been punctured by gaping wounds, new skin had formed as flawless as the rest of his body. She pressed against him, and he understood and rolled onto his back taking her on top.

Delilah pulled herself up to look at him. He was beautiful, if a man could be called beautiful. His shoulders were broad and muscular, his chest devoid of hair and ripped with muscles. She trailed her fingers along his torso. From beneath her lashes she noticed him watching her as she explored him. She discovered deep desire in them, yet he didn't move, but allowed her to take the time she needed to learn him.

For the first time she would make love to him with the full knowledge of what he was. A vampire.

Delilah still couldn't understand why an amazing man like he could fall in love with her, but she didn't questions it anymore. What she saw in his eyes told her that his love was real. Samson was hers. Her man. Her vampire. Her mate.

Her hand traversed the valley of his stomach to find the dark nest of curls surrounding his proud cock. Her lips followed the path her hands had traveled to arrive at the shaft she knew was yearning for her touch.

She felt him inhale sharply when her fingers touched the round velvet-soft head of his cock. Fully aware of the effect her touch had on him, she continued and ran her fingers from the tip down to the base.

Slowly, very slowly. She took a deep breath and inhaled the scent of his arousal.

Instantly she licked her lips, moistening them. "I want you, Samson," she whispered before her tongue touched the tip of his erection and started the long descent to the base.

"Delilah, I'm yours." His voice was almost unrecognizable. Deep and husky.

Samson dug his fingernails into the sheets to stop himself from pushing toward her. The sensation of her tongue on his cock almost shattered his control. What had he ever done in his life to deserve a woman like her? Delilah had accepted him wholeheartedly, and with every touch she showed him her love.

The moment she took him into her mouth, he, Samson, a strong and powerful vampire, was powerless in her arms. Vulnerable and at her mercy. Safe.

He moaned and moved his hips upwards, asking for a deeper penetration. And she heard his request, sliding her lips down along his hard shaft until he was completely buried inside her. Her warmth and moisture engulfed him, cradled him. In the shelter of her mouth he grew harder. Her sucking and her licking grew more intense, and he pressed his head back into the pillow, suppressing a scream of pleasure.

Samson felt his fangs itch, eager for her blood. How he had ever been able to hold back during the nights they'd spent together, he didn't know. Feeling her the way he felt her now, he realized he'd never had a chance to walk away from her after that first kiss.

His fangs extended as a roar left his chest. He called for his mate. "Delilah!"

He felt her hesitancy in letting go of his cock, but he pulled her up with his strong arms and looked into her eyes. "Take me inside you, now."

Her hand came up to touch his face, then she moved her finger and ran it over his fangs. He saw no fear in her eyes, only excitement.

Without breaking their eye contact, she positioned herself above him and bore down, slowly and steadily. The tip of his erection touched her moist center, and he groaned. Her body continued its

256 Tina Folsom

descent, taking him into her hot sheath, clenching tightly around him, pushing him deeper until he was inside her to the hilt.

For a moment he couldn't move for fear he'd spill instantly. She seemed to understand and remained completely still.

Samson turned his head to his nightstand. The ceremonial dagger glinted in the dim candlelight as he took it in his hand. Delilah's eyes followed his movements. He led the blade to his shoulder and pressed it down where his neck and his shoulder met. Drawing the dagger forward, he cut through his skin.

He felt the trickle of blood instantly and set the dagger aside. "Drink from me."

Delilah saw the blood spill from his cut and lowered herself over his torso.

"I love you, Delilah."

Without hesitation she placed her mouth over the open skin and suckled. The warm liquid ran over her tongue and down her throat, the taste surprisingly sweet. She latched harder onto his shoulder, wanting more. Delilah felt his arms around her, pressing her closer to him, his cock moving inside her, thrusting, pumping.

With a move she barely noticed, he flipped them, bringing her underneath him, now plunging his shaft deeper inside her.

"Now we bond," she heard his voice, before she felt his mouth at her neck. His tongue licked her skin, making it tingle, and then his fangs connected, breaking through her skin, burying themselves in her.

There was no pain, only pleasure when she felt his sucking motion and knew her blood transferred from her body to his. Then Samson's deep guttural moan reverberated in her body.

A lightheadedness spread within her as if she was floating on a cloud, and she took more of him. His blood streamed down her throat and warmed her from the inside, awoke every cell and made her entire body tingle. Like electricity it travelled through her veins, igniting sensations previously unknown, lighting a flame inside her.

Her womb clenched with need, wanting and accepting his body and soul and offering hers in return. Delilah felt his raw power and strength as his shaft drove deeper into her, filling her, completing her.

She ground against him, asking for more. Samson's body tightened even further under her demand, and his cock expanded in her already tight channel. With every movement, withdrawing, then thrusting again, he teased each nerve ending in her body and made the fire inside her burn hotter.

There was no need to speak, because she sensed everything he felt. How he needed her blood inside him, how his cock yearned for release, to spill himself and plant his seed. Her own desire to receive him grew with every second.

Delilah felt every cell in her body burn, hurtling her toward her climax. He was there with her, tumbling into the abyss as their bodies found their release within each other. Floating, carrying each other, connected.

When she released his shoulder, she felt him do the same. A moment later, his tongue smoothed over the area.

"Oh, Samson!"

He kissed her, catching her as she came down from her high. "I'm here, sweetness, I'm here."

She panted heavily. Had she even breathed during the entire time? She couldn't remember. "You didn't tell me it would be so amazing."

Samson chuckled softly. "The deeper the love, the more intense the bonding."

Delilah brushed her lips to his. "I could feel you."

"And I could feel you. Your heart is pure. I'm honored you gave it to me." He kissed her tenderly.

"I'm going to love living here with you," she said.

"We should talk to Amaury tomorrow to find us a new house though. This is going to get too small," Samson claimed.

Too small? Samson's house was a large Victorian. Her own tiny place in New York could fit into it at least five times. "This is large enough for us. It's just you and me. I don't need much space."

She noticed a rather sheepish grin build around his mouth.

"Yes, but it's not always just going to be only you and me. To start off we'll need a nursery, and then when the kids are a little bigger, they'll probably all want their own rooms and—"

"Kids?"

"Yes, our kids. I know you want them."

"But you told me you can't have any. Vampires can't have children."

"That's true, in general, but there's one exception. When a vampire male bonds with a human female the ritual changes their DNA. Once you complete your first cycle after the blood-bond, I can impregnate you."

"Impossible." She shook her head.

"Do you remember the mayor?"

Delilah nodded.

"I told you that he's a vampire, but that's not the whole truth. He's a vampire hybrid, a vampire born to a human mother and a vampire father. There are few of them, but they exist. They have vampire and human traits. They can subsist on blood as well as human food. They can be in the sun without burning and have the strength and speed of a vampire. They have strengths of both species, and weaknesses of none. Our children will grow up like human children, and when they reach maturity, they'll stop aging just like any vampire."

Delilah's eyes filled with tears. "We can have children?"

"As many as you want. I'll love every single one of them."

Delilah sniffed. "Why didn't you tell me before?"

Samson kissed her tears away. "I wanted to give you one last surprise. It's going to be pretty hard surprising you from now on."

She laughed. He was right. Already now she could feel other things about him, as if she was in his head. "So, when are we going to have that human wedding you're planning?"

Samson laughed out loud. "See, what I mean? I can't keep anything from you anymore. How did you know?"

"When you mentioned the mayor again your mind went to what he said to you at the shrink's office. That he wanted to do the honors. He offered to perform the marriage ceremony, didn't he?"

"If our kids are only half as smart as you are, we'll have a bunch of Einsteins on our hands. I hope you're ready for that."

"I'm ready for anything with you." She smiled and kissed him.

"Anything? I can think of a thing or two ..." His wicked grin coupled with his erection straining against her left little doubt as to his intentions.

"Only a thing or two?" Delilah teased him. "Do you think that's enough?"

"With you, never."

But for this night, a thing or two would be a start.

THE END

ABOUT THE AUTHOR

Tina Folsom is a member of the Romance Writers of America and writes predominantly paranormal and erotic romance. She lives in Northern California with her husband where she enjoys great food, changeable weather, and tolerates the occasional earthquake.

Her ideas for her books come from her many different careers – CPA/Accountant, Real Estate Broker, Chef, Secretary, Au-pair amongst others – as well as the many different countries she's lived in, and the people she's met over the years. And the vampires? Well, chalk them up to her active imagination.

For more about Tina Folsom, please visit her website: www.tinawritesromance.com

You can also follow Tina's blog: http://authortinafolsom.blogspot.com

Made in the USA
Lexington, KY
22 May 2011